NEVER LET HER GO

He returned to her, and, before she understood what he intended, he slid his arms about her waist and pulled her tightly against him.

"Sir!" she cried, aware suddenly that she did not even know his name. "Whatever are you doing? This . . . this is most shocking. I beg you will release me at once!"

Evelina could not have been more stunned. Her words, however, had little effect except to cause the gentleman to smile at her, but not a warm smile, rather the wicked expression of a man intent on devilment.

"I will not release you," he responded with roguish simplicity.

Astounded, she simply stared at him, her mouth remaining agape for a ridiculous length of time as she searched for the proper words with which to upbraid him for his conduct.

His smile broadened. "Hardly a ladylike expression," he murmured.

She clamped her lips shut, but this proved to be a terrible mistake, for in the next moment, he was kissing her.

BOOK YOUR PLACE ON OUR WEBSITE AND MAKE THE READING CONNECTION!

We've created a customized website just for our very special readers, where you can get the inside scoop on everything that's going on with Zebra, Pinnacle and Kensington books.

When you come online, you'll have the exciting opportunity to:

- View covers of upcoming books
- Read sample chapters
- Learn about our future publishing schedule (listed by publication month *and author*)
- Find out when your favorite authors will be visiting a city near you
- Search for and order backlist books from our online catalog
- Check out author bios and background information
- Send e-mail to your favorite authors
- Meet the Kensington staff online
- Join us in weekly chats with authors, readers and other guests
- Get writing guidelines
- AND MUCH MORE!

**Visit our website at
http://www.kensingtonbooks.com**

An Adventurous Lady

Valerie King

ZEBRA BOOKS
Kensington Publishing Corp.
www.kensingtonbooks.com

ZEBRA BOOKS are published by

Kensington Publishing Corp.
850 Third Avenue
New York, NY 10022

All Kensington titles, imprints and distributed lines are available at special quantity discounts for bulk purchases for sales promotion, premiums, fund-raising, educational or institutional use.

Special book excerpts or customized printings can also be created to fit specific needs. For details, write or phone the office of the Kensington Special Sales Manager: Kensington Publishing Corp., 850 Third Avenue, New York, NY 10022. Attn. Special Sales Department. Phone: 1-800-221-2647.

Zebra and the Z logo Reg. U.S. Pat. & TM Off.

First Printing: November 2004
10 9 8 7 6 5 4 3 2 1

Printed in the United States of America

The Five Riddles

Time is lost
A smuggler's weary end
The world is upside down
Walls that will not mend

Devil's Gate wat opens
Black the land will be
Down a path
A treasure ye will see

Ye olde well
Draws water deep
Of ale and mead
Made honey-sweet

Some stones flat
Others tall
A bridge in death
To any wat fall

Cross the stones
Cross one to dare
Pearl and gold within
Small and rare

Chapter One

Kent, England 1817

Lady Evelina Wesley lifted her lantern high. She stood spellbound before the tall, unruly hedge that separated her property from the Earl of Rotherstone's estate. The dense, overgrown foliage of blackthorn, hazel, dogwood, oak, and crab apple had almost completely obscured a heavy ancient gate. In mid-July a veritable tangle of creeping ivy clung like a veil to the farthest limbs of the oak and spilled like a waterfall in numerous places over the shrubs.

The gate, known as Devil's Gate on the map tucked into the pocket of her cloak, had been precisely positioned at the end of the walnut grove on the eastern edge of her estate. With a little careful search through the ivy, she had uncovered first a rusted iron ring and then the attached wooden gate. She wondered if Lord Rotherstone, her neighbor to the east, had been in the habit of using the gate to visit her uncle before his death some eight months earlier. Had either of the men known of the profound significance of the gate?

Evelina's chest felt crushed suddenly with the weight of her discovery. Earlier that day, she had been in the attics of her deceased uncle's house, now her house, and had found what appeared to be a quite ancient map. The map depicted a treasure buried on Blacklands,

Lord Rotherstone's estate. There was even a gate giving access to his property.

As she looked at the map now, she understood quite well that all she had to do was give a hard tug, open the gate and step through. Yet she could not. She felt anxious in a manner she could not explain, and her feet felt as though they were strapped to the earth below.

She lowered the lantern to the ground, trying to understand herself and her sudden reticence. Of course, crossing onto Rotherstone's lands without his permission was certainly an act of trespassing, but she knew in the deepest places of her heart that this was not why she had grown immobile in the last few minutes. No, something else, something unknown, was troubling her, and that so deeply that she could not bring the thoughts to the forefront of her mind.

She began to pace back and forth in front of the gate, the lantern the only thing separating her from the hedge. Back and forth, her long cloak sweeping at the dead leaves behind her, whispering to her as she marched.

How much her life had changed since her uncle's death. A few months past she had been an impoverished daughter of an earl. Now she was independent, wealthy and able to care for her invalid mother, as well as several of her younger siblings. She had all that she had ever dreamt of possessing. She had no need, none at all, to open the gate before her. She could return the map still couched in her pocket to the attics and bury it once more beneath the rotten wood of the floor from whence it had emerged. She could leave the map, and all its secrets and promises, for those who would follow after her.

She stopped suddenly and turned sharply to the gate. She swept around the lantern and laid a hand on the ring. She would open the gate tonight. This was her gate to open, no one else's. The map belonged to her as surely as

Wildings Hall belonged to her. Whatever secrets the map held, whatever treasure might be discovered because of the map, these belonged to her. This was her time, hers alone.

Her gloved fingers slid about the ring. She took a deep breath, preparing to pull very hard, when the words of her eldest brother, the present Earl of Chelwood, returned to her suddenly as from a nightmare.

Your heart is a rusted gate! What man will ever want you?

She drew her hand back as though the ring had been on fire. Why had this particular memory chosen to haunt her now?

Of course, Robert had been in his cups at the time, and the argument had been as old as it was familiar. He had been begging her to restore the family fortunes through an alliance he had forged with a wealthy family of trade. She had not had an objection to marrying for such a reason, since marriages of convenience were common enough. Her family was suffering dreadfully. She knew her duty and would have gladly done it. However, the man presented to her had proved, upon acquaintance, to be addicted to gaming just like her brother. The fortune she was to have wed would have disappeared just as the Chelwood fortune had disappeared.

Robert had been angry at her refusal, particularly since he had acquired new gaming debts on the expectation of the alliance. However, Evelina had had no sympathy for him. He had continued as their father had begun, running into the ground what had once been a fine, majestic estate.

That her uncle, Lord Bramber, had been free to leave Wildings estate to whomever he desired, and that he had chosen her, a woman, had been the most surprising, stunning event of her eight and twenty years. The inheritance had set her free forever. She had no need of a husband, no need to pinch every tuppence. She could live life as she desired, she could open any gate before her.

Yet for all that, she stood before the hedge, the light from the lantern casting shadows into the ivy-laden oak above, and her only thought was whether or not her brother had been right. Was her heart like an old rusted gate, stuck shut for eternity?

She began her pacing anew. Back and forth, her mind raced with confusion.

She should wait. She should press on. She should return to the house and the safety of her bedchamber. She should open the gate and see what adventure awaited her. She should think of her family and not do anything to endanger their security or fortune by offending her neighbor, Rotherstone.

She paused. Through the walnut grove, she caught sight of the distant flickering lights of Wildings Hall and a strange calm descended over her. Wildings had been a new hope, a new beginning for her and her family. Ended were her devastating fears of being forced one day to wed where neither her character nor her heart could dwell happily. Present was every possibility, so why did she hesitate now? What harm could come from a little midnight rambling at the edges of Rotherstone's property?

The decision arose from deep within her, from resources perhaps as yet untapped or unrealized, but she would open the gate tonight. First, however, she decided to consult her map again. She plucked it from the pocket of her cloak, and kneeling beside the lantern, studied the terrain just beyond the gate once more.

A sudden rustling behind her, from the direction of the walnut grove, sent a bolt of fear straight through her heart. She flipped around, landing on her bottom.

"Who's there?" she cried. The grove was heavy in shadow.

One of the family cats came trotting toward her. He was all black and barely visible against the mass of the walnut grove. He meowed and rubbed against her legs.

"You ridiculous creature!" she cried. "How you frightened me. Have you been following me and watching me this entire time? Well, I suggest you remain at Wildings. Rotherstone will not like that I am on his land, but if he should dislike cats in general, I have no doubt he will eat you alive!"

The purring sounds that returned to her, and the soft eyes of Frisky, gave no evidence that her warnings had been understood.

Evelina returned to studying the map, and once satisfied that she understood where it was she needed to go, she gained her feet, picked up the lantern and approached the gate. Though she was trembling, she would no longer permit her fears to deter her. With a single, hard, determined pull, she slowly opened the gate.

Creak, grate, groan. The poor old hinge had not seen oil in a very long time.

Passing through, Evelina sniffed. The air smelled very different but quite pleasant on Rotherstone's land. She closed the gate behind her.

Suddenly, a new fear arose. What if Rotherstone discovered her on his land? He was, by nature and by action, a hard man, unkind to his neighbors, reclusive, unknowable, reputed to be a hardened gamester who lived much of his life in London. Upon inheriting Blacklands some five years past, he had turned out two of his tenant farmers, a circumstance that had shocked the neighborhood. She had never even seen him in the eight months since she had taken up residence in Wildings Hall, just north of the village of Maybridge. Regardless, she knew enough of him to comprehend he would not like her moving about on his estate without his knowledge or permission.

Again she chose to ignore her fears. She traveled due east and was pleased that within thirty steps she came to a stream, for this, too, was on her map. Here the shrubbery grew surprisingly thin and a series of boulders tossed the water in a southerly direction with a cheerful bubbling sound. She realized this was the difference in the smell. The stream imparted freshness to the air.

She paused and looked about her, settling the lantern at her feet. The moon was high and the dark night sky full of brilliant stars. A lovely breeze soughed through the nearby beech trees, a sound so sweet and pleasant as to make her sigh.

Consulting her map again, she traced her path thus far with the tip of her finger. If she crossed the stream, there should be an old footpath not ten yards hence, one that would lead in a southeasterly direction toward an object described on the map as "ye olde well." The distance from the stream to the well did not seem overly great, and she thought it likely that given so much moonlight, she could reach it within a scant few minutes.

She did not deliberate long, but folded up her map and restored it to her pocket. She picked up the lantern and, making use of the flattest boulders, quickly crossed the stream. She found the old footpath easily, just as she thought she would, then hurried down it about a hundred yards until she reached a point at which the path diverged. This was on the map as well. The area was somewhat sloped, and a fallen log, aged by the weather, was blocking part of the upper path.

Exhilaration flooded her as she quickly took the lower path. Between this point and the avenue of Blacklands, the X marking the position of the treasure was firmly planted.

This trail was far less clear, and more than once she stopped, held the lantern close to the grass, trees and shrubbery, and peered all around her in order to reconnect with the path. She did this again and again, moving as swiftly as she could.

She came to a clearing and was a little startled to see a light, or rather several lights, visible from this new location. Her heart began to race. What was she seeing? Had someone espied her and was now marching in her direction? As she waited, however, she realized that the lights were stationary and that she must be looking at Blacklands, Lord Rotherstone's house.

She breathed a sigh of relief.

At the same time, she knew she must be closer than she had thought to the front avenue, which meant, if she had read the map correctly, that she had missed "ye olde well." A strong sense of disappointment overtook her. She realized she had been quite naively thinking that the process of locating each marker on the map would be accomplished in a trice. Where, she wondered, had she diverged from the proper route?

She lifted her lantern again, only this time she looked behind her at the path she had just traveled. There was nothing for it. She must retrace her steps and see if she had taken a wrong turn.

She returned slowly, investigating every line of the path with great care. She reached the place where the two paths converged, but so intense was her concentration that, until she heard the pronounced snapping of a dry branch, she had not the smallest notion that anyone had drawn near.

She whirled around, her heart once more in her throat, and lifted her lantern high. A veritable giant towered over her. She gasped, took three steps backward, then stopped. The giant jumped from the fallen log that partially blocked the upper path, and, though he had lost at least a foot of his height, he was uncommonly tall and quite broad shouldered.

"You do not look like the usual poacher," he began, his dark eyes scrutinizing her face carefully. "For one thing, such a person generally does not carry a lamp with him . . . or her. You also do not appear to be armed. Game is not your object, then?"

Evelina could not speak. His voice had stunned her, for it was as though a strong bow had been drawn across the deeper strings of a violoncello. Something within her warmed immediately to the sound. Who was this tall stranger whose eyes were as dark as night? He was unutterably handsome, and there was something in the set of his countenance that made her think of ancient warriors. Was it possible this man was Rotherstone? In response to his question, she merely shook her head.

"Are you mute?" he inquired in his gentleman's accents, his gaze never straying from her eyes.

"No," she said at last. "Not by half. Are you . . . that is, are you Rotherstone?"

His eyes narrowed. "No, I am not. I am at present visiting his lordship."

"I see," she responded, relieved.

"And yourself? Are you his neighbor, perchance? Lady Evelina Wesley?"

She did not know what prompted her to deny herself, but so she did. "I am a cousin to her."

"And your name?"

She paused and sought about for a simple appellation. "Arabella, er, Smith," she responded.

He bowed. "Well met, Miss Er . . . Smith. But I must ask, do you always take to trespassing when you visit your relatives, and that so late at night?"

She did not know why she had begun telling whiskers, but for some reason she could not keep from continuing. "Always," she responded with a challenging lift of her chin.

He watched her for a very long moment without saying anything. She had the strong impression that he was attempting in some manner to determine her disposition or perhaps her character.

He then closed the distance between them rather abruptly and took the lantern from her hand.

Though she was surprised, she found herself grateful, since the lamp had grown heavy. "How very thoughtful," she said. He then set the lantern on the grassy sward several feet away. She had thought he meant to carry the lantern and escort her back in the direction she had come, so she did not understand what he was doing.

"What are you about? I believe I must return to Wildings. I will have need of the . . . lantern. Why do you look at me so strangely?"

"You seem to be a very determined lady," he said. "I find the quality . . . intriguing."

Somehow she had the strong impression he was mocking her.

He returned to her, and, before she understood what he intended, he slid his arms about her waist and pulled her tightly against him.

"Sir!" she cried, aware suddenly that she did not even know his name. "Whatever are you doing? This . . . this is most shocking. I beg you will release me at once!"

Evelina could not have been more stunned. Her words, however, had little effect except to cause the gentleman to smile at her, but not a warm smile, rather the wicked expression of a man intent on devilment.

"I will not release you," he responded with roguish simplicity.

Astounded, she simply stared at him, her mouth remaining agape for a ridiculous length of time as she searched for the proper words with which to upbraid him for his quite horrid conduct.

His smile broadened. "Hardly a ladylike expression," he murmured.

She clamped her lips shut, but this proved to be a terrible mistake, for in the next moment, he was kissing her. Never would she have expected her adventure to culminate in this, a kiss from a stranger!

Her mind cried out to her that she ought to do battle with this wretched cur to force him to cease his ridiculous assault on her, but she was too stunned to do more than settle her hands on his arms.

He drew back.

"Release me," she whispered.

"Only if you tell me why you have trespassed on Rotherstone's lands."

"Very well," she responded. "Because I believe there is treasure buried in this vicinity."

"Treasure, indeed. Fascinating. So you paid a visit to Lady Evelina, who in turn told you of the local legends, and somehow you determined to explore my friend's lands and see if you might get the treasure for yourself?"

"Well, not precisely. I do not know if I intended to actually keep the treasure."

"How magnanimous of you," he returned sarcastically. "You know, I believe I have changed my mind. I shan't release you after all."

"How very ungentlemanly of you!" she cried. "I had heard that Rotherstone was not a man to be trusted. I see that his friends are cut from the same cloth."

"I will not answer for all his friends, but I suppose you could say I certainly am." Clearly, he was unmoved by her rebuke. If anything, his arms tightened about her waist.

This time, she struggled against him, twisting, pulling and kicking. But for all that, he held her firmly and laughed low in her ear.

"Unhand me, you brute!" she cried.

"Gently, Miss Ersmith, I beg you," he said in his mocking manner.

"And it is not Miss *Ersmith*, but Miss Smith, as you very well know!" she cried, shoving at his arms and twisting a little more.

"Then, gently, Miss Smith," he said, laughing again.

Finally, she grew weary. The hour was after all very late and she had been tramping about her property as well as Blacklands for over an hour. She stopped struggling.

"Much better," he murmured.

"Have your kiss then!" she cried defiantly.

"I shall, but what if I desire more than a kiss!"

She drew in a long, deep, sharp breath. "You would not dare!" she exclaimed.

"Whyever not? You are alone, unprotected, and you are trespassing. Although I might release you if you would at least pretend to enjoy my kisses."

She was seething. What a fine thing to have happen to her, even if he was wretchedly handsome and even if his voice did tend to tug at her heartstrings. "Oh, very well, if it will end this nonsense."

"There is nothing nonsensical about a proper kiss."

"You are nonsensical," she retorted.

He held her close and sighed. "I suppose I am." He leaned toward her and kissed her again.

This time she relaxed and let him take what he should not have taken. Her mind wandered first to how she would never trespass on Rotherstone's lands again. This led to why it was she had done so in the first place, and her mind became filled with thoughts of her map and Devil's Gate. All her earlier trepidation now seemed justified because of the stranger's embrace. Yet fear was not what possessed her now at all, for suddenly his kisses, which had grown sweetly tender, were not nearly so reprehensible. It would seem that all her initial feelings of exhilaration at having trespassed Rotherstone's woods were becoming entangled with the manner in which she was beginning to savor the stranger's kisses. She leaned into him, and his arms once more embraced her tightly.

She should not be enjoying his kisses, she thought, but so she was. She was drinking from a forbidden well and finding that never before had she felt so satisfied. She could not remember having experienced something so very sublime in her entire existence.

Without thinking, she slid her arms about his neck. The most passionate thought penetrated her mind that she wished she could remain in the stranger's arms forever.

The Earl of Rotherstone held the red-haired beauty, unable to comprehend what had prompted him either to lie about his identity or to kiss the lovely Miss Smith. He had reason to doubt that she was who she said she was, primarily because she had stumbled over her name. She had appeared wonderfully guilty in presenting herself as *Arabella, er, Smith,* and he had enjoyed teasing her about it.

Earlier, he had seen the dancing light of her lantern from the window of his library, a chamber that happened to be on the first floor of Blacklands Hall and which commanded a significant view of both the western and southern reaches of his property. His first inclination had been to set several of his servants in pursuit of the trespasser, but after a moment's pause he decided that giving chase himself might serve to relieve some of the boredom that had settled over his house during the past several weeks. Even the recent arrival of Sir Edgar Graffham, his good friend of many years, had not quite served to dispel a certain restlessness that had overtaken him.

Now, however, with such a damsel filling his arms so delightfully, these unhappy sentiments were wholly dispelled, and, as a faint moan slipped past her lips, he kissed her more deeply still. Was there anything so hopeful as a long, seductive kiss?

After a moment, he drew back slightly and gazed at her. The light of the lantern glanced off her red curls in a charming fashion but was insufficient to do more than cast her features in shadow. Nothing, however, could disguise the sparkle in her eyes. "You are quite beautiful, you know," he murmured.

She did not speak for a long moment, but merely gazed at him wonderingly. "How did you do that?" she asked.

"Do what?" He could not help but smile.

"Make me desire what I had no intention of desiring?"

This was very forthright speaking, and he found himself surprised. "Is that what I did?"

"As you must very well know," she returned archly.

"Well," he drawled, "you were a trifle reluctant at the outset. I suppose I felt challenged to change your mind."

She smiled and then laughed. "A *trifle* reluctant, sir?" she cried.

"I am given to understatement."

"So it would seem."

He was still holding her fast, yet she did not appear to wish to be released and he was quite content to continue holding her. "Shall I kiss you again, Miss Ersmith?"

"As I have said before, my name is Miss *Smith.*"

He shook his head. "I am not convinced, for I distinctly heard you say *Er*smith."

"I believe you are making sport of me."

"I am."

He felt her shiver.

"Are you cold?"

"Not by half," she whispered.

"Then why do you tremble?"

"'Tis your voice, sir." A sigh followed.

"Indeed?"

"Have you not been told as much before?" she asked.

He shook his head. His chest felt oddly tight, and he searched her eyes. Who was she really, he wondered? He had not yet become acquainted with Lady Evelina, though she had inherited Lord Bramber's estate some eight months past. He was not on easy terms with any of his neighbors, but if such a female were residing beneath Lady Evelina Wesley's roof, he thought it might serve him well to make himself known at Wildings Hall. "So, *Miss Smith*, shall I kiss you again?"

"Yes, if it pleases you."

"More than I can say," he responded.

He placed his lips over hers once more. How beautifully she kissed him in response. He felt her hands become laced about his neck again.

He was just about to draw back again and tease her a little more when a child's voice suddenly cried out, "Unhand my sister, you blackguard!" He released Miss Smith, but only in time to see a small blur race at him and strike him on the arm with what proved to be a wooden sword.

"William!" the lady cried out. "Oh, do stop at once, my love! You are quite mistaken—the gentleman was not hurting me!"

By the time she had finished speaking, Rotherstone had caught the boy up in one arm, taken his toy sword out of his hand and was now wrestling with a wildly wiggling child.

"Enough, William!" Miss Smith cried quite forcefully. "You must forgive him, sir. He is my brother and quite protective. Truly, Will, he did not hurt me, not in the least."

He finally desisted. Rotherstone held him over his hip as the boy, resting parallel to the ground, looked up at his sister. "But I saw him!" he cried. "He was holding you so tight you could not escape."

The lady's smile was both amused and yet painfully guilt stricken. "I know it may have appeared like that, my darling, but, indeed, the gentleman was, er, supporting me, for I had felt very faint of a sudden."

Rotherstone restrained a chuckle and, righting the boy, set him on his feet.

Young William craned his neck to look up at him. "Is this so?" he asked.

"Yes," Rotherstone returned gravely. "I came upon your sister and I could see at once that she had grown frightened, as lost as she was on Rotherstone's lands, for her face was the color of chalk. She tottered as I drew near. There was nothing for it but to hold her upright. Tell me, is she generally so cowhearted?"

William glanced at his sister. "N-no," he responded with an uneasy frown. "That is, I do not know. She has no fear of horses and will even take corners with her gig at a spanking pace. But I have never seen her lost at night. Perhaps she did lose heart."

"Miss Smith" knelt beside the lad, who Rotherstone thought could not have been more than six or seven. Slipping her arm about her brother, she said, "Dearest, do tell me why you are here. 'Tis very late, and you ought to be in your bed."

A smile, very much like the one he had seen on Miss Smith's lips, brought dimples to the boy's freckled complexion. "I saw you from my window when you crossed the lawn. I thought you might be having an adventure, and I wanted one, too."

"Were you near when I discovered the gate? In the walnut grove?"

He nodded.

"Was Frisky with you?"

He nodded again.

The lady smiled so warmly that something in Rotherstone's heart began to ache.

"I understand perfectly, but I do not think Nurse will be so forgiving, do you?"

"Of course not, for she is very old. But I left my bed stuffed with pillows, so she will not have known that I escaped."

He watched Miss Smith struggle within herself, and several times a new smile threatened her countenance. She was valiant to the end, however, and upon rising nodded seriously. "That was quite well done, and I hope it will serve, for I do not like the notion at all that Nurse should give you a dressing-down, and all for a little night's escapade." She then turned to Rotherstone. "We shall bid you good-night."

He retrieved the lantern and, handing it to her, addressed William. "Would you care to ride on my shoulder as far as the gate?"

William's expression brightened, but he wisely glanced at his sister for permission. She nodded, and without hesitation Rotherstone swept him up and perched him on his shoulder. "You may put your hand across my head for balance if you like," he suggested.

The boy did so, and after shifting his fingers away from his eyes, Rotherstone addressed Miss Smith. "Will you lead the way?"

"Of course."

Throughout the journey back to the stream, Evelina

took great care to keep Will from exposing their true identities. She spoke on any number of inconsequential subjects, such as the pleasures to be found in London and the current state of the July weather, so that he was kept from revealing inadvertently precisely who she was. But only as she passed through Devil's Gate did she realize she had not learned the gentleman's name. By the time she turned to inquire, he was gone.

Later, after having seen William to his bedchamber and tucked between the sheets, Evelina returned to her own room and slowly began dressing for bed. Her thoughts were full of Rotherstone's secretive guest, who had found her trespassing on Blacklands, who had taken her in his arms and who had kissed her oh-so-thoroughly. With her skirts falling in a heap at her feet, she pressed her hands to suddenly hot cheeks. The knowledge that in the end she had permitted so passionate a kiss suddenly dawned on her. Good heavens! How could she have allowed a complete stranger to kiss her so . . . well, so wondrously? What must he think of her?

Worse, however, was her fervent hope that she might meet him again very soon if for no other reason than to assure him that she was not in the habit of permitting such liberties to any gentleman, much less a perfect stranger.

She sat down on the bed, pondering the unusual nature of the entire adventure. Was there, for instance, a special meaning to the fact that only when she had worked up sufficient courage to open the gate and pass onto Rotherstone's estate, had such a wonderful kiss come to her?

But these thoughts were madness. There was no connection beyond the fact that in her wickedness at having trespassed onto Blacklands, Lord Rotherstone's guest had felt no need whatsoever to treat her like a lady. Her own iniquity brought that kiss down on her head, and she would be a fool to think of it in any other manner.

Her thoughts turned from the stranger to her pursuit of the smuggler's treasure. She wondered how it was she had not found the well that had been clearly marked on the map.

Picking up her gown and hanging it in her wardrobe, she moved to her cloak, which had been tossed across a chair near the door. Removing the map from the pocket, she unfolded it. She carefully avoided tearing the delicate and almost crumbling edges as she once more examined the crude drawing.

The well was clearly marked on the map, but she had seen nothing of it on Rotherstone's property. The map was dated 1652, so it was possible that an old well could have been torn down decades ago. She wondered if there was someone living who would know of an old well.

One thing for certain: She did not feel she could continue her search on her own. She needed Rotherstone's support, and because she was not acquainted with him, she would have to involve someone who was. Any of her neighbors would do. Besides, she wanted to include them. She had many friends among the local gentry, and she knew quite well, because of all the local legends about a smuggler's buried treasure, that many of them would take great delight in participating in a hunt for the treasure.

As she scrutinized the map, she could see that all the local estates were very well delineated. The major ones were marked, those belonging to Sir Alfred Monceaux, Mr. Crookhorn, Mr. Rewell, Mr. Fuller and Colonel Carfax.

There was only one thing to be done: She must bring all her neighbors together and present them with her extraordinary find. She debated whether or not to tell them that she had made an initial exploration of Rotherstone's property, but in the end thought she would only do so if she felt it necessary.

She would certainly not tell anyone of having kissed Rotherstone's handsome and quite wicked guest! Only, who was he, she wondered, and how soon would she meet him again?

Chapter Two

On the following day, Evelina sat in her drawing room surrounded by a significant representation of the local gentry. She had summoned them all for the purpose of sharing the ancient map with them and could scarcely contain her excitement.

From the time she had risen from her bed that morning, she had been aware of a change within herself. Ever since she had opened Devil's Gate and ventured onto Rotherstone's property, a sense of adventure had begun to envelop her like a warm cape on a blustery March day. Though she could not explain it precisely, she felt more like herself than she had on any day before.

Clutching her hands tightly together, she glanced from one visage to the next, noting the shock on each face, for she had just told them that she had discovered a most valuable clue as to the whereabouts of the smuggler's treasure, though she did not say precisely what.

"You believe you know where the treasure is buried?" Sir Alfred queried, his brow furrowed in disbelief. "I am all astonishment. Where? How did you come by such knowledge?"

"As to the location," she responded, "the treasure appears to be buried somewhere on Blacklands."

The expressions of those present turned to despair. She thought she understood the nature of the combined hopelessness and said, "But surely if there was sufficient proof, Lord Rotherstone would support our efforts to find the treasure."

Lady Monceaux said, "There has always been speculation that Blacklands is the location of the treasure. Every tale I have ever heard suggests as much. But if you think our neighbor is in the least disposed to be of use to us, then you have not been listening to our opinions of his, well, his obnoxiousness!"

Evelina was surprised. In general, Lady Monceaux did not speak so heatedly on any subject.

"What is your opinion, Sir Alfred?" Evelina asked. "Do you think he will be completely disinclined to be of use to us?"

He shook his head. "He is an impossible man."

"Is there no one here who can give me hope?" she asked, half-smiling as she glanced round the group.

George Fuller snorted. "He would help us just as swiftly as he would swim to France on the next tide."

Annabelle Rewell, quite shatter-brained, sighed heavily. "He has the broadest pair of shoulders in three counties."

Her brother, Stephen Rewell, younger by a year, gave her a hard nudge. "What a ninnyhammer you are!"

Their father, Henry Rewell, interjected, "Enough, the pair of you!" He then addressed Evelina. "Rotherstone is unfortunately a very hard man. I wish I could offer you some encouragement, some hope, but I cannot. You would have better luck persuading an eel."

Evelina pondered Rotherstone for a moment. She realized he was an earl and therefore used to traveling in the first circles. As the daughter of an earl herself, she fully understood the impact such an exalted rank could have on any setting. What she could not understand, however, was why Rotherstone had expressed so much hostility toward his neighbors, or why he had shunned their society generally.

Her enthusiasm began to wane.

Mary Ambers shuddered. "I hope none of you are expecting me to ask him for his assistance, for I shan't do it. The last time I requested a donation for the orphanage, he nearly bit my head off."

"I daresay he was not so polite as that, either," James Crookhorn suggested.

"Well, he did ask what he had to do with a lot of useless brats!"

A murmur of disapprobation flowed about the disenchanted neighbors.

Oh, dear, Evelina thought. *This is not at all a propitious beginning.* "But he should be approached. Would not you all agree as much?"

Faint shrugs and grimaces returned to her.

"The task must fall to someone, I suppose," Lady Monceaux murmured.

"I think you have interjected your opinions quite enough," Sir Alfred said, addressing his wife.

"Yes, yes, of course," she returned.

Evelina was irritated by this rebuke and watched as Lady Monceaux tightened her lips, a faint blush rising on her cheeks. She had been in company with Sir Alfred and his wife several times since taking up residence at Wildings, and it seemed to her that the baronet was not always kind to his spouse.

Sir Alfred was the acknowledged leader of the local gentry. He was much older than everyone else present, being near fifty. His black hair was streaked with silver, and many years of hunting out of doors had lent a weathered appearance to his countenance. His jowls sagged a trifle over what she had always thought was a mulish jaw.

"I am inclined to think," Evelina said, addressing him,

"that you ought to be the one to speak with Lord Rotherstone. Yours is the largest consequence of our small party. Surely he would give you an audience were you to request one."

"You think so?" he queried, clearly unconvinced. "Let me remind you that the last time I tipped my hat to him at the Bull in Maybridge, he lifted a brow and stared at me as though I had just sneezed on his best coat."

With that, Colonel Willoughby Carfax, cousin to Lord Rotherstone, laughed heartily. He was of an age with the earl and had attended Oxford with him, but Evelina already knew enough of their history not to bother placing this particular obligation on him. "Do not even ask," he said, smiling. "Everyone here knows that my cousin has taken an incomprehensible dislike of me."

Evelina smiled in some sympathy upon the colonel. He was a handsome man of perhaps two or three and thirty years and possessed one of the most generous dispositions she had ever encountered. Though she had only known the Earl of Rotherstone by way of his reputation, his treatment of one of his closest relations certainly did him no honor at all.

She could only wonder, however, just how she was to gain Rotherstone's cooperation. She had more than once determined to seek him out herself but had quailed time and again by recalling all the accounts she had heard of him. He was, if the general report of him was to be believed, a wholly unapproachable man.

Mrs. Rewell sighed, drawing all attention to her. She was a small, rather spiritless woman who had never had even the weakest command over her offspring. "He was not always so very bad," she said, her blue eyes drooping sadly. "I recall quite well that before Miss Punnett broke off her engagement with him, he was a friendly sort of young man. He is very much changed from that time, and now his character seems quite fixed. I only wish he had sold off his property when his father died; then we might have secured a better neighbor, certainly one more obliging, who would be interested in bettering our community."

"That is my point, exactly, Mrs. Rewell," Evelina said. "We do not know whether he would be disinterested or not, and I daresay we shall never know if we do not make a push."

"Perhaps you had best speak to him, then," Mr. Rewell suggested. "He does not know you, except through the idle gossip of servants, and he might be persuaded by someone younger and, dare I say, quite pretty."

Evelina thought this ridiculous in the extreme. "If Miss Ambers, who is by far the prettiest lady in the entire vale, could not persuade him to give a tuppence to a few starving children, I doubt he would be moved in the least by my request that he permit his neighbors to invade his lands."

"Only tell us," the colonel said, "why it is you are so intent on making a push in the first place. You seem quite confident of success. What is it you have discovered that you have not yet told us?"

Evelina could not help but smile. The moment had come for which she had been waiting from the time the entire group had assembled. "Last night, I happened to be in one of the attics used for storage, sorting through trunks. I had found a very old bottle of brandy, which told me that the contents of this attic were quite old indeed, and that the attic itself belonged to the original structure."

"Brandy, you say?" George Fuller interjected, sitting up a little straighter in his seat.

Evelina smiled but shook her head as she rose to her feet. "Mr. Fuller, it is not yet two in the afternoon."

Mr. Fuller pretended to be mystified. "What is your meaning? I do not take your meaning."

"And what a ridiculous man you are," she cried.

Everyone laughed, including Mr. Fuller, who, at nearly thirty and giving great evidence of becoming a confirmed bachelor, showed on most occasions a predilection for strong drink.

Miss Ambers sat forward in her seat. "But what is it, Lady Evelina? What did you find in the attics? Was it something in one of the trunks?"

"As it happens, I did not find this clue in the trunk. Through an unhappy accident, I discovered that the floor is quite rotten in several places. Merely walking from one trunk to the next caused my foot to break through several boards—no, I was not in the least injured—and that was when I found this."

She moved to the table nearest the entrance hall in order to retrieve the map that she had rolled up in a length of dark blue velvet. Taking up a place near the hearth, she slowly unveiled the map. Every pair of eyes was fixed on the document, and more than one brow rose in some interest.

"It is a map," Miss Rewell stated, her eyes wide.

"Any dolt might see as much," her brother cried, much disgusted. "But what is it a map of?"

Evelina felt her heart begin to race. "It is a very old map of our neighborhood," she returned. "Indeed, the date is set at 1652."

A round of faint murmurs and gasps passed through the drawing room.

She continued, "Many of you have told me about the smuggling traffic along both coasts lining the English Channel that began centuries ago. As many of you know, one of these notorious smugglers was supposed to have buried a portion of his treasure somewhere betwixt

Summersfield to the north and Studdingly to the south."
She gestured to these places as indicated on the map, each
with a large scrolled S. "I believe this to be a genuine map
indicating the exact location of the treasure."

Another outbreak of murmuring and gasping traveled
about the assembled guests.

Mary Ambers left her seat at once and came to peer
closely at the thin, yellowed parchment. Mrs. Huggett,
her companion, joined her.

Mary Ambers was a beautiful young woman who
resided in Victory Cottage in the village of Maybridge.
She had taken up residence there less than a year prior
with her much older cousin, Mrs. Huggett, known to be
a widow. Both ladies were well received in local society
and were invited everywhere. Mrs. Huggett was a sensible, genteel but impoverished woman with a cheerful
countenance.

"Do but look, Eugenia," Miss Ambers began, "even
Maybridge is indicated."

"Mm," Mrs. Huggett responded quietly.

As Miss Ambers touched the map very lightly, Evelina
said, "Yes, all of you please have a look and give me your
general impressions and opinions. It is possible, after all,
that I may be mistaken."

As one, the remainder of the group left their seats and
stations and converged on the map. A chattering
erupted that did not cease until Colonel Carfax, his
complexion rather heightened, suggested that the map
be placed on a table for better viewing. Since this notion
was approved of at once, Evelina took the parchment,
along with the length of velvet, and returned it to the
large table near the entrance. She weighted each corner
with the nearest objects she could find, including a small
ormolu clock and a green rock Will had dug up from

the garden in recent weeks. Once more the crowd gathered round.

The next hour was spent by one and all scrutinizing Evelina's find. A variety of opinions were expressed concerning the authenticity of the map, but most agreed it had to be genuine since the state of the paper itself was so very fragile.

Stephen Rewell said, "These must be riddles of a sort, and there are five of them. Does anyone have a notion as to what they might mean?"

The entire group fell silent, all eyes intent on the map.

Miss Ambers said, "I believe there are six."

"I thought as much at first," Mr. Rewell said, "But one of them is repeated. It appears at both the top and the bottom of the map."

"So it does," Miss Ambers cried. She then read that particular riddle aloud. "'Time is lost, a smuggler's weary end, the world is upside down, walls that will not mend.'"

Mr. Crookhorn said, "Perhaps he was referring to that period of time when the smugglers were being hunted. His world may have been ending, nothing known or certain, upside down in fact."

"Perhaps," Evelina said. "I have looked at all of them again and again, but I cannot really make sense of them, except the one that begins with 'Devil's Gate,' which would again support the long-held tradition that the treasure is buried somewhere on Blacklands."

"You refer to this riddle," Miss Rewell said. "'Devil's Gate wat opens, black the land will be, down a path, a treasure ye will see.'" She sighed, "I wonder what is in the treasure."

Mr. Fuller touched the riddle on the east side of the map. "Perhaps this is a clue. 'Cross the stones, cross one to dare, pearl and gold within, small and rare.' Pearls and gold perhaps."

"Oh," she murmured, sounding disappointed. "I was hoping for rubies and diamonds and emeralds."

"What a sapscull you are!" her brother cried.

Evelina tapped the riddle to the southwest. "'*Ye olde well, draws water deep, of ale and mead, made honey-sweet.*' Would anyone know if there is a well, or used to be a well, on the southwest portion of Rotherstone's property?"

No one had an answer for her.

Lady Monceaux said, "But this last one, here," she pointed to the northwest, "I believe may refer to a grave-yard. '*Some stones flat, others tall, a bridge in death, to any wat fall.*'"

"That is ridiculous," Sir Alfred said, directing a scathing look at his wife. "I believe it refers to a bridge. You may fall from a bridge, for instance, and perish. You could hardly be hurt falling from a gravestone."

"I was venturing an opinion only," his wife said.

Sir Alfred whispered, "It might be best to keep your opinions to yourself."

Lady Monceaux again said nothing, and Evelina wished she could reprove Sir Alfred for his unkindness. However, nothing could be gained by doing so in the midst of a large group of people, so she asked for more ideas concerning the possible meanings to any of the riddles.

What evolved from this was a lengthy debate, but in the end nothing was decided as to a final meaning for them except the one making very specific reference to "black" and "land."

"It is no wonder," Sir Alfred ventured after a time, "that you were so adamant about involving Rotherstone. If this map is authentic, there simply cannot be another opinion as to where the treasure is buried. Each of our estates is clearly marked." Using his finger, he gestured first to Rotherstone's home. "Blacklands, of course, and here is my home, Pashley Court, and in the northeast, Slyes Manor," at which time he nodded to Mr. Crookhorn. "Carfax's estate, Darwell Lodge, is here south of Blacklands, and to the west, Fuller's Ewehurst Manor. And of course, marching along the westerly borders of Blacklands is Wildings. All the major streams, as well as the River Rother, are marked, and I must say, if the treasure was not to be found on Blacklands, then I would be greatly shocked indeed. Everything seems so clearly marked and recognizable."

"Just so," Evelina said, "which is why one of you must take this obligation on yourself to seek an audience with Lord Rotherstone and somehow gain his cooperation."

The excitement of the group abated like a hot-air balloon deflating all at once. Mary Ambers returned to her seat not far from the table. Mrs. Huggett followed suit. Annabelle Rewell also sat down, though her brother moved to stare out the window. Sir Alfred cleared his throat and slung his hands behind his back, his brow marred by a deep furrow. His wife continued to peer at the map, as did George Fuller and James Crookhorn. Colonel Carfax seemed most affected and began marching to and fro from the window to the table and back again.

Evelina glanced from one unhappy visage to the next and found herself somewhat appalled. "How can one man have treated you all so badly, and without the smallest consequence to himself?"

"Except that he is invited nowhere," Mrs. Rewell said, glancing at Evelina and sighing in her melancholy manner. "For some that is a very great consequence."

Evelina took up her seat near the fireplace, her thoughts fixed on a man she had never met. She could not imagine what had happened in the course of Rotherstone's life that he would so completely have exiled

himself from all good society. Rumors among the tradesmen in Maybridge indicated that he was working very
hard to restore Blacklands to its original fine, elegant condition, a telling circumstance in its own right. Evelina
believed it spoke well of him that he should be conscien-
tious where his property was concerned. However, even
Sir Alfred said he thought it all a hum. Nothing known of
Rotherstone's character indicated to the smallest degree
that he would have integrity toward his inheritance. Why
would a man who treated his neighbors so abominably
have the smallest capacity to be a proper husbandman of
his lands? Had he not ejected two families from their
farms? Was he not a gamester?

Her own brother, the Earl of Chelwood, was of a similar
ilk, as had been her father in his time, neither giving a fig
for what had at one time been a splendid estate until all
that was left was but a shell of a house. Even much of the
furnishings had been sold off to pay gaming debts.

Mrs. Huggett said, "I think it a good thing he does not
go about in society. I heard recently from Mr. Fuller that
he is known to take frequent trips to London in order
visit the East End gaming establishments."

Evelina knew perfectly well the meaning of Mrs.
Huggett's statement. The places she spoke of were
known in more vulgar usage as the East End Hells. Both
her father and Robert were known to have lost much of
the family's fortune there.

"Is this true, Mr. Fuller?" she inquired.

Mr. Fuller turned toward her. "I fear it is well known
he enjoys gaming more than most."

Evelina repressed a heavy sigh. Because of her father
and brother, she knew only too well how insular the habit
of gaming caused a man, or even a woman, to become. If
it was true that Rotherstone was just such a man, then she
believed she understood why his neighbors had grown to

dislike him so very much. He had no interests but his own at heart and probably never would.

Already it seemed to her that in every sense Lord Rotherstone was going to be difficult.

Her thoughts were drawn quite naturally to the stranger who had found her trespassing last night and who had kissed her. Although he had been a quite determined gentleman, stubborn in his way, he had also proved himself to be a kind, thoughtful person. He could have parted company with them at the fallen log. Instead, he had carried William on his shoulder as though he had been a bag of feathers instead of a sturdy lad of seven, escorting them both back to Devil's Gate. She admitted to herself that she had liked this man very much. She had even approved of him, which made her wonder just how a man she thought well of could also be a friend to Rotherstone. Regardless, she truly wished that she might have an opportunity to know him better.

"I was given to understand," she said, once more addressing the company, "that Lord Rotherstone presently has a guest at his house. Does anyone perchance know his name?"

"A guest?" Lady Monceaux queried, raising herself upright from the map. "I had not heard that anyone had come recently to Blacklands."

"Nor I," Mrs. Rewell said. "Although I learned yesterday from the baker that Sir Edgar Graffham would be joining him quite soon but was not expected for a day or so."

"Sir Edgar is coming to Blacklands?" Miss Ambers queried.

So Rotherstone was to have a guest. Evelina realized that Sir Edgar Graffham must have arrived earlier than expected, something that would not at all be unusual. Surely he was the gentleman she had kissed last night.

She turned to Miss Ambers and was surprised to see

that her complexion had paled a trifle. "Are you acquainted with him?" she asked.

"A little," she responded.

Evelina chanced to glance about the party and saw
that more than one countenance had grown uneasy. She
wondered if Miss Ambers was perhaps a little better acquainted with Sir Edgar than what she had indicated.

So many questions, she thought, even about Sir Edgar.
The sense that she had just stumbled into a quagmire took
hold of her. Well, Sir Edgar would not have been the first
gentleman to end an attachment. How that should affect
her now, she was not certain. What she did know was that
she still wished very much to see him again.

Her heart fluttered suddenly in her breast. Whatever
his former connection to Miss Ambers, last night he had
kissed a *Miss Smith*. Sir Edgar Graffham. How wonderful
it was to have a name to attach to such a handsome
countenance, to so resonant a voice and to so sweet a
pair of lips.

She gave herself a quick mental shake. It would hardly
do to be exposing the true nature of her feelings to any
of her neighbors. After all, Sir Edgar had kissed her,
nothing more, and it was likely that his association with
Rotherstone would make it impossible for her to see him
during the remainder of his visit. Unless . . .

There was before her a perfect way to insinuate herself
into Rotherstone's house, and she concocted her plan
swiftly. Oh dear, when was it she had become so conniv-
ing?

"I suppose there is nothing for it," she stated, her heart
now beating strongly in her breast. "I must call upon
Rotherstone myself." How audacious! She could not credit
she was being so very brazen, and that with no one the
wiser as to her true motives. As much as she would like to

see the map's secrets revealed, in this moment she was thinking only of meeting Sir Edgar again.

All eyes were now turned upon her, and given the guilt of her thoughts she felt a blush climb her cheeks. Knowing that she would soon reveal herself if she did not divert this unwelcome attention, she rose to her feet and crossed swiftly to the map. "After all, do but look at this map! It is old and crumbling, and therefore it must be genuine. It gives a precise location to the buried treasure. Who could fail to be intrigued by such possibilities?"

Several of her neighbors intoned as one, "Rotherstone."

On the following morning, just past ten o'clock, Evelina stood in the doorway of Rotherstone's drawing room and glanced about. She was stunned at the sight before her. Because of all that her neighbors had said about Rotherstone, she had imagined that his house would reflect his unhappy, ungenerous character. At the very least, she expected austerity and meanness in the nature of the décor, or perhaps no furnishings whatsoever given his purported addiction to gaming. Instead, she did not know when she had been in so rich and warm a chamber.

With the butler's footsteps echoing down the hall, she took a few tentative steps into the long receiving room. The wainscoting was a beautiful dark mahogany. A chair near the fireplace appeared to have been covered in buckskin. The adjacent sofa of burgundy velvet surprised her completely. Other chairs about the chamber were in gold or brown patterned silks. An extremely large vase of flowers had been placed on a round, inlaid table near the entrance to the chamber.

A panel of windows overlooked an extensive lawn to the south and the west and, to the extreme west, a steep rise of hillside that a month or so earlier must have bloomed with a fine display of pink and purple rhododendrons, since a few of the blossoms yet remained. Interspersed

were blackthorn shrubs and elm trees. The latter were
now fully leafed, and the vista was so beautiful she found
herself drawn to the window, where lovely summer sun-
light poured over her. The faint warmth was nearly as
delightful as the sight of black swans strolling across the
lawn, heading toward a pooled stream and island in between.

None of what she beheld was what she had come to
expect from the general reports she had heard of
Rotherstone. How could so much beauty reside at
Blacklands when the owner was a hard, miserly man?
She was utterly mystified. Was he really the tyrant and
gamester his reputation suggested?

She was drawn from her reverie quite suddenly by the
sound of whistling coming from the direction of the entrance hall. Could this be Rotherstone, she wondered,
sounding so cheerful as he came to meet her? If she were
hearing Rotherstone, this would be a second occasion
within the space of a few minutes that had shocked her.

She turned and waited, swinging her reticule ner-
vously as it dangled from her wrist. She could hear his
steps now. What would he say to her? Would she be able
to convince him to allow his neighbors onto his lands?
Her heart began to thrum in fearful anticipation. How
was she ever to persuade such a man?

A gentleman appeared in the doorway, still whistling,
his hands thrust deeply into the pockets of his coat. This
must be Rotherstone, she thought, only never in a hundred years would she have pictured him with curly blond
hair and of rather slight proportions. She recalled
Annabelle Rewell saying only yesterday that he had the
broadest shoulders in three counties. The only way in
which this gentleman could be said to be in possession
of such shoulders was in Miss Rewell's dreams. He was
fearful handsome, however, so she could only suppose

that Miss Rewell had a *tendre* for him and in her fancies endowed him with attributes he did not truly possess.

She frowned suddenly. There was nothing particularly intimidating about this gentleman. Perhaps he was not Rotherstone after all. Perhaps another guest had arrived at Blacklands in addition to Sir Edgar.

Realizing that her position so far away from the entrance to the chamber had not allowed the gentleman to perceive her presence, she took a step toward him and cleared her throat.

He turned startled blue eyes upon her. "I say!" he cried. "You gave me a fright! I did not know anyone was here."

"I arrived but a handful of minutes ago. I am here to see Rotherstone."

"Ah," he murmured, a crooked smile twisting his lips. "I feel obligated to warn you that he does not like to be disturbed before eleven."

She could not resist saying, "I have been given to understand that he does not like to be disturbed at any hour of the day."

The gentleman issued a crack of laughter and crossed the room to her. "I am Graffham, Sir Edgar Graffham."

Evelina realized she had been right: this man was not Rotherstone. "Lady Evelina Wesley," she said. She dropped a small curtsy, inclining her head to him at the same time. He in turn offered a practiced bow.

She realized she was feeling a quite profound disappointment. She had since yesterday afternoon so nurtured the notion that Sir Edgar was the gentleman who had kissed her that to learn he was not the man was quite lowering. Of course, the next question that rose to mind caused her stomach to draw up in a knot. Who, then, was the man who had kissed her? He was not Rotherstone. The stranger had denied such an identity, and he had spoken as if he was only a guest at Blacklands. She could not therefore resist asking, "Tell me, are you one of several guests his lordship is presently entertaining? I realize the question must seem impertinent, but I have a very particular reason for asking."

"And I have no disinclination to give you answer. To my knowledge, I am the only guest at present."

Evelina did not understand, not in the least.

"Are you absolutely certain?"

"Yes, I am."

"Well, it is all very odd," she murmured, not meeting his gaze. She found she was twirling her reticule again and desisted the moment he glanced at the spinning, beaded object.

"Odd? In what way?"

Evelina felt utterly disinclined to enter into a subject that must force her to admit to having been on Rotherstone's property at a very indiscreet hour of the night two nights past. She shook her head. "It does not signify in the least," she responded with a smile. "Now, tell me, Sir Edgar, just how long have you known his lordship?"

Rotherstone attempted to tidy several folds of his neckcloth but was not wholly successful. Generally, he enjoyed the ritual of preparing a perfected *trone d'amour*, but at the moment the sanctitude of his morning ablutions had been utterly desecrated. Instead, his irritation at the presence of his butler, still awaiting an answer as to whether or not he would receive Lady Evelina Wesley, had completely destroyed whatever pleasure he had been experiencing in the tying of his cravat.

As he tucked, pinched and pulled on the fine white linen, therefore, his ire rose. What the deuce did the lady mean by calling upon him at such an hour! What the deuce did she mean by calling upon him at all? Had she no sense of propriety, no common courtesy? He had no wish to see her or any of his worthless neighbors, and he certainly had no respect for a female who would call upon a bachelor at all, much less without an invitation. The fact that a maid had not accompanied her furthered his unhappy opinion of his newest neighbor.

"Shall I tell her you are not at home, my lord?" his butler called across the lofty chamber.

"Yes!" he shot back. "No! That is, hold a moment, if you please."

"Of course, m'lord," was the trained response.

Rotherstone paused for a long moment, considering not so much Lady Evelina but the young woman presently visiting in her home.

Since his adventure with Miss Smith of two nights ago, his mind had frequently been caught up in the memory of the shared kiss. What a surprise that kiss had been, when she had initially struggled against his advances. Never would he have expected so incensed a young woman to give herself a few minutes later so thoroughly to his embraces. Yes, she had surprised him.

Even more so, however, she had become fixed in his head. Yesterday, for instance, he had thought of her with such frequency that he had actually been tempted to call at Wildings in order to see her again.

"And Lady Evelina did not have a companion with her, a friend perhaps, when you admitted her to the house?" he inquired. He began unwinding the now ruined neckcloth from about his neck.

His butler cleared his throat. "No, m'lord."

He became suspicious suddenly, and his suspicions afforded him a great deal of aggravation. Good God, what if his delectable Miss Smith proved in truth to be Lady Evelina?

"Tell me, Hardwick, what color was her hair?"

"M'lord?" his servant inquired, clearly surprised by the question.

He turned to look at Hardwick. "Her hair, was it red?"

Hardwick cleared his throat again. "I beg your pardon, m'lord, but I fear I cannot say. It might have red, perhaps brown. She is wearing a bonnet, and I was not attentive to her appearance."

"Yes, of course," he mumbled.

He attempted another neckcloth but found he was far too agitated to achieve an adequate result.

There was an art to the careful arranging of a cravat. In the course of his career, he had perfected the Mathematical and the Mailcoach, the latter of which he had worn exclusively in his salad days. The Rothersfall, his own particular creation, he had abandoned a year ago but knew it was still aped by the younger set. In recent times he had favored the *trone d'amour*. Today, it would seem, he would be fortunate if he achieved even a modest rendition of any of them.

In the end, as aggravated as he was, he chose another neckcloth and made a simple bow with two or three folds.

"You may go, Hardwick. I shall receive the lady."

Without another word to either his shocked valet or his butler, he shrugged on his waistcoat and coat and fairly stomped from the chamber.

The distance from his bedchamber to the drawing room was considerable, since Blacklands was a long, rambling Elizabethan mansion. As he made his way, his thoughts turned to his neighbors. He could never think of them without his temper pounding at the top of his head. They had served him sufficiently ill to be barred from his home forever. That the latest to take up residence must now plague him only served to inflame his temper, for he could not help but suspect she had come to represent their community.

Arriving at the threshold of the drawing room, the harsh words he was about to speak fell backward into his throat, for there, seated opposite Sir Edgar and playing at piquet with him, was the young woman he had kissed only two nights past. She was laughing, a smile so warm and friendly suffusing a countenance so beautiful he felt all his ire melt away like frost beneath a strong sunshine. Just as he had told a whisker about his identity, so had Lady Evelina. How strange to think that his first encounter with his newest neighbor had involved two lies and a quite passionate kiss. She was as beautiful as he remembered. She was gowned in a charming dark green bonnet, a matching riding habit and wore fine leather gloves. Tucked into the wrist of her right was a cluster of yellow daisies.

"Lady Evelina," he called to her, stepping into the room. "Or should I say, Miss Ersmith?"

She rose quickly to her feet, a sudden blush suffusing each cheek.

Sir Edgar rose as well. "Good God, Gage!" his friend cried out. "What did you do to your neckcloth?"

Lord Rotherstone glanced apace at his friend, then quickly reverted his attention to the lady whose expression of astonishment still had possession of every lovely feature. A gasp parted her lips. Faith, but she was a beautiful woman, exquisite in every perfect feature, but what the deuce was the matter with the chit that she would ignore society's dictums and call on him in this wholly improprietous manner?

"You . . . *you* are Rotherstone?" she asked.

"The very one," he said.

"Then I am the greatest simpleton in all of Christendom."

Chapter Three

Rotherstone was amused that she would speak of being a simpleton. "I shall not argue with you," he said, without the smallest sympathy. He then bowed as was expected.

She responded with a slight curtsy and a proper bowing of her head as well.

"I suppose you have come to ask something of me," he stated.

She blinked once. "I have," she responded succinctly.

Well, he would give her that; she did not simper or demur. He could appreciate her direct, open manner. On the other hand, his suspicions were wholly confirmed by her simple admission. She wanted something from him, just as did most of the eager ladies of his acquaintance.

A familiar boredom, laced with his former irritation, descended on him. He had known dozens of young ladies just like the one before him—confident, pretty and, to varying degrees, avaricious. Her presence on his land last night became painfully obvious. He had little doubt that in some secret place in her heart she one day desired to be the countess of Rotherstone and mistress of Blacklands.

"But I am being remiss," he stated coolly. "Will you not sit down?" He ignored Sir Edgar's rather fierce scowl.

His friend hurried to Lady Evelina's side, taking her

elbow and guiding her in the direction of the sofa. "Yes, do be seated, and I beg you will not pay the smallest heed to Rotherstone's ill humors. He is not himself at this hour of the day." He glared at him anew.

She took up a seat on the sofa, settling her hands primly on her lap. She was still frowning. He could not imagine what thoughts had taken hold of her mind, but he sincerely hoped she was regretting her decision to call on him today. Perhaps in the future she would refrain from indulging whatever impulse had brought her to Blacklands.

He followed Sir Edgar, taking up a seat opposite them both, for his friend, clearly delighted with Lady Evelina's company, chose to settle beside her on the same sofa.

"And what is it you would ask of me, I wonder?" He purposefully lifted an imperious brow, an expression he used for just such audiences as this, when he wished to dampen pretension in every form.

Evelina regarded Rotherstone in some bewilderment. So many thoughts rampaged through her head that she hardly knew which to address first. Of course, she was still not in the smallest degree used to the notion that the man she had kissed last night had turned out to be the enemy of every inhabitant of this part of Kent. From the moment he had made his presence known in the drawing room, she had been beset by the worst disappointment. How much better if Sir Edgar had been Rotherstone! Instead, all the very private hopes that last night's extraordinary kiss had raised in her breast were completely and utterly shattered. She could no more hope for even the smallest romantic entanglement with a man of Rotherstone's stamp than she could with a fish.

She had understood his character nearly from the day of her arrival at Wildings, since anyone she questioned on the subject of her neighbor gave a very poor account of the hard, reclusive earl who had a horrid love of gaming. His kisses may have been as sweet as honey, but there was nothing good in the man now seated opposite her, staring at her as though he wished she would take herself off to the farthest reaches of the kingdom.

All these thoughts and considerations, however, still vied for position in her mind with the undeniable truth that the moment his voice had drawn her gaze from Sir Edgar, she had experienced the worst presentiment that she had already tumbled in love with him. How had this happened? If only she had not been held so firmly in his arms two nights past, and if only he had not carried William on his shoulder the entire distance back to the border between Wildings and Blacklands. And if only he did not look so dashing in daylight, even if his neckcloth looked quite odd! Despite the unusual appearance of the ill-tied cravat, she admitted to herself that he was quite possibly the handsomest man she had ever before seen, and her experience had been sufficiently wide and varied to have met many who approached Adonis in beauty.

His hair was thick, black and wavy. His cheekbones were high and strong, matched by a powerful jawline that presently appeared quite stubborn. His eyes were nearly as dark as his hair, and as he met her gaze, she had a powerful sensation that he was peering into the deepest recesses of her mind. This was ridiculous, of course, but even so, a sudden spate of gooseflesh raced down her neck.

"Do not tell me," he said, interrupting her reveries, "that you have suddenly grown shy of me?"

Evelina gave herself a strong mental shake. She had been silent far too long and responded firmly, "Not in the least. I am merely trying to make you out."

"Hence the frown and pouting lips."

"Yes, I suppose so. I do not mean to be uncivil. It is merely that I did not expect you to be Rotherstone. After all, you told me a whisker the other night, very boldly, too, I might add."

"I heard one as well, *Miss Ersmith.*"

"You confound me," Sir Edgar cried, addressing Rotherstone. "Why do you speak of her as Miss Ersmith, and how is it you have already met?"

"As it happens, Lady Evelina wandered quite by accident onto my lands, not last night but the night before, and I chanced upon her."

"Indeed?" he cried. "A rather marvelous circumstance, I think."

"It was. But for reasons unknown to me still, she presented herself as a Miss Ersmith."

"Indeed," Sir Edgar said. "Well, this is rather curious."

Evelina disliked immensely the self-satisfied expression on his lordship's face. She could not imagine why he was so irritated by her visit, particularly when he had kissed her so warmly not so very long ago. The two circumstances made no sense to her in the least. Perhaps he was addled, dicked in the nob as her next-youngest brother, Harry, was wont to say. Somehow these thoughts elevated her spirits and she felt better able to proceed with her purpose in coming to Blacklands in the first place.

"I suppose I was merely having a bit of fun," she explained, though she did not smile. "But that is not of the least consequence. As to why I am here today—" she began.

"I am intrigued beyond words," Rotherstone said, the sardonic tone of his voice not lost on her.

"As it happens, I have come on a matter of some import, which, as it again happens, pertains to my having trespassed upon your lands two nights past. I was not there by accident."

"As you said at the time." He appeared at his most bored, save that his nostrils flared. "I believe you told me you were hunting for buried treasure."

"Yes, you have remembered correctly, and if I recall our conversation equally as well, you spoke of the local legends, so I must conclude that you are aware of them."

His expression grew slightly arrested, and she felt hopeful. "I am," he said, "but only a trifle."

Despite Rotherstone's hostile attitude, her heart began to hum with excitement, and she could not help but smile. "Well, as it happens, I have found a map which I believe to be quite genuine."

"You have!" Sir Edgar cried. "Do you mean one that indicates where the treasure is buried?"

"Yes, precisely so!" she responded enthusiastically.

"By Jove, but this is famous!"

"Sir Edgar," Rotherstone interjected, a hard light in his eye. "If you please."

The baronet rose hastily to his feet. "Tell me you do not mean to be mulish about this, Gage. She has a map, and even I have grown sufficiently familiar with the tales abounding in your neighborhood to know of its significance."

"That is hardly the issue."

"Then what is?" Evelina asked firmly.

Rotherstone narrowed his eyes. "That I strongly suspect you intend to incommode me with the object of the map, which no doubt places the treasure somewhere on Blacklands. But mark my words, my lady, I have no intention of digging up even a square inch of my property merely to serve your curiosity or that of my neighbors. Besides, I rather suppose that you have in some manner been wretchedly humbugged!"

Evelina could not help but glance at Sir Edgar. For one thing, she wanted to see just how he had responded to his friend's outburst. But she also wanted to determine if she might have an ally in him. Sir Edgar, however, had returned to the table where they had been playing piquet. He was now placing the cards in a neat stack, his back to both of them. It would seem she must fend for herself.

Turning to Rotherstone, she asked, "Will you not at least discuss the matter with me?"

"No," he responded.

"Do you even care to look at the map? I have brought it with me."

"I have not the smallest interest."

"Then there is nothing I can say or do to persuade you on any score?"

"Nothing."

Evelina regarded him frankly for a long moment. She was not in the least deterred, though she could not say precisely why. He was clearly not to be moved, yet she must find a way to deliver him out of his mulish position. But how? Only one course of action came to her, but Sir Edgar's presence made such a notion impossible to execute. She thought it possible that, had they been alone, she might have offered another kiss in hopes he would acquiesce. In her experience, gentlemen became quite agreeable when permitted to hold a lady in their arms.

This was not to be, however, so she rose to her feet. "I suppose I must take my leave then and beg your pardon for having inconvenienced you."

"I suppose you must," he responded, also rising.

He did not even smile, the beast.

She huffed an impatient sigh. "Permit me to say, my lord, that your attitude toward your neighbors is completely incomprehensible to me. Indeed, I would like to think that were you to relent in your isolation, you might find a friend or two in Kent."

Rotherstone regarded Lady Evelina closely and tried

to determine precisely her motivation for saying such a thing to him. He thought it likely she was hoping that if she enlightened him, he would agree to allow a great deal of digging on Blacklands. He knew, however, that she had no notion just how disinclined he was to oblige any of his neighbors. "Though I will disappoint you, I daresay we will never be of a mind in that regard."

She frowned slightly. "But are you entirely certain that you do not wish to see the map? I assure you, it is fascinating and is dated from 1652."

"Since, as you have said, the treasure appears to be on my lands, why do you not give me the map and be done with it?"

She appeared quite shocked.

"I see," he responded, smiling. "You want the treasure for yourself."

She seemed unable to speak. Her mouth opened and closed several times.

"Just as I thought."

Finally, she said rather heatedly, "I can see that you are disgusted with me, but I believe you have mistaken my hesitation. In truth, I have not thought at all about the actual treasure, merely the finding of it. However, if I did have command of the treasure, I think I would make certain that it belonged to the community."

He barked a fairly substantial amount of cynical laughter. "You are quite naïve if you think your neighbors will simply permit a treasure of any value to be given to a local charity or good work. I am fully persuaded there is more than one of your acquaintance who will want the treasure for himself."

"I cannot pretend to know all the intentions of our neighbors, but I am not so unhopeful as you."

"So you will not give me the map?"

"The map, my lord, is one thing I do believe belongs to me, since I found it in my own attic."

"Very well, but you may tell our delightful neighbors that I have no intention of allowing even one of them to set foot on my property."

Evelina watched him closely. She could see that he felt confident this would be the end of the matter, but regardless of his present stubbornness, she was not cast down. She had begun this adventure, and she would see it through to a proper end. She would gain his support and cooperation. She would find the buried treasure.

Therefore, she offered him a smile, thanked him for his time, bid Sir Edgar a good-day, then quit the chamber. Leaving the house, she approached her mount wondering how it was possible she had ever enjoyed kissing such a horrible man!

Rotherstone moved to the window overlooking the drive and watched as his recent guest mounted her horse, gathered her reins and encouraged her gelding to begin at a walk down his long drive. He felt strangely uneasy about his encounter with Lady Evelina, but he could not understand why. He had conducted himself with her as he had with any of his officious neighbors who dared to call on him uninvited. He had made his dislike of her presence clear, and he had thwarted her plan to invade his lands. Yes, he should have been well pleased. Instead, something nagged at him.

Sir Edgar drew near. "She has an excellent seat," he commented.

"Yes, I suppose she does."

"Do hold back your enthusiasm," he retorted. "I am embarrassed by such an excessive display."

At that, Rotherstone smiled. "You are right. I am hardly being fair. She sits her horse uncommonly well."

"Much better, only will you please explain to me how it came about you treated possibly the most beautiful lady in the entire world in such a cowhanded fashion, as though you have not a particle of wit in your brain?"

"I believe our Lady Evelina has quite turned your head."

"Damme, I liked her very much indeed," he responded. "And it was not just her beauty. I thought her quite an unusual female. Did you not think so?"

"Unusual in that she paid a call on a bachelor's establishment without a maid in attendance?"

"No, unusual in that she did not attempt even once to throw herself at your head. You must give her that. I did not hear one word of flattery pass her lips. Although perhaps she was too frightened to do so when you were being so high-handed."

"I must disagree with you there," he said, frowning. "I daresay she was not frightened of me a jot."

"No, by God, she wasn't! Well, then, I do like her. Only why did you not let her show you the map? I vow I was all agog to see it myself."

"You cannot possibly believe for a moment that it was anything more than a hum, do you?"

Sir Edgar shrugged. "I suppose now we shall never know."

Rotherstone turned to face his friend, who appeared rather forlorn. "Is it possible you have tumbled in love with her?"

Sir Edgar ran a careless hand through his blond locks. "No," he drawled. "I think not, though I will admit she was excessively pretty. But it was something else. Do you know, she quite put me in mind of Emily Cowper. That same gentle spirit but with a determination underneath, almost of adventure were the right circumstance to present itself.

I had not been in her company but two or three minutes before she knew more of my history than many of my friends. Yes, I liked her very much indeed."

Rotherstone watched her trot down the drive. "Perhaps you ought to court her."

Sir Edgar glanced at him, a speculative light in his eye. "Maybe I shall, by God!"

"You cannot be serious! You heard her quite impertinent suggestion that I allow her to hunt for treasure on my land, and this from a stranger. Only one motivation sits at the bottom of that lady's heart—a desire to be mistress here."

At that, Sir Edgar burst out laughing. "You have been far too long in possession of your rank if that is what you think. I never saw a lady less interested in a house or, indeed, in you, once you came the crab with her. However, I shan't complain, for were you to charm her, I daresay I should not have even the smallest chance of winning her. In fact, I beg you will excuse me."

"Of course."

Sir Edgar quit the chamber on a run, and a moment later Rotherstone watched him emerge from the house onto the drive and call after Lady Evelina.

The lady drew her horse up, turned the black gelding about and began walking her mount at a quick pace back to Sir Edgar. A conversation ensued that resulted in the lady laughing, nodding several times and at last resuming her course. Rotherstone found himself quite irritated. There could be no doubt that Sir Edgar had just arranged to call on her.

He should have felt completely indifferent. He had no true interest in Lady Evelina, since he had already taken her measure regardless of Sir Edgar's protests. However, memories assaulted him quite suddenly of just how she had felt in his arms the night he had found her trespassing. He felt a dreadful sinking sensation in his heart. She had been a small miracle that night, a gentle surprise. He had meant to punish her by kissing her, and instead the kiss had transported him out of the doldrums of his present existence. He had entered a place that reminded him of his youth, when he was full of hope and even excitement for the future. He admitted now what he had been striving to deny since his first encounter with Lady Evelina: that when he had kissed her, he had felt fully alive for the first time in many, many years.

He only wished she had not been so very determined about the map and about the supposed buried treasure. He did not like her determination, not in the least. And as for her denial that she had thought nothing of the treasure itself, he simply did not believe her. He was five and thirty and had had a great deal of experience in the world. His betrothed of several years ago, the beautiful Angelique Punnett—with whom he had believed himself to be deeply in love—had broken their engagement to marry a wealthy marquess. She had been a masterful teacher, and he had promised himself that he would never forget the lessons learned under her tutelage.

No, whatever Lady Evelina's protests, he could not believe she was indifferent to the treasure.

A half hour later, Evelina left her horse at the Wildings stable and returned on a brisk step to the house. She was smiling, and it was Sir Edgar who had placed the smile on her lips. He had given her such hope, and wouldn't Rotherstone be shocked were he to know that his friend meant to be of use to her!

Before she had crossed the gallery, William came racing up to her, throwing his arms wide. He was still small enough—but not for long, no doubt—to enable her to catch him up in her arms. She did so now and swung him in several circles until he was giggling and calling for more.

"I must stop!" she cried. She released him and struggled to keep her balance. Pretending to be far too dizzy to do so, she sank into a heap, at which time he launched himself on her. This afforded a perfect opportunity to commence a lengthy tickling. More giggling ensued, and before two minutes had passed, Mia, Alison and Sophy entered the gallery to see what all the laughter was about.

"Dear ones!" Evelina cried.

Mia, just sixteen and feeling every year, refused to join in the fun, but neither Sophy nor Alison held to the smallest speckle of propriety and took to tormenting their brother quite happily as well. They were twins, just two years Will's senior.

Mia, however, stood by and occasionally reached down to give her brother's arm a tweak.

The melee did not cease until the soft tones of Lady Chelwood's voice intruded. "What news, Evie?"

The children untangled themselves at once, and Evelina rose to her feet. Her bonnet was hanging by a loose knot and her neat curls had come undone, unleashing a waterfall of her curly red hair. "Good morning, Mama. How are you feeling?"

"Quite well since Bolney put a little oil in the wheels." The dowager Lady Chelwood was an invalid and confined most of the time to a Bath chair. She was still a lovely woman even though she was some years past fifty. Her red hair was only slightly graying, and when she smiled, as she was now, her green eyes still sparkled. "But enough of me. Has Rotherstone agreed to permit you and our neighbors to explore his lands? I would not have thought it possible, but you could not appear happier than in this moment."

Evelina huffed a sturdy breath and crossed the room to her quickly. "He has not agreed . . . not yet."

"But you are hopeful?" Lady Chelwood sounded entirely disbelieving.

"I refuse to be unhopeful," she responded, bending down to kiss her mother's cheek. She then twirled the chair about and began pushing her mother back into the drawing room that connected to the gallery.

Her mother remonstrated at once, insisting that if she were not permitted to manage her own chair, she would soon grow too weak to be of use to anyone. Evelina refused to listen and did not cease pushing her until she was settled near the fireplace. "Why is there not a fire built up in here?" she demanded.

"Evelina," her mother complained. "You must not coddle me. I am perfectly well."

Evelina lifted a brow and crossed the chamber to give a tug on the bellpull. "I am mistress of this house," she said with a smile. "And while you are here, you will do as I say." She had meant for the words to be playful, and she was certain they sounded as such, for even Mia and the twins were smiling, but Lady Chelwood merely released a very deep sigh.

Evelina was not certain she would ever quite understand her mother. She had brought her to Wildings, as well as the youngest of her siblings, for the happy purpose of tending to them. In no way had she ever felt obligated to do so. She loved her family more than anything on earth, and given the truly wretched fact that her eldest brother, now the Earl of Chelwood, was in *dun territory*, she had supposed her mother would be content. Perhaps her illness was affecting her more deeply than she had thought.

When Bolney arrived, she asked that a fire be built and tea brought.

The twins played spillikins with Will on the carpet near the table while Mia took up her embroidery that their mother was supervising. "Was Rotherstone as disagreeable as everyone says?" Mia asked, threading her needle with blue thread.

Evelina took a tour about the chamber. She pondered her sister's question but at the same time let her critical eye survey the décor. The house was taking shape, but some of the fabric on the chairs and sofas still needed to be replaced. Lord Bramber had allowed every piece of brocade from the prior century to become threadbare.

As for Mia's question, she was not certain how to relate her experience of Rotherstone to her family. "Our neighbor was not the most convivial host, but then I had not been invited to Blacklands, so I suppose he had reason to be put out."

"Did he offer an insult?" Alison asked, her large eyes wide. She was a sweet, soft-spoken girl, boding well to become a great beauty. Her hair was a light brown, her eyes as blue as spring bluebells and already she was so accomplished on the pianoforte that she would soon exceed even talented Mia in her abilities.

Evelina at last took up a seat not far from the group on the floor. "No, he did not. He was merely unwelcoming."

"And he refused your request?" Mia asked.

"Yes."

"What gives you hope then?" Lady Chelwood asked.

Evelina glanced at the plasterwork on the ceiling, then averted her eyes at once. There was still so much work to be done at Wildings that dwelling on it overly much tended to lower her spirits. "It was not Rotherstone who gave me hope, but rather his friend, Sir Edgar Graffham."

At that all eyes turned upon her. "Who is Sir Edgar?" Sophy asked. She was a keenly intelligent child, more interested in the study of nature and fossils than music.

Evelina smiled down at her. "I believe he is a very great friend to Lord Rotherstone, a man I liked very much."

"Are you in love with him?" Will asked suddenly.

Evelina was surprised by the question. Glancing down at him, she responded, "No, dearest."

He searched her eyes in the way a child does when he is trying to solve what seems to him a very great mystery. "Is that because you are already in love with that other man?"

"*What other man?*" four female voices intoned as one.

Evelina knew precisely to what Will was referring. She was horrified by her present predicament, for she might be able to humbug Will or the twins, but certainly her mother and sixteen-year-old Euphemia were awake upon all suits!

She chose to ignore her sisters and mother. "You mean that gentleman who carried you on his shoulder?"

"Yes, the man who was hugging you. He was hugging you, was he not?"

"*Hugging!*" the four voices cried out again.

Oh dear, there is nothing for it, she thought. She could hardly prevaricate now, especially since a blush was already heating up both cheeks. "As it happens," she said, "the man who assisted us two nights past was Rotherstone."

"*What?*" the ladies cried.

Will scowled. "That man was Rotherstone?" he cried. "But I liked him, yet everyone says such bad things of him."

"Yes, I know," she continued, still addressing him exclusively. "He was very kind to us that night, for reasons of his own, I must presume. But in general, I fear, he is not so beloved in our community."

"But why?"

"That is a question I believe you must put to him, perhaps the next time you see him."

"When will that be?"

"Well, if Sir Edgar is to be believed, very soon indeed."

"Oh, Evie," her mother cried. "You are making my head swim. Why does Sir Edgar believe as much, and to what are you referring about Rotherstone's kindness to you and William? Why did none of us know of it? And was it Rotherstone who was, er, *hugging* you?"

Where to begin? "I suppose I must tell you all."

"Indeed, you must!" Sophy cried.

"Well, two nights past I very unwisely crossed onto Rotherstone's land just past midnight. I had found the map so recently, and truly all I had meant to do was to look for the gate in the hedge. But having found it—"

"*You found it!*" the ladies once more cried as one.

By now the twins were standing in front of her. "Did you also find the buried treasure?" Sophy asked.

"Will you not take us to it? Were there many jewels and crowns?" Alison cried.

"My dears, do sit down and pray do not ask so many questions, at least not yet." She then related the rest of the adventure and, except for giving her mother and Mia a brief, penetrating glance, said that the reason Will thought Rotherstone had been hugging her was because she had fallen and he was helping her up and afterward ascertaining if she had been injured.

"On your lips?" he asked, appearing quite bewildered.

Mia pressed a hand to her mouth, but Lady Chelwood could not keep a gasp and a laugh from escaping hers.

The twins appeared equally confused, until a knowing look came over Sophy's face. Her sister whispered, "What do you know that I do not?"

"Enough!" Lady Chelwood finally commanded. "So, after Lord Rotherstone so obligingly came to your aid, what happened next?"

"Will came to my rescue, if you must know, for he was under the mistaken apprehension that Rotherstone was doing me some injury. And I must say," here she grew thoughtful, "Rotherstone was ever so considerate toward William, even though he was quite nasty to me today. Why, he carried Will on his shoulder all the way back to the hedge."

Evelina glanced at Will, as did all the ladies. The scowl deepened on his face.

"Are you angry that the man who helped us was Rotherstone?" she asked.

He shook his head. The scowl became a serious pout. "Now Mama knows," he whispered, as though Lady Chelwood would not be able to hear him.

Evelina did not know to what he was referring. "I do not take your meaning, dearest. What does she now know?"

He rose from his knees and drew near in order to whisper in her ear. "That I was not in my bed."

Evelina could not help but laugh. "I suppose she does, but I do not think she will be much aggrieved with you."

The look of surprise on his face was quite precious. "Truly?" he queried.

Evelina nodded. "I strongly suspect she will be thinking even now that a little adventure would serve you no harm."

He slid onto Evelina's lap and looked at their mother. Evelina thought that no more tender expression had ever existed on a mother's face than in this moment as Lady Chelwood regarded her youngest son.

"Are you angry, Mama?" he asked.

She shook her head. "I should not be a proper mother if I objected too strongly. Besides, I know you would not make a habit of it."

"No, Mama, of course not. I only stole from the house because I saw Evelina leave."

"Just as I thought. If I have any disappointment in this moment, it is in your sister."

Will twisted around and smiled broadly up at Evelina.

"I suppose you are satisfied," she cried, "now that *I* am in the basket!"

When he nodded, there was nothing left to do but to begin tickling Will all over again.

Chapter Four

The next day, Sir Edgar made his promised call. Evelina introduced him to her family, and much to his credit, he offered to play a game of cribbage with Will.

After Sir Edgar had permitted Will to win his third game in a row, Evelina suggested a turn about the gardens, for the day was very fine. Sir Edgar agreed at once.

Once among the roses, Evelina began, "I consider it a great kindness, Sir Edgar, that you have attended to Will this morning as you have. He misses his elder brother, Harry, very much. After his last term at Oxford, we expected him to come home, but he is at that age when his acquaintance is expanding, and though I can understand his desire to be yachting at Plymouth, William cannot."

"Your brother is delightful," Sir Edgar said quite sincerely, "as are your sisters. I have always thought it most unfortunate that Rotherstone grew up in such a lonely house. No brothers or sisters. I have seven myself and have quite the opposite problem as my friend. I could never escape them, even when I have wanted to. With four sisters desirous of seeing me wed to any number of their acquaintance, I find that I often seek refuge at Blacklands."

"Something, I am beginning to believe, that must be of great benefit to our solitary neighbor. I do not know how he manages without the benefit of society."

"He does go to London a lot, however, and he does have a great deal of acquaintance there. Still, I must say he was not always so bad as he is now."

"That is very frank speaking."

"Do I sound disloyal?"

"A little, perhaps."

"Regardless, I thought he used you abominably yesterday."

"Quite disloyal, but in a most charming manner."

"My friend was quite rude, and you and I were having such a pleasant conversation."

"Did he repair his neckcloth sufficiently to please you?"

"Of course. In truth, he is generally a great deal more fastidious. I was merely shocked that he had entered his drawing room in such a state. He never does, you know."

Evelina laughed. "He was aggravated that I dared to call on him."

Sir Edgar smiled broadly. "I was very right about you."

"I do not take your meaning."

"You have no fear of him, and that is a very good thing, for both of you. However, I can see that I have put a blush on your cheeks, and rather than distress you further, let us turn to a different subject."

"One moment, Sir Edgar," she said, then called out to her brother, "Will, hold steady or you will put a tear in your sleeve! Mia, do help him. He has been snagged by a rose."

Euphemia turned about. "Will, do not tug on it!" she cried and came to his assistance.

Evelina begged pardon for having interrupted her guest.

"Completely understandable."

"Now, tell me what it was you wished to say."

"Only that I have not ceased thinking about your map. Do you believe it to be genuine, indeed?"

"I do."

"And that somewhere on Blacklands is a buried treasure?"

"So it would seem, at least by all indications, particularly since I found 'Devil's Gate.'"

Sir Edgar laughed. "Do not tell me one of the places was actually named such. I must confess it rather sounds like a *made-up* name, a bit theatrical."

"Perhaps," she mused. "On the other hand, it is very likely that the smugglers of two centuries past were as set against the owner of Blacklands as are Lord Rotherstone's neighbors today."

Sir Edgar chuckled. "But what of you? Do you dislike my friend so very much?"

"No," she drawled. "Not precisely. I will admit his conduct yesterday was quite ungenerous, but I am afraid it supports quite dreadfully how he is perceived by our community."

"He has made himself so unwelcome?"

"I am sorry to give you pain, but so it is."

She saw by his present frown that he was attempting to understand the situation. "But is there something specific that has occurred to bring about such animosity? For I promise you Rotherstone has said nothing of a past incident that would explain either why he is contemptuous of the local gentry or why they have reason to dislike him."

Evelina thought for a long moment. "I do not recall anything of a specific nature," she said. "However, I had not been in Kent but a day before I was warned against Rotherstone. That I have not even seen him these many months did nothing to dissuade me against the opinions of the surrounding gentry. He even refused Mary Ambers's request for a donation to an orphange."

He seemed astonished. "Mary . . . that is, Miss Ambers resides near Maybridge?"

Evelina heard the slip of his tongue, but even if she had not, the sudden gentling of his tone bespoke a certain affection. She found herself intrigued. "Why, yes, at Victory Cottage in Maybridge. I believe she took the house a month before my arrival. I apprehend that she is known to you, and I can only wonder that your friend said nothing of her presence in our community."

"Mary in Maybridge," he murmured beneath his breath. Giving himself a slight shake, he said, "I daresay he must have had his reasons for not telling me, although I believe them to be high-handed."

Evelina remembered that Miss Ambers had also had a visible reaction when she learned Sir Edgar was to stay at Blacklands. She could not help but wonder at their shared history. She did not, however, feel she could discuss it with him, a circumstance that left her feeling profoundly curious.

"I see her frequently in society," she stated grandly, more for his information than anything else. "She is a very fine young woman, much given to good works. Whenever my sister and I call on her, she is engaged in sewing for the poor. I like her and admire her very much."

Sir Edgar sighed. "And Rotherstone refused his assistance. What a hopeless fellow he is become, but I promise you he is the very best friend I have ever had."

"How do you explain him then?" she asked, surprised at her own audacity in even posing the question. "For I, too, have witnessed his kindness, but then in the next moment he behaves like a perfect cretin."

Sir Edgar laughed heartily. "Do you know, yesterday, when you were speaking with Rotherstone, I had the profound sense that you were the right woman for him. Indeed, I came here today to ascertain as much. Though

I believe I may set you to blushing anew, I am now convinced I am right. Consequently, I wish to encourage you not to let his ill humors discourage you overly much. At his heart, he is a good man, no matter what is said of him, and at times he is even a great man. I have had my own experience in the matter."

"And will you tell me in what way?"

"No," he said, smiling and shaking his head. "For if you knew, I daresay you would refuse to acknowledge our acquaintance further, and for the present, I am come to believe my happiness may depend on securing your friendship."

She felt certain he was referring to Miss Ambers.

"And now," he said, "I wish to ask a favor."

"Of course."

"Will you show me your map?"

"With pleasure," she cried.

"You were certainly gone a very long time," Rotherstone said. He was seated in the library enjoying a glass of sherry and the latest Waverly novel when Sir Edgar finally made his appearance. He had been expecting him to return hours ago.

"I suppose I was," Sir Edgar said, glancing out the window as though he was just noticing the hour. "Lady Chelwood asked me to stay for nuncheon. I would never have refused. I daresay the afternoon slipped away."

"Lady Chelwood?"

"The dowager, Lady Chelwood. She is an invalid, and it would seem your neighbor has taken the younger members of her family, as well as her mother, into her house."

"Indeed?" he murmured. "That was quite good of her."

"Yes, it was, and you all but chased her from your home."

Rotherstone narrowed his eyes at his friend. "You know very well I do not countenance the interference of my neighbors—any of my neighbors!"

"So you have said," Sir Edgar stated. "At any rate, they are quite a happy lot. Lord William asked after you. You seem to have made a friend in the boy." He moved to the table where the sherry sat and poured himself a glass.

Rotherstone nodded. The mere mention of William brought several memories strongly to mind. One in particular he set aside as quickly as he could. "How is the lad?" he asked.

"In excellent spirits, though he seems to be missing his next-eldest brother, Harry, not unexpectedly. Harry is yachting near Plymouth. Of course, the whole of the arrangement is a reflection on Chelwood."

He took up a seat adjacent to Rotherstone and stretched out his legs.

"Chelwood is cut from his father's cloth, by all report," Rotherstone said, "and the estate is very nearly sold off by now, I would suppose."

"So I have heard."

"Did Lady Evelina speak of her eldest brother?"

"No. She seems to be a loyal sort of person, very devoted to her family. Do you know, I now recall that Chelwood tried to marry her off to that Wadly fellow, the one who has a fortune in trade."

Rotherstone frowned. "How odd, for I met a man by that name in London, Monday last. He was quite foxed, and I believe he had lost a thousand pounds at hazard by the time I had entered the establishment."

"Then I would say our Lady Evelina did very well in rejecting the match, although I imagine Chelwood was not happy about her refusal."

Rotherstone laughed. "I am certain he was not. There can be no doubt that the settlement for her hand in marriage would have been extraordinary."

"A very pretty tuppence, no doubt."

"At least she appears to be a woman of some sense."

"Indeed, I believe she is," Sir Edgar said. "She spoke at length of the many improvements she is determined to make at Wildings, beginning with repairs in the attic. Do you know that she found the treasure map because her foot went through a rotten board?"

"Indeed?"

Sir Edgar chuckled and sipped his sherry. "Shall I tell you more of my visit, or are you bored of the subject already?"

In truth, Rotherstone found himself far more interested than he felt he ought to be, and only with the strongest effort had he refrained from asking all the questions that slipped into his mind. He had no cause for such strong curiosity, except perhaps that he was having some difficulty in keeping a certain red-haired female from taking possession of his mind two minutes out of three. Worse still, his conscience had been prickling him all morning about his conduct toward her of the day before. He had been rude, which was not precisely an unusual mode of behavior for him when it came to dealing with his neighbors, but his initial encounter with her had somehow made his abrupt discourteousness less than acceptable.

Sir Edgar sank further into the chair and sipped his sherry a little more. He appeared profoundly content. "I like this room very much," he said.

Rotherstone glanced about the four walls. The library was one of the first chambers Rotherstone had refurbished when he took possession of Blacklands. He had been acquiring books for a very long time, and the addition of his own private collection to the books purchased by his forebears had filled every shelf to overflowing. The air was redolent of snuff and fine leather, for there was not a piece of silk, muslin or brocade to be found in the room. Even the windows bore only simple shutters to keep the western light from damaging any of the precious volumes.

This was his room, a gentleman's room. "In that, then, we are in perfect agreement," Rotherstone said.

Sir Edgar sipped again. "Faith, but Lady Evelina is beautiful. I vow I could look at her for hours. Would you not agree?"

"Would I agree that you could look at her for hours? I could not possibly say."

Sir Edgar chuckled. "So, what do you mean to do?"

"About what?" Rotherstone queried, although he had a strong suspicion just which direction this conversation was headed.

"About the buried treasure. You will certainly not be allowed to keep your neighbors at bay forever."

Rotherstone sighed and finished his sherry. "I suppose not, although I have a right to do so. This is my property."

"But what if the map is correct and there is treasure buried somewhere on your land, would you not wish to find it?"

Rotherstone shrugged. "It is an old country legend. I hardly put the smallest store in it, and what of the map? A few clever drawings, soak the paper in tea or at least throw tea on it, wrinkle it up, hold a candle beneath it in a few well-chosen places and you have an antiquated parchment."

"I can see your reasoning, Rotherstone, and I commend your imagination, but in this case I believe you to be wrong. I have seen the map."

"She showed it to you?"

"Whyever not? Of course, she had something to gain in

doing so, since I am your friend and perhaps might be able to persuade you to change your mind. Although I must say, I did not give her much hope that you would do so, since I have never known a time when I had the smallest influence on your mulishness."

"Thank you."

"I was not offering a compliment. I think it no great attribute of yours that you do not allow your friends to be either of use to you or to hint you in better directions."

"I prefer to determine my own course."

"As well I know."

"So you thought the map genuine, then?"

"It crumbled as though it were."

At that, Rotherstone began to wonder. From the first he had thought the whole business a ruse of some sort to entangle him in the neighborhood's comings and goings. A crumbling map, however, would not have been so easily constructed.

His friend sighed. "We took a turn about the rose garden. She wore a pretty bonnet of straw, but the scarf was embroidered with little green apples."

"Good God, I do begin to think you are smitten with her," he cried.

He watched his friend shift in his seat and cross his legs, but he did not meet his gaze.

"Perhaps I am. Oh, but I nearly forgot." He reached into the pocket of his coat and withdrew a missive. "Lady Evelina asked me to give this to you."

Rotherstone took it. "An apology, I suppose."

"What a hopeless fellow you have become!"

Rotherstone merely grunted and turned the letter over in his hands.

He broke the seal and read:

Dear Lord Rotherstone,

I have invited Sir Edgar to dinner tomorrow night at seven. You have no particular obligation to join us, but Will has asked after you most particularly and insists you come as well. It seems, despite knowing of your ridiculous conduct yesterday, he is still determined to hold you in some regard. If you are of a mind, therefore, I have no great objection to your joining us for dinner as well, though I hope your manners will have improved by then.

Yours, etc,

Lady Evelina Wesley

"The impertinence, the incivility, the rudeness!" he cried.

"What is it?"

"She has asked me to dine."

"Good God!" Sir Edgar cried facetiously. "What sort of wretched person would ask a neighbor to dine?"

He wore a familiar expression of imbecility that always caused Rotherstone to laugh. "The devil take you!" he cried. "Read this for yourself!" He flung the note at him.

"Well, I don't know," Sir Edgar drawled. "She has caught your likeness so nearly in these few words that I think you ought to be flattered. Certainly had she been obsequious or even polite you would not have even considered going."

"What makes you think I am doing so now?"

"Because you have many flaws, but the chiefest is the absolute inability to restrain yourself from giving a deserved set-down to a beautiful woman."

"At least we agree on one thing then."

"And what would that be?"

"That Lady Evelina Wesley deserves a set-down!"

* * *

The next day, with the sun on the wane, Rotherstone sat beside Sir Edgar in his traveling chaise. He knew precisely what his friend was thinking: that he had succeeded in maneuvering him into accepting Lady Evelina's invitation.

The truth differed significantly, however. Somewhere in his discussion with Sir Edgar, Rotherstone had begun to ponder just how Lady Evelina's arrival in Kent, as well as her treasure map, could be the exact opportunity he had been awaiting since the death of his father five years past. For a very long time he had had a scheme in mind by which he could redeem a great wrong done to his father two years before his death. Sir Alfred had succeeded in cheating his father of forty thousand pounds, but because it was done in the name of gaming, the local gentry upheld his claim, several of them having been present that terrible night, albeit heavily foxed.

For himself, he had not learned of the incident until after his father had died and the diminished wealth of the estate had been explained to him by his solicitor. Rotherstone could not remember having been so angry as in that moment when he learned of the gaming loss. His father had never been known to gamble large amounts, yet suddenly he had thrown away such a large fortune.

There had been nothing he could do, however, for the law had not been violated in any manner. He had known at the outset that his retribution must be a different sort altogether. For that reason he had taken up gambling, not for the sport of it or for the possible winnings, but for the purpose of learning to excel at the business. One day he meant to take back what was his. It was just possible that day was now on the horizon.

Therefore, as the coach drew up to the front door of Wildings Hall, Rotherstone felt a sense of excitement. He had waited a very long time indeed to have his justice.

Taking in the stone front of the ancient Tudor house,

he tried to recall the last time he had visited Wildings. Lord Bramber had invited him only once, and to the best of his recollection that would have been nearly three years ago now. In his opinion, the baron had been a useless, irritable creature who welcomed no one and whose penurious nature had caused the beauty of the old house to disintegrate during the thirty years he had been in residence there.

Descending the vehicle, he glanced about, his eye critical to the general nature of estate management, and found himself pleased by what he saw. He recalled from his previous visit a great deal of thick, dark shrubbery that had encroached on the drive badly. All that undergrowth had been cleared out, revealing a beautiful bank of rhododendrons on the west side of a neatly scythed lawn. Opposite was what appeared to be an extensive grove of walnut trees that he knew extended to the edge of his property. Despite his wish otherwise, he found himself impressed.

Once inside the entrance hall, a square staircase, heavily paneled and smelling of beeswax and turpentine, rose up to a first floor. An enormous basket of flowers was displayed on the central table, beyond which was a settee draped with some sort of peach-colored knit shawl. The effect was not unpleasant, just surprising. In Lord Bramber's day, the large fireplace to the right had been blackened, the ashes old and smelling damp from a breach in the chimney. The odor had been less than inviting. Today, only the fragrance of the flowers filled the now-sunny chamber.

"Hallo!"

Rotherstone turned to find young Will standing in the doorway of the drawing room regarding him intently.

"Good evening, Lord William," he said.

Will made his best bow, which the gentlemen returned quite formally.

"My mother and sisters have bid me fetch you, for we
are to dine beneath the apple trees this evening."

"How charming!" Sir Edgar cried. "I should like nothing better."

"Come along then," he said, turning about and waving them forward. There was nothing left to do but
follow after the boy.

The remainder of the journey through the house and
the gardens to the apple orchard confirmed Rotherstone's opinion that Lady Evelina was a very attentive
landowner. Even a pond just beyond the rose garden was
clean, stocked with fish and several water plants that
floated attractively upon the surface. Nothing, it would
seem, had been left unattended.

When he greeted her, he complimented her on her
house.

"Thank you," she responded, clearly surprised. "But I
must confess that I have an extraordinary housekeeper
and a head gardener, both of whom have a passion for
their labors, which account for most of what you see."

"Even the basket of flowers in the entrance hall?"

She smiled, a lovely, summery smile. His breath
caught despite his intention of remaining unmoved by
her beauty. She was gowned in white muslin embroidered and trimmed in a pale apricot. She had a ring of
small yellow roses in her fiery red hair. Strangely, his
heart ached a little as he looked at her. "No," she responded, still smiling. "I am not so clever in arranging
flowers. The basket in the entrance is the work of my sister, Euphemia. May I present her to you, my lord?"

"With pleasure."

The introduction of Lady Euphemia, Mia to her family, was followed rapidly by a presentation of Lady

Chelwood and the twins. He complimented the dowager on her family.

Will, who had not moved far from his side, added, "I have two older sisters who are married. They live in the West Country, and I am an uncle five times over."

"I congratulate you," he said, smiling down at his young friend.

"I also have a brother, Harry, but he would rather be sailing than spending time at Wildings."

Lady Evelina interjected, "Harry is not yet twenty and feeling his oats. We forgive him, since he is doing what a young man ought to be doing at his age, but we miss him terribly."

Rotherstone watched her put her arm about Will's shoulder, and he saw at once the depth of the boy's disappointment. He began to understand the family's situation, the mother in her Bath chair, the father deceased, the eldest son a worthless fellow like his father, the married daughters living far away and Lady Evelina doing apparently what most of the ladies of his acquaintance would never have done—tending to them all.

His chest felt like a balloon expanding with warm air.

Was this lady different, he wondered?

Unlikely, his mind answered firmly. Still, an unfamiliar feeling of hope drifted through him. He took care to remind himself that he knew perfectly well just why she had invited him to dine at Wildings. He was not for one moment going to engage in self-deception on that score.

Evelina gave Will's shoulder a second squeeze, then released him. She offered the gentlemen sherry, which was settled on a nearby covered table.

Rotherstone took his gratefully.

Sir Edgar, however, demurred, saying he would be happy to partake of a glass just as soon as Miss Alison and

Miss Sophy showed him their pony. "For I understand he is a recent acquisition."

"And so he is," Lady Evelina said with a smile. "He is from Mr. Crookhorn's stock."

"May we?" Alison asked.

The stables were not far, so Evelina agreed readily. "Only, you may not ride him, either of you, for our dinner will be served in about an hour, and Cook, as you know, has been slaving in the kitchens since dawn."

"We will not!" Sophy cried. "Come, Sir Edgar. You will like Gwinny; she is the very color of chestnuts! Will, you may come as well, if you like."

With that, the younger set and Sir Edgar marched in a line on the footpath leading to the stables to the west. Will raced ahead, picked up a stick and began beating at any rambling branches that might impose on their progress.

"I do hope your cook has not overtaxed herself on our account?" Rotherstone queried politely.

She laughed at him. "Of course on your account. Well, not yours precisely, but Cook has for so long believed herself superior to your own cook that she cannot bear the thought of even one of her dishes remarked upon as inferior to those served at Blacklands."

"Then my mind is wholly relieved."

"Evie, I am going to take Mama for a turn about the rose garden," Mia said.

Evelina addressed her mother. "I hope you are not grown fatigued," she said.

Lady Chelwood shook her head. "Not in the least. But I intend to persuade Mia to allow me to walk about the gardens for a minute or so. Now, now, do not scowl at me, dearest. Remember that Dr. Dungate said I might do so if the weather was fine, and have you seen such a lovely evening?"

Evelina forced a smile. "I suppose I have not."

Mia pushed her mother up the path leading back to the house. Evelina sighed more than once. Even Lord Rotherstone remarked on it.

"Am I doing so?" she queried. She turned around fully, her back now to the house. "She was not always thus, not even a year past."

"You love her very much."

"Indeed, I do," she said, meeting his gaze and smiling.

A breeze ruffled her red curls and swept the gauzy skirts of her gown in a gentle arc in front of her. Again, her beauty caught him, teasing his heart. What was it about a beautiful woman that tended to take hold of a man's admiration and not let go?

"So, tell me of your mother, my lord."

"Ah, I wish that I could. She died when I was quite young, not yet six."

"I am very sorry to hear it."

He heard the sincerity in her voice and wished that she was not being so kind. She disturbed him. "Were you well acquainted with Lord Bramber?" he asked.

"My great-uncle? Not by half. I only met him once, when I was thirteen. Apparently he was much struck by me, and I can see by your expression you are wondering how I came by the estate. His was not a hereditary title, and his fortune having been made in trade—some say the smuggling trade as much as in any legitimate business—permitted him to confer the estate upon anyone he preferred. Since he was childless, he chose me. Do not ask me why he did not select either Harry or Will, for I cannot say, although I suppose by then Harry had already shown . . . well, that is not in the least important. I merely consider myself greatly fortunate."

"You are something of a mystery to me, you know," he said, offering a smile.

"In what way?" she asked. She poured herself a glass of peach ratafia.

"You are hardly an antidote, yet you are unwed. How is it that you have thus far escaped the connubial knot?"

"I ought to refuse to answer so impertinent a question."

He smiled again. "Come, come, Lady Evelina. From the beginning, we have each chosen a less civilized form of exchange. You trespassed on my land."

"You kissed me. And that, quite boldly."

"You invaded my home without an invitation, without a chaperone and for the strict purpose of annoying me."

"And you spoke like a brute to me."

"So I did, but you sent me an invitation that I should have tossed in the fire. So why, in this moment, should we proceed in a wholly proper manner?"

She giggled and sipped her ratafia. "Indeed, my lord, I can think of no reason. So you have no objection to plain speaking today?"

"None whatsoever."

"Very well, but just remember that I am intent that you will very soon be served with your own sauce."

He nodded, finding himself surprised. He may have had his own reasons in coming to Wildings today, but he had not expected to enjoy himself so very much. "Will you tell me then how it is that you are as yet unmarried?"

"As to that, I think it simple, really. I have never been in love."

"Yet you have had offers."

"Several, yes."

"How is it that I have not seen you in London?"

She shrugged faintly. "Our family situation cannot have escaped your notice, and I am certain the entire *beau monde* is well acquainted not just with my brother's present habits but with what my father's had been before him. It was therefore requisite, with so many children to be provided for, that our mother keep a keen eye to what little remained of the family purse. Trips to London were for the most part out of the question. We often went to Bath, however, and enjoyed a fortnight or two in the spring, which is the primary reason that my sister Elizabeth is settled in Somerset and that Sarah now resides in Devonshire." She regarded him thoughtfully, swirling her ratafia in her glass. "There is something I would ask you."

"About buried treasure?" he inquired with what he hoped was an imperious lifting of his brow.

She chuckled. "I do wish to discuss that with you, but at the moment I desire to know something else."

"Go on."

"Your cousin, Colonel Carfax. Why do you cut his acquaintance?"

Rotherstone took a sip of his sherry and withheld an impatient sigh. "He is not a man I can admire, not by half."

She tilted her head. "Why?" she demanded. "And pray do not think of refusing to answer when I have spoken to you about my spinster state."

He smiled. "Very well. I believe my cousin never grew out of habits formed at university and which even then I found . . . distasteful." When she opened her mouth, he cut her off. "No. You must not inquire further, for I could not in good conscience offer specifics."

Evelina held Rotherstone's gaze firmly. She wanted to know more, but she could see in the expression of his eye that he was not to be moved. "I have always thought him a quite amiable gentleman," she said, wondering what he would say in response.

"His manners can be very pleasing."

She was curious. Before her was an acknowledged

gamester who had isolated himself from good society, at least in Kent, and yet he dared to hint at a darkness to the colonel's character. She thought Rotherstone would be wiser to look at himself in the mirror instead.

"I suppose I have but one mystery to solve," she began.

"The buried treasure?"

She shook her head and smiled. "I was not thinking of that, but rather of you. Can you tell me just how it came about that a man of your education, birth and rank should have alienated so many persons of distinction without the smallest qualm of conscience?"

"You must ask your friends. They know the answer as well as I do."

"That is all the response I will get?" she inquired.

"Yes," he responded simply.

"Here is my last, then. Why did you elect to accept my invitation this evening when it was less than civil?"

"It was, was it not?" He smiled and sipped his sherry.

"You know, Sir Edgar helped me compose that missive."

"Ah, I begin to understand. My friend has used me ill. I can see now that he manipulated my coming."

"Indeed? He said you would not be able to resist so wretched a note. I argued with him, but in the end allowed his knowledge of you to prevail. He was right."

"He said I could never resist the opportunity of giving a beautiful woman a set-down."

"Do you intend to do so now?" She realized she was vastly amused by the entire conversation.

"I have changed my mind," he said. "You have shown yourself to be a rather superior woman, at least with regard to your family."

She placed a hand at her breast. "Have you offered a compliment?" She fluttered her eyes and pretended to swoon.

"Now you are making sport of me."

"You deserve nothing less, although I might be willing to forgive the past entirely were you to offer an apology."

"I ought to," he returned. "But I seem to have forgotten how. That, or I lost the will to do so many years ago."

"You are a very cynical creature, I see. You are grown so used to being disappointed in your fellow men—"

"And ladies," he interjected.

"And ladies. So much so that you have given up seeking good society altogether."

"That's the rub. Define 'good' society, for I have seen little of it in recent years."

"Very cynical. You distrust me equally?"

His silence and the arrested expression on his face gave her the answer she sought.

"So very bad? Oh, dear," she murmured. "Perhaps you should have another sherry, then I might improve in your opinion."

He chuckled as he handed her his empty glass.

So he thought meanly of her, but why? "Is it because I broke with propriety and called on you as I did?"

"Coupled with your request, yes."

"Another case of plain speaking. Well, I suppose I did put the question to you."

"Yes, you did."

She glanced about. "Have you been to Wildings before?" she asked.

"Only once. Your great-uncle and I had a lovely quarrel, and I have not set foot on the property since."

"Would you care to see a little more of the estate? There is a grotto."

"Indeed?" He seemed surprised.

"A very pretty one. It faces north, and the water is nearly as black as the sea on a moonless night."

He nodded in acquiescence, but there was a strange

light in his eye. She realized she had blundered . . . badly. In her naïveté, she was thinking she was showing him some of the property. However, a grotto viewed as the sun was on the wane, and in the solitary company of a gentleman who had already stolen a kiss from her could be seen, and was undoubtedly being seen, as an invitation to a little dalliance. How could she have been so foolish?

Chapter Five

Evelina walked beside Rotherstone as she directed him down a path through the apple orchard. "Did Sir Edgar tell you he has seen the map?"

"Yes. He mentioned it."

She glanced up at him. "Are you not in the least curious?"

He shrugged. "Perhaps a little."

"Well, that is a beginning, I suppose, though I must confess I do not understand why you are not completely intrigued by the idea."

"That there may or may not be a smuggler's treasure on my land?"

"Of course."

"Perhaps because I am uninterested in the treasure generally, or perhaps I am still bothered that you came to me uninvited in order to beg to be allowed onto my lands."

"Yes, that was audacious of me," she said brightly. Perhaps she should have been distressed that he had rebuked her again, but somehow she was not. Her spirit seemed to rise to his provoking remarks.

"I have known any number of ladies like you; determined, placing your pursuits above everyone else, selfish in fact."

"These are hard words, my lord," she said. "Is that how you see me, then? Determined and selfish?"

"Is there any other way to consider your actions? You found a map, and somehow you now feel it perfectly acceptable to charge into my home. Ah, you are frowning now. You must know I am right."

Leaving the orchard, the path ended at a thick hedge running east and west. Evelina directed him to the northeast, where a path was visible climbing up a low hill.

Once on the path, he glanced at her. "You are not answering me, which tells me that you are in agreement."

"Of course I am not," she cried. She lifted her skirts a trifle as they began the climb. She had a new reason for regretting she had offered to show him the grotto, since it had rained recently and the ground was still muddy in low places. Her leather slippers, of a fine York tan and tied prettily at the ankle with blue ribbons, were hardly serviceable for such a climb. However, she had said she would show him the grotto, and she would not turn back now.

"The reason I have not yet refuted your criticisms," she continued, "is because I am considering the initial accusation. I must confess I do not understand in full my own enthusiasm, at least not entirely, but perhaps it is very simple. I found the map in a house I now own, and therefore I ought to see where the map leads."

"You see it as your property, then."

"No," she drawled, minding her steps. "Rather, I see the map as my particular responsibility, though I cannot tell you precisely why."

She wished she could offer a greater explanation, but she did not know what else to say. She thought for a long moment, picking her way along the path, up the hill, her skirts still in hand. The map had come to represent something very important to her, if not wholly defined in meaning. She had spoken truly when she had told Rotherstone of her life before coming to Maybridge. Her existence had been very small; indeed, almost sheltered. Without funds, it had been impossible for her family to enjoy a wide variety of amusements, much less the pleasures of a vast acquaintance. Wildings had quickly become a place of grace and comfort in her life, but the map had emerged as a symbol of what her life could be. So powerful was this now, that the mere thought of giving up the map caused her heart to constrict painfully. Somehow relinquishing it would be akin to returning to a time before Wildings.

She decided to turn their conversation upon him. "I was given to understand that you actually ejected two tenants when you arrived at Blacklands."

"Do you always heed the local gossip?"

"Generally there is some truth to be found in it, and since your discharge was spoken of as scandalous in the extreme, I hoped to hear your version."

"You mean to be large-minded, I see."

"Perhaps I do. Only tell me, how do you account for your actions?"

"I had several reasons: drunkenness—no, not mine; inattention to planting and harvest times; houses in disrepair though funds were sufficient; refusal to adopt farming methods proven to increase yield; and mistreatment of laborers. I believe I had cause."

She turned and stared at him. "Is all this indeed true?"

"I see I have given you a shock," he said sardonically, a knowing light in his dark eyes.

For the barest moment as she stared at him, her breath caught in her throat. Why was it she kept forgetting how handsome he was and how his black gaze seemed to cut through her? "Yes, I am quite astonished," she agreed, bringing her senses to order. "I only wish I had some reason to disbelieve you but your frankness with me generally has made the use of lies quite unnecessary."

"How you flatter me!" he cried.

"What an enigma you are," she returned. "Well, I do

have some intuitive sense of you, especially having seen the current, meticulous state of your home, so I suppose I must credit you with speaking the truth."

"You sound quite disappointed."

She chuckled. "Very much so."

He laughed outright. "What a baggage you are to speak to me so. I am your guest, you know. You ought at least attempt to be civil to me."

"You have Sir Edgar to blame if I am not," she said, turning around, picking up her skirts and once more continuing her ascent. "He recommended that if I hoped to gain your support with my treasure hunt, I must speak forthrightly with you, and, if the truth be known, I rather like it."

He grimaced. "I can see that you do, but as for Sir Edgar's advice, I shall punish him later for having set your bulldog's teeth into me."

"Oh, what a dust you are kicking up to speak so. If I desired to draw blood, I promise you I would do more than tell you what you already know."

"I begin to think I was quite mistaken in you. Sir Edgar said you were unusual, but I believe even he did not know just how much."

"Did he say so indeed?" she queried, pleased with the compliment, or so it was to her. "I like your friend very much. He is just what a gentleman ought to be."

"Yes, he is," Rotherstone agreed.

"He told me you rendered him some sort of assistance."

"Scarcely anything. A roof for a time. Something I could easily spare."

"And are all your kindnesses extended by such a measure? What you can easily spare?"

"You would like to think so, no doubt, and I certainly do

not intend to boast of my good deeds in hopes of altering your opinion."

"This is fun," she stated, climbing a rise of stones that led into the grotto.

He grunted. "Making sport of me?"

"That, too, I suppose," she responded, turning to flash a smile down at him, for he was now several steps below her. "I was, however, referring to the ease with which we are conversing. I am rather put in mind of the first night we met. That is, how we chatted all the way back to Wildings." She winced inwardly. She should not have referred to that event, for she hardly wanted him thinking about the kiss he had forced on her, one that she had received far too willingly.

She was, however, too late, for he caught up with her quickly and took her elbow. "The rise is steep. May I assist you?"

She glanced up at him, saw the glitter in his eyes and knew full well what he was about. "I think not," she responded archly, but it did not help that she immediately tripped over the next mossy stone step. If he had not been holding her elbow, she would have plunged onto her face. "Oh dear. I suppose now I must thank you."

"Yes, you should, and I must continue to hold your arm. It would be quite remiss of me to do otherwise."

"Oh, very well. I did not expect the stones to be so slippery." He released her elbow and offered his arm, which she took. However, she lifted her chin to him by way of warning. She had no intention of allowing him to take advantage of her again.

The grotto appeared around a bend in the path, a pond settled against a natural stone wall. Over the embankment, vines hung low, almost kissing the water. The pool, as she predicted, was black, especially in the growing twilight.

She released his arm immediately and moved away from him.

"Are there legends attached to these waters?" he asked.

Evelina pondered his question. "You mean has this pool been known to heal lepers or to offer up magical swords or perhaps to shelter a water nymph or two?"

He nodded, smiling broadly.

Evelina sighed. "I fear not, though I should have liked it very much were there some mystery or secret attached to the pond. Alas, I have heard of none."

He drew close, standing just behind her. He leaned over her shoulder. "Is it perchance a place meant only for lovers?"

She heard the subtle shift of tone, and her heart picked up its cadence. His breath against her neck sent a shiver down her back. She must, she absolutely must, keep him properly settled in his place. "As it happens," she returned cheerfully, stepping away from him. "I believe it is! Should a lover prove false, one is allowed to have him dunked a score of times, until he is properly chastened, which is to say *drowned.*"

He was not deterred and moved swiftly behind her again, snaking an arm about her waist. "Surely not," he whispered. "Not in such a pretty grotto!"

What a beast he was! She slid away and turned toward him, holding up an imperative hand. "You shall not kiss me again, Rotherstone! I shan't permit it."

The smile that had been playing over his lips deepened suddenly. "Not even were I to promise to *consider* your request of yesterday? A kiss can be very persuasive."

"Oh," she groaned, "that is quite unfair of you! Blackmail and nothing less!" She recalled that she had actually been contemplating such a course the very day she had initially called on him at Blacklands. Had Sir Edgar not been present at the time, she believed she might have even offered one. Yet somehow these circumstances seemed very different to her. In the beautiful grotto, she suddenly felt quite vulnerable.

"You ought to think on it," he said, advancing toward her again. This time, she remained facing him.

"To do so would be utterly improper," she cried, but something inside her began giving way. He was quite handsome, and his voice always seemed to work so magically on her senses.

"Are you certain?"

"No . . . that is, I meant to say 'yes,'" she cried.

He took a step toward her. "But it would be a very pleasant way to negotiate what you desire."

She felt a sudden urge to run from the grotto. What a terrible man he was to beset her in this fashion. On the other hand, would it be so terrible to acquiesce? After all, were she to get him to agree to let their party march about his grounds for an hour or two, she was convinced she would be able to find the buried treasure. She backed up slowly.

"Are you certain?" he wheedled.

"You should have only one motive in agreeing to my request—to be of use to your neighbors, your community."

He remained silent.

Evelina could not help but wonder again why Rotherstone disliked his neighbors so very much. "I wish I might understand you better," she said suddenly. She saw that she had surprised him in saying so and continued, "Though I do not comprehend the animosity between you and your neighbors, do you think it possible it is time to forgive them for whatever misdeeds they might have committed against you?"

His eyes darkened. As black as they were, they grew blacker still. She took another step away from him. She felt his rage as he clenched and unclenched his fists, striving to master his feelings. "'Tis no concern of yours," he said at last, drawing in a deep breath.

Evelina was stunned. She had expected him to complain of some slight or other; instead, she could see that whatever circumstance had to so set him against Sir Alfred and the others had not been of an insignificant nature. She tried to recall anything that her neighbors might have said that would indicate just why Rotherstone felt so aggrieved, but nothing specific came to mind. How little she knew of him after all.

"You are right, of course," she said. "I am being impertinent."

"*Impertinent* is too mild a word."

She decided to press him. "But what of obligation? I am convinced it is your duty to allow us to find the treasure if we can."

"I do not think much of duty, especially when it involves my neighbors."

"Do you never tire of your solitary existence, living as you are, alone in your house?"

"I am not alone," he answered in his most reasonable voice. "I have Sir Edgar with me, and I am thinking of getting a dog."

She could not help but chuckle. "Will you not at least think on what I have said? I believe it might do you some good."

"Perhaps I shall."

She did not see anything in his expression that gave her hope, but she chose to be hopeful anyway. "Good."

"For now, however, all I wish for is a kiss." She gasped and would have protested, but he spoke hastily. "I promise to give you a quite generous compensation." His smile was utterly wicked.

"And what would that be?"

"If you allow a kiss, I promise to take your request

seriously." When she tried to begin her arguments again, he stopped her. "No more, my lady, for I fear you are blushing too charmingly to make me think of anything else of the moment but your kisses. If I may say so, you appear just like a water nymph among these ferns and boulders."

"You are being quite absurd." She moved backward, fairly certain of the pond's edge. "I will not kiss you no matter what your offer."

"Do you not want to find the treasure?" he asked in all innocence.

"What a devil you are to tease me so when you know I do."

She took another step and another, and suddenly he grabbed her arm. "Whoa!" he cried.

The next moment, she felt her foot slide away beneath a sinkhole of mud. "Oh!" she cried aloud as she grabbed for his shoulder.

"I have you!" he responded, pulling her toward him and out of harm's way.

"My slipper is ruined," she cried. Mud rimmed the entire heel up to her ankle.

"Sit down," he commanded, pointing to a large rock nearby, one she had sat on many times over the past several months. She often came to the grotto to be very quiet and to enjoy the day. She had never thought in a million years she would be here with Rotherstone, who was now bent on one knee as though offering a proposal of matrimony and lifting her ankle to examine the hapless shoe.

"Not so very bad," he proclaimed, removing his handkerchief from the pocket of his coat. She was about to order him to refrain from staining his kerchief, but then she thought better of it. He deserved to have his kerchief ruined for so torturing her and fairly forcing her into the muddy bank.

He wiped the slipper gently until most of the dirt was

gone, then carefully folded the kerchief up and returned it to his pocket. Only then did she realize that he was holding her leg and now rubbing her ankle. "Were you injured?" he asked, looking up at her.

She blinked as all thought and certainly all ability to comprehend his question deserted her. "I beg your pardon?"

"Your ankle. When you slid backward, did you twist your poor ankle?" His fingers swirled over her skin in a truly terrifying manner, for she suddenly wished he would never stop.

"N-n-no," she stammered, watching his fingers. They looked like little snakes moving over her skin, sneaky little things that were keeping her from putting two thoughts together, until suddenly one hand slid up her calf.

She was on her feet in an instant. "Rotherstone!" she cried. "What do you think you are doing?"

"Nothing you would not like," he returned, also rising.

She cast him a scathing glance and tried to turn away, but once again he caught her about the waist. Her heart hammered in her chest as she met his gaze. He leaned very close. "If you allow a kiss, I will consider your proposition. I will allow you to offer every argument you can think of without once coming the crab. One kiss and I will promise to listen to you."

This entire speech had been breathed most unhappily against her neck. She did not know which was worse, the exploring fingers against her ankle or his breath on her neck. Both sent chills up and down her body and gooseflesh popping up everywhere. He was a terrible man, just as all her neighbors had said, but how was she to have known he was terrible in just this way! She understood now that he was a seducer of maidens, and yet she was not pulling away from him!

"Well," she murmured slowly. Was she actually contemplating his offer? Oh dear, what was she thinking? This would not do. She tried to stop the next words from leaving her mouth, but she was wholly unsuccessful. "I suppose one kiss would do no harm, and . . . and I suppose I owe it to my neighbors to do all that I can . . . and . . ."

He waited for no further invitation but took her nearly as forcefully in his arms as he had that first night. His lips were on hers in a hot flame of passion that so took her by surprise that she drew back and called his name. "Gage," she whispered.

"I like how you speak my name."

"This is truly dreadful!"

"So it is," he responded with a new smile.

Again he kissed her and held her, his arms a vise. Of all the situations she had imagined arising this evening, the possibility of again kissing Rotherstone had never once crossed her mind. Yet, in a world that had thus far been unpredictable, she suddenly felt incomprehensibly safe.

Other gentlemen had kissed her over the years, usually because she had been considering the acceptance of a proposal of marriage. She did not like admitting as much to herself, but she had refused three offers because the ensuing kisses had been so . . . well . . . paltry. How could she have wed a man who did not even know how to kiss her?

There was nothing paltry in the kiss that followed, for his tongue was soon searching out the depths of her mouth. She was shocked and quite wickedly delighted!

Oh dear, oh dear, her mind cried. What devilment was this that she must find so much pleasure in the kiss of a man she otherwise did not trust and even had an inclination to dislike? She had previously wondered if Rotherstone was addled. Now she wondered if she was.

Regardless of the reason for the kiss, she held him close, treasuring the feel of his strong shoulders beneath her arms.

He drew back slightly. "You should have been wed long before this," he murmured, teasing her lips anew.

"I rejected enough suitors, I suppose," she said. "Had I been sensible, I would have been married ten years by now."

"Particular, eh?" he asked, searching her eyes.

"Very. I have two sisters wed, as you already know."

"Happily?"

"Exceedingly."

"Will you kiss me again?"

She lifted her chin defiantly, but her heart was beating warmly. "Only because you said you would consider listening to my supplications."

"Of course," he said. He smiled at her, a tender expression that reached to his eyes. How was it, she wondered, as he pressed his lips against hers, that he was considered so villainous among his neighbors when he could appear so very loving?

Finally, she withdrew from his arms, and he allowed her to go. She stared at him, striving to catch her breath. His expression was warm, even affectionate. Good God, she had kissed Rotherstone again. She was breathless, and her brain seemed not to be functioning very well at all. How was it she had come to allow another kiss? What was the reason that seemed to escape her? Oh, yes, he had promised to listen to her arguments.

After a moment, she swallowed hard. "As to the former subject," she began, arranging her thoughts as best as she could. She then regaled him with all the facts, the general belief that the map was genuine, all the legends that pointed to his land as being the location of the treasure, the long history of smuggling throughout the southerly coastal counties, the desire of the neighborhood to pursue the hunt and her own belief that she had been given this task by some dictate of fate. "Will you not please allow it? We would of course abide by any restrictions you might require."

He appeared to be pondering all that she had said, but she could not like the deep furrowing of his brow. He seemed almost angry, something she did not understand in the least. How could he be in the smallest degree overset when she had allowed him a kiss because he had promised to hear her reasonings?

Rotherstone had listened to her arguments just as he had promised, but the intensity of her present expression disturbed him and her apparent indifference to his kisses he found quite appalling. After having shared so passionate a kiss, how could she launch so easily into her speech? Had she no feelings at all? Again, he became convinced that she was in the mold of most of the ladies he knew: determined on their own ends, their hearts inaccessible.

He smiled to himself. What Lady Evelina could not know, however, was that he had already decided to allow his neighbors access to Blacklands, but for reasons that had nothing to do with her arguments.

As he faced her now, however, he felt she ought to be punished a little. He decided that since he was to allow an invasion of his property, she ought to pay for it.

"I will allow your use of my land," he said, "but I have a condition."

"Yes?" she asked, her green eyes brightening.

"I want the right to claim three things of you, at any time I desire, one or all of them, and with no stipulations as to what these three things may be. I will only assure you that you will prize what I take from you quite deeply."

A scowl quickly descended over her face. "I believe this to be completely unfair," she complained.

"And so that we do not misunderstand one another, let me say that I do not give a flying fig whether you think it unfair or not. 'Tis what I wish if I am to allow my neighbors onto my land."

"Will you give me any hint as to what I will be required to relinquish?"

"No," he responded coolly.

She shook her head as one bewildered. "I do not understand you. Why are you being such a brute?"

He shrugged. "Again, I do not give a fig for how you might feel about what I require."

"You would not hurt my family, would you?"

He ground his teeth. What sort of monster did she believe him to be? "I suppose you must now ask yourself whether you trust me enough, upon our short acquaintance, to be reasonably decent. You have heard the gossip about me, you have been in my arms, you have been in my home, you have seen me with your family, you have heard my justifications for ejecting two families from their homes and now you must decide for yourself just how well or how ill I would use you."

He could see that she was distressed. He continued, "You do not have to give me your answer now. And if I do not much mistake the matter, we should return to the apple orchard. As you said before, Cook will not like to have her food grow cold before it can be served."

Evelina regarded the man before her and did not know which she felt more, anger or disgust. She knew Rotherstone to be a gamester, to be harsh, even ruthless. He took what he wanted. So how was she ever to trust him? "You are asking me how much I wish for this hunt to proceed."

"I suppose you may view it in that manner."

"I can view it in no other."

"This is my only offer," he stated.

She had not the smallest doubt that he meant precisely what he said.

She held his gaze steadily. No, she did not trust him. How could she? At the same time, there seemed to be no alternative before her but to acquiesce. Swallowing hard, she said, "I do not need to wait. I agree to your condition."

"Excellent," he said, smiling, but there was nothing warm in his expression. "And now we should return lest we offend Cook."

That night, long after Evelina had bid her guests farewell, she reflected on just what a terrible thing she had done by agreeing to Rotherstone's condition. Climbing into bed and blowing out her bedside candle, she stared into the shadows of her chamber. Moonlight shone in a dim patch through muslin draperies. Had she truly agreed to permit the earl to demand three things of value of her without the smallest foreknowledge on her part as to what, or when such things would be required? She could not credit she had done so. What idiocy had so taken possession of her that she would agree to such an arrangement? She knew little of Rotherstone that would give her even the smallest hope that he would be generous or even kind in his demands.

She trembled in her bed. What manner of mischief had she set into motion by submitting to his desires in the situation? She should have been stronger with him. She should have been willing to relinquish her quest the moment he proposed so high a price. And then he had even had the audacity to say that she must determine for herself if she could trust him. This from a gamester!

Good God, what on earth had she been thinking? She felt as featherheaded as Annabelle Rewell.

Well, her die was cast. She had made her decision. She had accepted his terms. There was only one thing to do now. She must abide by her word.

With that, as she stared up into the canopy covering her bed, she ordered her troubled mind to cease thinking, and after a mere two hours of tossing about on her bed and more than once becoming tangled in the bedcovers, she fell asleep.

On the following morning, as Evelina reclined in bed and sipped a steaming cup of hot chocolate, a missive arrived for her from Blacklands. She broke the red wax seal, read the message and felt a swift blush climb her cheeks.

Rotherstone had written,

> *Dear Lady Evelina,*
>   *Thank you for dinner. I must say I enjoyed myself prodigiously last night, particularly our enlightening tête-à-tête at the grotto. I should be happy to accompany you there any time you are wishful for a little "adventure."*

"What a dreadful man," she cried aloud, then continued reading.

> *Concerning our agreement, I beg you will meet with my bailiff at two o'clock this afternoon. He has information of great value to impart to you, and I wish as well that he might have a look at your map. I will join you when I am able. Yours, etc, Rotherstone. P.S. I am having a great deal of fun pondering just what I shall demand of you.*

"A dreadful, horrid, odious man indeed!" she again cried aloud.

Chapter Six

As requested, Evelina met with Rotherstone's bailiff in the morning room of Blacklands at two o'clock.

Mr. Creed proved to be a surprise. Evelina had not been five minutes in his company when she realized she was conversing with an extraordinary man.

He was short in stature, but what he lacked in height he made up for in understanding. He was a curious creature with blue eyes that seemed in her opinion to be lit with wisdom. His penetrating expression at first unnerved her until she realized there was nothing but kindness in his heart. His hair was white and his complexion dark from many years traveling about Blacklands on the back of a horse. He knew all the tenants and their respective families by name. He was humble but not obsequious, which gave her the impression that once he formed an opinion, he could easily dig in his heels.

"So, you have found a map, have you?"

"Yes, Mr. Creed," she responded, smiling. She liked him very much indeed.

"And you have cause to believe 'tis real?"

"Aye."

He smiled. "And will you be showing me this map?"

She laughed and opened the satchel at her feet, withdrawing the map still wrapped in blue velvet. She would have displayed it on the table, but he stopped her.

"Not here, I think," he said. "Bring it to the sideboard, and I shall light some candles."

Evelina did as he instructed. The sideboard was higher than the table and afforded both of them a much easier posture by which to peruse the document. With the candles lit, Mr. Creed began a silent investigation of the map and the five riddles.

Once or twice he grunted. Beyond these gutteral sounds, he did not open his mouth. He reviewed every portion of the drawing, read and reread the riddles and traced each river and stream.

"And where did you propose starting your search?" he asked at last.

Evelina pointed to Devil's Gate.

"Aye, there is some logic to your choice, and that one ought to be investigated. '*Black the land will be*' seems clear enough."

Evelina saw no other possibility for the location of the treasure. "Do you recommend another?" she asked, wondering just what he would say. In her opinion, the map was quite straightforward. The treasure had to be somewhere in the southwest portion of Blacklands property.

He thumbed his jaw, scratching a little at his chin and wrinkling up his brow. "I suppose it is as good as any."

"You must have another thought. Pray tell me what it is you see that I may not."

"'Tis an instinct only. I do not hesitate to say that I am very much surprised, but I do believe the map to be genuine. The smuggler's treasure has been such a large part of our local legends that it would be quite a significant event to have it discovered at last. With that said, you may want to be careful, m'lady." A small smile played at his lips.

"How is that?" she asked, a little shiver coursing through her.

"What he means," Rotherstone said, "is that there may be some who desire to possess the treasure."

Evelina turned sharply and saw that the earl was standing in the doorway and must have been for some time, since he was leaning negligently against the doorjamb. He left his post and entered the chamber.

"How do you go on, Lady Evelina?" he asked, drawing close to the sideboard.

"Until this moment, quite well. Now, however, I do believe you and Mr. Creed have quite filled me with dread." Turning to the bailiff, she queried, "And do you believe I am in danger?"

"Any that look for the treasure, I would think, or have you not heard of the curse?" Mr. Creed asked solemnly.

Oddly enough, Evelina's heart began to thrum with excitement. "A curse, indeed? No, I have not!" she exclaimed. "Oh, but this is too wonderful! A treasure and a curse!"

Mr. Creed scowled and grimaced. He appeared at his most foreboding, no doubt exclusively for her benefit. He was not, however, all that convincing, since his blue eyes twinkled with laughter. "Madness, murder and mayhem," he said. "Nothing less."

"Oh dear," she whispered, but she could not repress her smiles.

"Her ladyship is not convinced," Rotherstone said in a very low tone.

"I can see that she is not, but m'lady, I shall whisper a name to you that I believe not a single person in Maybridge may know."

Evelina listened intently.

"Jack Stub."

She frowned. "You are right. I have never heard his name spoken before."

Mr. Creed nodded slowly. "That is because 'twas a

great secret passed down through my family. A secret told and kept, until now."

Evelina wondered if she was being humbugged, but she did not care. The name, Jack Stub, was far too intriguing to be dismissed. "If this is true, Mr. Creed, why do you break now with your tradition?"

He met her gaze and smiled, if sadly. "For the simple reason there is nought of my family left. I am the last. I had thought to marry, but 'twas not my good fortune. I had therefore supposed the telling of these tales would have died with me, but when my master told me that you had found a map, I knew there would be at least one more recounting."

"I feel honored," Evelina said sincerely. "Thank you."

"And now, shall I tell you of Jack Stub?"

"Indeed, of the moment I wish for nothing else. But first, do you believe he created this map?"

Mr. Creed nodded again.

Evelina shivered. "But how wonderful to think that the smuggler legend would involve a man with such an evocative name!" She shifted her gaze momentarily to the earl. "Is it not extraordinary?"

"Quite," Rotherstone returned, but there was nothing but amusement in his face.

"To the unbeliever," Mr. Creed continued, "the curse doubles in strength." He paused for effect.

"Do go on, " Evelina cried. "Or can you not see that I am in the worst suspense to hear all that you have to say?"

Mr. Creed laughed heartily. "Very well. The legend has it that in 1650, a band of smugglers worked the coastline betwixt Kent and France. Up and down both coasts they traded in forbidden goods but eventually took to piracy as well, taking life where they pleased and stealing what they could find. The worst of smugglers they were, blackguards and thieves to the last man.

"There was not a maidenly soul that could sleep in safety while these bands ruled the coasts and several miles inland. Doors and windows were barred shut at night and bloodhounds sent to patrol every hamlet, farm and empty country lane. But so fierce and cruel were these villains that nothing could stop them. Nothing, that is, that was allowed by the King's law.

"In due course, good and honest men, some of low birth, some of high and a score in between, formed an army to be rid of the legion of brigands that had seized control of the coastline. One by one, the dastardly fellows were seized and hanged, not through the process of any court but by the natural law found on the branch of a tree, as has been done since the beginning of time.

"Fear began to penetrate the hearts of the smugglers. Many disappeared with their fortunes, never to be seen again, perhaps setting up honest lives in ports unknown, others perhaps to perish when caught by those they had robbed. The numbers diminished slowly as booty was seized and given to the poor, and order returned to the vales of Kent and Sussex.

"But there was one notorious band called the Seven Brothers, a villainous collection of thieves and murderers feared by even the worst of the smugglers, for they killed anyone thought to be a traitor to their own. The leader was a vile fellow by the name of Jack Stub, so called because he had lost his hand as a lad stealing from a butcher who took his vengeance in a gruesome manner. The band operated from the coast directly east of Maybridge, though some miles distant, of course.

"It was this fellow, when the army of honest folk was preparing to blow up this vile nest of villains, who was said to have buried his treasure somewhere within a ten-mile reach of Maybridge.

"These legends I heard first from my great-grandfather, and now that I look at this map I can tell you 'tis a true one, because do you see this mark, a seven with a sword crossing over it?"

"Indeed!" Evelina cried. She thought she knew precisely what it meant. "The Seven Brothers."

"You've the right of it. Brothers of the sword and no less."

A shudder of pure exhiliration went through her. "And you truly believe this map was created by Jack Stub?"

"None other."

"Do you actually think he was able to write?"

Mr. Creed smiled. "Perhaps not him, for he was a thief since a child and therefore probably orphaned and without education. But not all the smugglers were of low descent. Some had a fair scrawl, as the one who wrote these riddles did. I only wonder if, once the map were complete, the fellow survived to see the next sunrise."

"What a horrible thing to say!" Evelina cried.

Mr. Creed's smile broadened. "And if you do not take offense, Lady Evelina, I begin to think you are not in the least offended by such histories."

"No, I am not," she responded a little sheepishly.

"Then you are worthy of being in possession of the map. I wish you good fortune in seeking the treasure of Jack Stub. I only hope the curse attached to any who search for the treasure does not come true."

Evelina gulped. "What is the nature of the curse?"

Mr. Creed leaned close to her. "Death," he whispered.

"Now you have gone too far, Mr. Creed," Rotherstone interrupted. "You are frightening Lady Evelina."

Evelina glanced at him and could not help but giggle.

"Only in the most delicious manner, I assure you," she said.

Rotherstone looked at the lady next to him, and though he had already steeled himself against her willful determination to pursue the treasure, he still could not help but be struck by the sparkle in her green eyes. Almost, he found himself smitten, but this would not do in the least, so he gave himself a small shake. "Regardless," he said, "a little more fact and a trifle less fancy might be of use, Mr. Creed, since my neighbors are intent on attempting to unearth Jack Stub's treasure from my estate. Though I must say, you tell your tale admirably."

Mr. Creed's blue eyes twinkled anew. "I told it as my grandfather did. I knew many a sleepless night, I promise you."

"I have no doubt you did," Lord Rotherstone returned.

Evelina gestured to the map. "So you would agree then that to commence at Devil's Gate would be a proper beginning."

"As good as any, I expect," he responded. "Although I should warn you not to be thinking the map is as straightforward as it appears."

"And do you have any particular thoughts as to just how it might be deceptive?"

He shook his head. "Nay, but something is amiss. I just cannot say what. I will think on it, however, as should you."

"I shall heed your words." She then turned to Rotherstone. "I intend to recommend to my neighbors that we begin at Devil's Gate. Is this acceptable to you?"

He inclined his head. To his bailiff, he said, "I think for the moment I shall permit this new band of adventurers to wander about at will. I would prefer that you and Lady Evelina decide on a proper day and time for the hunt so that the estate laborers will know when to expect them."

"Very good m'lord."

"Will that suit you?" Rotherstone asked Lady Evelina.

"Very much indeed," she said. Turning to Mr. Creed, she added, "When I have met with our neighbors, I shall send a servant with a suggested time, and you may tell me if it is suitable for you."

"Very good, m'lady."

"You may go now, Creed, and thank you very much."

Mr. Creed bowed and quit the room.

Rotherstone watched Lady Evelina begin rolling up the map and blue velvet slowly and carefully. She seemed pensive, though what she was thinking was lost to him. "You seem rather deep in thought," he said.

"I suppose I am."

"You are thinking about the treasure, then?"

She turned toward him. "Actually, I was wondering if you meant to make one of your three requests today."

He was surprised, for he had not given the matter the smallest thought since the day before. "No," he responded succinctly.

"And do you truly feel it necessary to hold by such a condition?"

He saw the concern in her eye and could not help but smile. "When did you decide I was such a complete monster?" he asked.

He could see that the question startled her, for her eyes opened very wide. She remained silent for a long moment. "What gentleman other than a monster would behave as you have? First, you kiss me entirely against my will. Then, in the face of an innocent request, you exact another kiss, as well as the right to demand three things of me. Why would I not have an unhappy opinion of you?"

"Let us review further," he suggested. He could not help but smile, though he supposed it was not an entirely warm expression. "Both kisses appeared to me to have been equally enjoyed by you, or was I mistaken in that?"

She shook her head. "You are far too skilled to make the experience less than," she looked up at the ceiling as though searching for the right word, "pleasant."

"Pleasant?" he asked, amused. "Is that all you felt when I held you in my arms, how pleasant it was to be kissed by me? If this is true, I believe I should practice a little more."

"Now you are being absurd," she cried.

"As are you, my lady. I did not invade your home. You have invaded mine. I have responded and made demands. How does that truly make me a monster? Oh, I see what it is. You believe every gentleman should simply bow to your wishes. Is this not so?"

"Of course not," she cried. "I hope I am not such a vain, ridiculous creature. But why have you not been willing to be generous with me and with your neighbors?"

He wanted to give her a sharp answer, but since he had already decided the time had come to engage his neighbors in a new game, he held his tongue. Instead, he took a deep breath and said, "You are right. I have not acted the gentleman as I should have."

"Then will you relent and release me from these three demands?"

"No," he returned softly. "I have come to adore the notion of having an excuse to see you again." He watched her shiver. "However, I will try to do better with our neighbors."

The effect these few words had on the lady before him was rather marvelous. Her complexion grew heightened and a smile set her features in a beautiful glow. She had never appeared prettier, and his heart actually hurt just looking at her. "You have made me happy today, and that was unlooked for."

A silence mounted between them, and he found he

could not shift his gaze away from her. He had previously thought that her acquiescence to his demands had given him some power over her, but in this moment he was completely powerless to do more than look deeply into her eyes. He wondered what she was thinking.

Evelina thought that never had a man been able to so easily capture and hold her attention. She had every reason to be angry with him forever, and perhaps she would have been, but she had heard in his words and now saw in his countenance a gentleness that commanded trust. She did not want to trust him, but she did. "I shall take my leave now," she said. "I intend to share with our neighbors what you have agreed to."

He was still looking at her, still holding her gaze tightly within his own. Without thinking, she leaned quickly up to him and placed a kiss on his cheek. "Thank you," she said, tears sparkling in her eyes. With the velvet-encased map tucked beneath her arm, she quit his home.

By the time Evelina set her feet in the direction of Wildings (for she had walked the distance this afternoon), she found she was trembling, though she could not comprehend why. What had changed, she wondered, that she would be so affected by this last conversation with Rotherstone? Yes, he had softened his attitude somewhat, but he still held to his original demands, so she should not be so ecstatic. However, she was: wondrously so.

As she walked briskly down the drive, she strove to gather her reeling senses and to remind herself that this man, by his actions, was not to be wholly trusted. Why, then, had she kissed his cheek?

Rotherstone made his way up to the library. He moved swiftly, thinking he would have a sherry and read a book, but when his feet took him directly to the south window, he understood precisely what he was doing. Some part of him, the part that had felt completely undone by the sweet kiss Lady Evelina had placed on his cheek, had needed to see her once more. There she was, already halfway down the drive, so fast was she walking. There she was, a woman who had already changed so much for him. He should be thinking of her in an entirely different sense, as the one who had disrupted his home and in doing so provided him with the perfect excuse for taking revenge on several of his neighbors. Instead, his senses were fixed solely upon the warm imprint of her lips against his cheek. Was it possible he had finally met a woman whom he could trust?

Two days later, Evelina drove her gig to Pashley Court, Sir Alfred's home, in order to meet with her neighbors. Though she had wanted to begin the hunt for Jack Stub's treasure immediately following her conversation with Mr. Creed, this was the first occasion upon which the entire group could assemble together. More than once over those two days, she had longed to venture again onto Blacklands by herself, but her conscience forbade her. She felt her neighbors must be included in the search for the smuggler's fortune. As much as she felt the map belonged to her, she did not believe the treasure did.

Entering the drawing room of the ancient manor, she was struck again by how dark and relatively unwelcoming Lady Monceaux's drawing room was. A bank of narrow diamond-paned windows that extended the length of one wall was the only source of light, and the wainscoting was dark, nearly black, as were the old smoke-stained beams that lined the low ceiling overhead. Although Lady Monceaux had attempted to lighten the chamber by covering the chairs and sofas in a light green silk damask, little could be done to entirely allay the gloom that pervaded the poor chamber.

Regardless, she could see that spirits were high in view of her excellent news.

Lady Monceaux helped her display the map on a table opposite the fireplace.

"I cannot credit 'tis true," she whispered to Evelina, "that we are to begin the hunt. My dear, I congratulate you. Only, however did you achieve it? How did you persuade Rotherstone?"

Evelina controlled the blushes that threatened to overtake her and responded quietly, "With some difficulty, I assure you."

Sir Alfred cleared his throat and frowned his wife down. "So," he began, a disbelieving grimace on his face, "Rotherstone has actually given his permission." His arms were folded across his chest.

"Yes, he has," Evelina said, taking up a seat next to Lady Monceaux. "When we are ready to proceed, I am to consult with his bailiff, Mr. Creed, in order to arrange the day and time of our first exploration. I had a lengthy conversation with Mr. Creed two days ago. He knew a great deal of the legends surrounding the smuggler's treasure, and of course he knows Blacklands better than anyone."

"That would be true," the elder Mr. Rewell said. "For he was employed first by Rotherstone's father many, many years ago, and Mr. Creed is now quite old."

Evelina said, "Mr. Creed told me his version of the smuggler's legend, and I believe parts of it may be unknown to you all, for his stories have been kept a secret for generations."

The entire group stared at her. Miss Ambers leaned forward in her chair. "Are you at liberty to tell us these tales?"

Evelina felt certain Mr. Creed had related them to her

strictly for that purpose. She nodded and revealed to the intently silent group all that Mr. Creed had told her.

"Upon my word," Mrs. Rewell murmured at the end of her tale. "And the smuggler's name is Jack Stub?"

"Incredible," Mrs. Huggett said, shaking her head.

"I believe I might faint," Annabelle Rewell said, "but it was most exciting."

Similar comments passed round the remainder of the group.

Sir Alfred, standing near the fireplace, grunted and shook his head. "This is all very interesting and it may or may not be true. What I wish to know, Lady Evelina, is how it came about that so selfish an individual as Rotherstone was ever made to agree to our treasure hunt?"

Evelina regarded him closely for a long moment. She recalled the degree of hostility between him and Rotherstone and again had the impression that more lay behind such crossness than mere dislike.

Having anticipated his question, Evelina responded, "I may be mistaken, but I have a sense that Lord Rotherstone may be interested in making amends. He did not say as much, but his tone generally has become increasingly agreeable. He even dined at Wildings, as some of you know, and he was perfectly amiable to my entire family."

A round of whispered astonishment traveled swiftly through the dark chamber.

Colonel Carfax rose from his seat and crossed to the table where the map was displayed. "Though I find this discussion interesting, and I do hope my cousin is at last coming to his senses, the real question remains—where do we begin?"

Evelina smiled and rose to her feet. Joining him, she said, "You are a man whose interests reflect my own quite to perfection." She pointed to Devil's Gate and continued, "And now I will tell you something that I believe I should have confessed at the outset. The same night I found the map, I did a very quick exploration of this vicinity of Blacklands, but without success—in part because Rotherstone discovered me and escorted me back to the border between our properties. No, he was not entirely enchanted that I had trespassed, but as events have proved, perhaps our meeting in this way has opened the door for all of us. In any event," she gestured to Halling Stream, "this is the area I previously explored. I promise you all that regardless of how sorely tempted I may be in the future, I shall do no further explorations by myself."

The colonel smiled at her. "You will hear none of us make the smallest complaint. I do believe we are all indebted to you for being included in the first place. After all, you have the map in your possession and the treasure would appear to be buried on Blacklands. Do any of us truly have a claim upon it otherwise?"

Evelina glanced around the group that was now gathered loosely about the table. "I believe that such a treasure, should it actually prove to exist, ought to belong to our community. Though I admit I am protective of the map, any results of our search I lay no claim to whatsoever."

"You are being greatly generous," Miss Ambers said.

"Indeed, you are," Mrs. Huggett intoned.

"Yes, yes," Sir Alfred said, frowning. "That is the proper attitude."

"I believe you are being far more generous," the colonel said, meeting her gaze, "than most of us would be."

"Hear, hear," Mr. Fuller agreed.

Evelina met Colonel Carfax's gaze. He was smiling, his expression wholly friendly. His blue eyes, she realized, were thickly fringed with dark lashes. He was a very handsome man, and she knew him to be a favorite with all the ladies about Maybridge. He was an excellent dancer, always had an interesting anecdote for those moments when an occasion grew dull and never refused an invitation to a game of cards, chess, backgammon or cribbage. He was an avid sportsman, enjoyed his snuff and frequently went to London for the amusements only the capital could provide. Since her arrival in Kent, she had never quite understood why she had not tumbled in love with Colonel Carfax, even though it was quite the usual thing for all the ladies to do. Yet his society had not evoked even the smallest flutter in her heart.

The colonel said, "I am still mystified that he agreed to dine at Wildings."

"As was I," she said, "but I believe Sir Edgar had something to do with that."

"Ah, Sir Edgar," he murmured. She could not mistake the expression of quick disapprobation that twisted his lips.

"You do not respect him?"

"Anyone who knows the details of that man's history cannot claim even the smallest friendship with him."

This time, Evelina was properly shocked. "I must confess I am astonished. I met him for the first time but a few days ago and found him to be all that was gentlemanly and worthy."

The colonel inclined his head. "Perhaps he has changed. It has been known to happen."

Remembering that Miss Ambers had blushed the last time Sir Edgar's name was brought forward, she chanced to glance at her and saw that the young lady was quite distressed.

Immediately, she turned the subject. "But enough of gossip," she added hastily, still addressing the colonel. "So, what is your opinion? What do you think of the riddles?"

Colonel Carfax shook his head. "I only wonder how easily we will find the treasure. Surely so many riddles must indicate that though there is a large X on the map, perhaps the treasure will not be found so easily as we all hope."

"That is what Mr. Creed said. Indeed, he spent a very long time quietly perusing every inch of the map. He seemed somewhat puzzled, though he could not say why."

"And what of my cousin? Did he seem hopeful having seen the map?"

"Generally, he seemed quite disinterested." Curious suddenly about his relationship with Rotherstone, she asked, "Were you never friends with him?"

"Of course, when we were younger, for we are of an age. We were at university together. I had a great fondness for him then. I was for the army, however, and our paths diverged greatly. When I sold out after Waterloo, I found him greatly changed."

Miss Ambers tapped the map and brought the conversation back to the matter at hand. "What do you think this means?" she asked. "'*Ye olde well, draws water deep, of ale and mead, made honey-sweet.*'"

The younger Mr. Rewell said, "It must refer to a well to be found somewhere on Blacklands, surely?"

"That is a question I believe I must put to Mr. Creed," Evelina said. "On my initial exploration, I did not find one. However, wells are often knocked down and filled in, so I do not rely overly much on that particular clue."

Colonel Carfax shook his head. "Surely if the well were quite ancient, some remnant of it still might be on Rotherstone's estate." He tapped the large X located on what everyone believed to be the southwestern portion of Blacklands.

"I would agree with you, so I am hoping that our search is more conclusive than my previous one."

The next hour was spent with each of them perusing the riddles again, as well as the map, and offering all manner of suggestions as to the meaning of the riddles. A very lively, at times witty and at other times quite silly, discussion followed as to the whereabouts of Jack Stub's treasure.

In the end, little could be made of the possible meanings of the riddles without first beginning to explore the path indicated on the map that began at Devil's Gate.

At this time, Lady Monceaux provided refreshments for her guests: a platter laden with fruit, another with biscuits and sweetmeats, and as much ale and ratafia as was desired.

When everyone was seated and appearing quite content, Evelina explained how the hunt would be conducted: that once the date and time were arranged, they were free to explore Rotherstone's property.

"It would be better," Sir Alfred said, "were we all to meet with Mr. Creed. I for one should like to hear him tell his tale just in case some clue or other might be hidden within. Would you ask Rotherstone if he would allow us all to consult with his bailiff?"

"Yes, of course," Evelina said. "I think it an excellent notion." Privately, she doubted very much that he would agree to it. She had seen for herself just how angry he became at the mention of his neighbors.

His wife, however, lifted a tentative finger and said, "I have a suggestion."

Sir Alfred immediately stared her down. She seemed to shrink into herself and would not have said anything further, but Evelina wished to hear what she had to say.

Ignoring Sir Alfred, she said, "I value everyone's opinion and hope we may all contribute. What were your thoughts, Lady Monceaux?"

She avoided meeting her husband's gaze and said, "You mentioned earlier that you thought his lordship seemed to be more amenable to rejoining our society. Perhaps if we extended an invitation to him, say to the assemblies on Saturday, he might find we are not as disagreeable as he seems to think we are. In such an environment, surely he would have a greater likelihood of embracing our treasure hunt."

Sir Alfred barked, "He will never attend the assemblies, not in a hundred years, were he to live so long."

Evelina regard the baronet for a long moment. She thought he was uncommonly disposed to think Rotherstone would always be unwilling to embrace the local society. She was more convinced than ever that the breach between the earl and the Maybridge community had occurred primarily between the two men. For that reason, she queried, "I have been in company with Rotherstone several times now, and I have grown to wonder just what it was that set him at odds with our neighborhood. Can anyone enlighten me as to the particulars?"

The entire group fell silent. Mr. Crookhorn and Mr. Fuller turned pale, Sir Alfred's scowl nearly brought his eyebrows over his eyes and Colonel Carfax turned away to stand by one of the windows. No one said a word.

As Evelina glanced about, she saw that the ladies did not seem to be informed in even the smallest detail. Annabelle Rewell was playing with her reticule, twirling it in ever-enlarging circles, Mary Ambers and Mrs. Huggett both appeared bewildered, Mrs. Rewell stared at a fly on the table at her elbow and Lady Monceaux frowned at her husband.

"Is there no one present," Evelina queried, "who can tell me the basis for his rejection of society?"

Finally, the colonel spoke. "I believe it was a gentleman's affair," he said kindly. "Something having to do with his father. Beyond that . . ." He said nothing more, his intention clear. She was not permitted to probe further.

"I see," she murmured.

The colonel continued, though addressing the previous

subject, "I would, however, agree with Lady Monceaux that if my cousin is expressing even the smallest interest in taking his place in society, he ought at least be invited to the assemblies. There could be no harm in proffering the invitation."

Evelina could see that there was a general agreement about the idea, but she could not help wondering just what Rotherstone's response would be. He had been so varied in his reactions thus far that she honestly could not predict whether he would say yea or nay. "We should definitely ask him," she said. "However, I feel it absolutely necessary that his houseguest, Sir Edgar Graffham, be invited as well."

At that, Lady Monceaux pressed a hand to her lips and glanced at Miss Ambers. After a moment, she said, "I believe I forgot all about Sir Edgar in offering my suggestion. Naturally, we cannot invite one without the other. However, given present circumstances, I now see that an invitation to the inmates of Blacklands is quite out of the question."

Evelina could not keep from glancing at Mary Ambers as well. The young woman's gaze was pinned to the black, gold and green carpet at her feet. Her cheeks were quite pink. Mrs. Huggett as well appeared deeply distressed.

"I am sorry to hear that there is an objection to Sir Edgar," Evelina said. "I can only presume then that he has committed some infraction that has placed him beyond the pale. We shall consider the subject closed."

"No, pray do not," Miss Ambers said abruptly.

All eyes turned upon her, and more than one expression appeared quite shocked.

Miss Ambers swallowed hard. "Sir Edgar has committed no gross impropriety that must exclude him from society. Of that I am certain."

"This from you?" Colonel Carfax asked, his eyes

searching. "But are you certain, Miss Ambers? It is my understanding—indeed, I believe everyone's understanding—that he used you quite ill."

"He . . . he never importuned me. The circumstances . . . that is, it is very difficult to explain. He was in his altitudes at the time and not himself, a state of being I believe not a gentlemen present has failed to experience at one time or another."

Evelina wished she knew to what Miss Ambers was referring. Even Annabelle Rewell seemed apprised of the event, and she was the youngest member of their party present, not being three and twenty.

"But Miss Ambers," Miss Rewell queried, "did he not force you to remain with him *all night* at his rooms in Half Moon Street?"

"Annabelle!" her father cried.

Being the youngest lady present, and featherheaded, it did not occur to Miss Rewell that to ask such a thing was quite improper. Lady Monceaux offered her a reproving scowl. Mr. Rewell shook his head severely at his daughter, stunning her to silence. "I beg pardon," she murmured, her eyes wide.

Miss Ambers, however, appeared to take a different view of Miss Rewell's inappropriate question. She straightened her shoulders and gave all the appearance of one gathering her courage. She began to speak of the event, addressing Miss Rewell. "I am grateful you have brought the subject forward. Indeed I am, and unless there is an objection, I should like to address your concerns."

Evelina glanced round the dark chamber, but no one present seemed disposed to stop her. Far from it, since all eyes were fixed on Miss Ambers and more than one visage filled with curiosity.

"I chose not to leave him," she said, lifting her chin. More than one gasp filled the air. She continued, "He was violently ill, you see, and I remember being with my brother once in such a situation. I have been convinced from that time even until now that Sir Edgar would have perished had I not stayed with him. I believe it was not just that he had imbibed too much champagne at Lady Jersey's soiree, but that something he had eaten had not agreed with him as well. He had a violent fever."

"The scoundrel should have had the decency to marry you!" Stephen Rewell cried.

"Hear! Hear!" his father agreed.

"He offered, of course," she stated, seeming confused. The entire chamber fell silent, and Miss Ambers glanced from face to face. "Surely everyone knew as much? Tell me I am not mistaken in that!" she exclaimed, the color draining from her face.

"No, I think not," Lady Monceaux whispered, a kerchief clutched to her bosom.

"But . . . but I told Mama most particularly how it was, and that he offered but I could not accept of his proposals. She must have misinformed all of our acquaintance, and I was too reticent to speak of it. I must say I never quite understood until this very moment why he received the cut direct from so many. All, except . . . Rotherstone."

Silence pervaded the chamber. Evelina was put forcibly in mind of Sir Edgar's reference to his friend having acted with great kindness on his behalf.

"Lord Rotherstone did this?" Lady Monceaux queried. "I mean, of course he did, for they were always great friends." She then looked at her husband with a serious frown in her eyes. "Did you know of this, Alfred? Of the extent to Rotherstone's kindness?"

"Of course not. I thought, as everyone else did, that Rotherstone enjoyed snubbing all of society whenever he had but the smallest opportunity. In this case, it meant giving shelter to a libertine."

Lady Monceaux appeared not to believe her husband, but she said nothing further.

Evelina, suspecting that Sir Edgar was not indifferent to Miss Ambers, braved asking another question. "I can see that it is painful for you to speak of it," Evelina began softly, "but may I inquire why you refused him?"

Mary smiled faintly. "I was not indifferent to him, if that is what you are asking, but I could not bear the thought of being wed to a man so addicted to . . . to such useless ways. Perhaps I was wrong, but no good could have come from our alliance, at least at that time, of that I am convinced."

Evelina did not know when she had seen a more courageous young woman than Miss Ambers. She found herself grateful that she had broached a subject that affected more than one of the households present. George Fuller in particular stared at the ceiling and tapped his foot at an alarming rate. There were far too many gentlemen among the *beau monde* given to drinking to excess and to gambling far beyond their means.

"Do you think I was wrong?" she asked.

"Not in the least," Lady Monceaux stated firmly.

"I quite agree," Evelina said.

"Does not Sir Edgar have five thousand a year?" Miss Rewell queried.

James Crookhorn nodded. "He does, and a very fine Elizabethan house in Surrey."

"Well!" Miss Rewell cried, staring hard at Mary Ambers. "He could have cast up his accounts for a week, and I should not have refused such a tidy offer."

Her brother, sitting nearby, leaned over and pinched her very hard on the tender underneath portion of her arm. She yelped and would have pounced on him, but her father stayed her with a sharp, "Enough! The pair of you. Bella, you owe Miss Ambers an apology. She has shown a great deal more character than I have ever seen you exhibit in the course of your life."

Mr. Rewell glared at his daughter until she finally laid her feathers and addressed Miss Ambers. "I do beg your pardon. I am sure you are very worthy."

"Yes, she is!" Colonel Carfax cried, his laughing gaze fixed on the beautiful Miss Rewell.

"We have certainly strayed from point," Sir Alfred said. "If it pleases you, Lady Evelina, I think it an excellent notion that both of the gentlemen at Blacklands be invited to the next assemblies. And if it would not be too much trouble, would you inquire again if we may all be in consultation with Mr. Creed?"

"I shall be happy to do so," Evelina said. She then glanced about her friends and neighbors and felt her heart grow very warm. This was the first time she had ever been so nearly involved in a community, and she was finding she enjoyed it very much. She felt as though her own efforts were spurring the society forward, giving a unified objective to the group in the form of the treasure hunt and thereby creating opportunities for interesting exchanges. Even Lord Rotherstone was being affected.

She watched as Colonel Carfax began pacing the chamber. She had seen him do so at her own house not a few days past when she had first presented the map to everyone. She thought his conduct curious and said, "Is something distressing you, Colonel?"

He stopped abruptly. "Have I been marching to and fro again?"

"Indeed, you have."

"Well, I suppose it is because I have had a thought of my own by way of hoping to add some merriment and opportunity to our party."

"What is on your mind, Carfax?" Sir Alfred called out in his blunt way.

"I am thinking of giving a ball."

Another gasp arose, mostly from the ladies.

Miss Rewell cried out, "A ball! I should love a ball! It is so boring in Maybridge. Nothing ever happens!"

"Boring?" her brother cried. "How can you say so when we are very close to finding Jack Stub's treasure?"

Annabelle rolled her eyes but refused to say more.

"And lest I be accused of forsaking the proprieties," Colonel Carfax added, "I would like to know, Lady Monceaux, if you would oblige me in hostessing my ball?"

Evelina saw the expression of gratitude on her face and thought the colonel's actions showed great kindness.

"I should like nothing more," Lady Monceaux returned happily, once more ignoring her husband's frowns.

In the end, it was agreed that the colonel's ball would take place on Tuesday in one fortnight and that two days hence everyone would assemble at Wildings for the first hunt for the treasure. There was nothing left to do but for Evelina to arrange with Mr. Creed the time of the hunt and to lay her requests and invitations before Lord Rotherstone.

Chapter Seven

"The chapel ruins?" Evelina queried uneasily. She had been awaiting Rotherstone in his drawing room, but when he arrived on the threshold, instead of taking up a seat, he asked if she wished to accompany him on a short walk to the chapel ruins located on his estate. She had meant to settle all her matters of business with him quickly because she feared the longer she was in his company the more likely she was to succumb to one of his wretched flirtations. Apparently, there was to be nothing short or succinct about this visit. "You have a folly, then?" she asked politely.

"No, not a folly," he responded. "These ruins are real, several centuries old. 'Tis a lovely setting, and because the old chapel was built on a hillock, parts of each of the surrounding estates can be viewed from there. I thought you might enjoy the vista."

Ordinarily, Evelina would have delighted in nothing more, but her previous experience at the grotto told her Rotherstone was not to be entirely trusted in private, sylvan settings. On the other hand, she felt she risked offending him by refusing to go.

"Although," he mused, glancing out the window and frowning a trifle, "the clouds have gathered rather thickly in the last hour. It could rain."

Evelina smiled suddenly. She had her answer. Rain

would drive them back to the house, and betwixt times she felt there would hardly be sufficient time for him to make any improper advances. She did not think even the most determined gentleman would kiss a lady who was being pelted by a rain shower.

The chapel was situated on a hill north of the great house and must have been six hundred years old but was presently little more than several unrecognizable piles of weathered stones. An ancient sundial was cracked nearly in two and faced the wrong direction to be of any use. A lovely green grass had grown up around the ruins. She found herself grateful Rotherstone had suggested the excursion.

"How lovely," she cried. "And you were very right. The prospect affords an excellent view of the surrounding country. And look how busy your laborers are, like watching bees near a hive."

Rotherstone's estate was a bustle of activity below. Several gardeners could be seen pruning shrubs, cutting out dead branches from among a variety of trees and cleaning the flowerbeds of debris. A number of upper servants could be seen in several windows of the expansive house tending to the various rooms. The nearby farms were also full of laborers employed in midsummer tasks, repairing dry stone walls, digging ditches and generally preparing for the forthcoming harvest.

A sudden breeze swept over the vale, carrying a strong hint of rain.

"Oh dear," she murmured. "We have just lost all our sunshine. I believe you are right. It may rain very soon." The clouds to the west had now grown quite dark. "But nothing could be prettier, just as you said."

She let her gaze travel the ridges of the surrounding heavily wooded hills. In an area to the east that must have been near Pashley Court she noticed something on the hillside. "That must be the old windmill." She gestured in the direction of Watcombe Hill. "I would never have thought it could be seen from here."

"That would be Sir Alfred's estate," he said.

"And which church tower is that, the square one?"

He peered to the east. "The gray tower belongs to the hamlet of Gildstone."

"Gildstone? I do not recall it."

"Near Carfax's estate. There are scarcely more than two or three laborers' houses there."

"I see. That would explain my ignorance then." Her gaze traveled west. "And these hills to the southeast must be near your cousin's northernmost borderlands."

"I believe so. Just south is the village of Maybridge. You can see the tower of the church if you try very hard."

Evelina struggled for a full minute.

He drew close and directed his arm along the sight of her gaze. "Between those two monstrous oaks, just there."

" I see it!" she cried. He lowered his arm and she suddenly became aware of how near he was standing to her. She swallowed hard, recalling how tender was their last parting, when she had kissed him on his cheek. She felt a flush of something very near to affection bloom over her face and warm her heart. She wanted to step away from him but felt she would offend him in doing so or, worse, expose how she was feeling by arousing his scrutiny.

A cold, damp wind swept over her and the sensation passed. She breathed a sigh of relief. Glancing to the southwest, she said, "I did not know Wildings could be seen so clearly from anywhere on your property, but you can see a very large portion of the house from here." She moved away from him as though wanting to see more, but her real design was much more critical, for she found it unnerving to stand so close to him.

When he moved with her, she decided to offer a new subject, one she hoped would set him on his heels a trifle. "You asked me a few days past why I was not married. I have been wondering ever since how it is you are not. You must be past thirty, or am I mistaken?"

He nodded. "I am five and thirty."

He was therefore seven years her senior. She thought he looked quite well for his age and wondered if he would simply grow more and more handsome with the years. But this would hardly do, to be thinking such hopeless thoughts about him.

She brought her errant thoughts to order. "A bachelor for so long," she continued, "will not willingly surrender his life of command."

The wind again swept across the hillock, tugging at her bonnet and pressing the skirts of her walking gown against her legs.

Rotherstone crossed his arms over his chest. "So, I do have the right of it, that a man gives up that which he values most upon entering the married state."

"His freedom to do as he pleases?" she queried.

"Precisely."

"Just as a woman does," she countered.

"But you ladies seem far more inclined to the prospect than most men."

"I cannot speak for all women, only myself, and I promise you that the last thing I have ever desired is to be obligated in such a way to a man."

He narrowed his eyes and appeared pensive. "I believe you may have come to hold such an opinion given the former and quite harsh circumstances of your life. Yes, I know I am speaking plainly, so do not ring a peal over my head. My intention is not impertinence but rather to let it be known that I am aware that your eldest brother has not cared for either his estate or his family as he ought. That you have brought your mother and siblings beneath your wing is a trait in you I admire exceedingly. So let me pose this question to you: Could a gentleman in possession of good character and who would be properly attentive to you, could such a man tempt you to tie the connubial knot?"

His long speech had silenced her. She was shocked both that he had spoken as a man of sense and that he had actually shown compassion for the difficulties of her past. She could not, however, give him an entirely serious answer. "I daresay I should marry such a man in a trice," she responded gaily, "were I ever able to find one."

He laughed. "I never suspected you were a cynic."

"Then you hardly know me at all."

The breeze quickened suddenly.

"Rain it shall be," he cried. "We should return at once. Look how dark the clouds are become."

Since Evelina was wearing a new bonnet of yellow silk and had not brought her umbrella with her, she agreed at once. Taking his proffered arm, she let herself be led quickly down the path. The breeze became brisk, tugging once more at her skirts. Just as she entered the orangerie, a barrage of large raindrops struck the glass roof so loudly that it sounded like an entire regiment of drummers had begun pounding away.

"That was very close!" she exclaimed, laughing. "A minute more and we would both have been wet through."

"Yes, we would have. Now that we are here, however, would you care for some tea?"

"Yes, very much. Then we might discuss the matter at hand."

"Ah," he murmured. "The matter at hand. Do I apprehend that your calling on me today involves something more than setting a date for your hunt for Jack Stub's treasure?" he queried, eyeing her suspiciously.

"You have guessed correctly," she returned.

Rotherstone led her from the orangerie to an antechamber overlooking the north lawn. The expanse of green bouncing with raindrops had been recently scythed. A sprawling rose garden ambling to the east was in bloom with shades of pink, red, yellow and white flowers. After ordering tea, he led her to an upholstered chair near the French windows.

Evelina sat down gladly, spellbound by the beauty of the garden, the play of the clouds across the sky and the increasing rain. Without thinking, she curled up in the chair and watched the rainstorm unfold. A flash of lightning and a subsequent crack of thunder made her jump in her seat then laugh.

Rotherstone took up a chair opposite her, his back to the garden, his gaze fixed to her face. He had been in her company five times now, yet each succeeding time she seemed to become more beautiful. As he looked at her, he tried to determine just what it was that made her so lovely. Her eyes were a pretty almond shape and an exquisite shade of green. Her cheekbones were well defined and her nose fairly perfect in symmetry and definition. Her chin had the faintest cleft, and the line of her jaw completed what he now saw was a charming oval in structure. Yet he would swear that was not why she was so heartachingly beautiful.

Another flash of lightning and rumble of thunder, and she jumped in her seat. A smile suffused her face, and his breath caught. There it was, a joyful expression in her countenance that frequently lit her complexion. He could feel his heart quicken, and he restrained a strong impulse to reach toward her, to pull her from her chair, to draw her onto his lap and to hold her once more in his arms.

How the devil had she remained unwed these many years even if she was a cynic?

At length, the tea arrived. She poured cups for them both in the manner that had become a tradition in elegant homes. He realized they were not speaking. She was still mesmerized by the weather, he by her beauty. Even her hands were a delight: long fingers, creamy texture and a shape that begged to be held. He sipped his tea. Were he ever to court her, he would hold first one hand then the other, kissing them both over and over until she understood just how much he treasured them.

He liked that she was perched on the chair as though she had been in his house a hundred times instead of twice. How comfortable she looked draped over the arm slightly. She sighed several times, then glanced at him.

He met her gaze, perhaps more forcefully than he should have.

"Is something amiss?" she asked, a frown quickly marring her perfect brow as she took a sip of her tea.

He chuckled and shook his head. "No, not by half, I assure you."

"You appeared so . . . so serious. I thought perhaps I had offended you."

"Not in the least." He sipped his tea a little more. It would not do for her to comprehend even a particle of his thoughts. How easily she could manage him then if she knew just how strongly her beauty worked on his heart and how he wished he were back in the grotto with her.

She appeared perplexed, a frown on her brow in a beautiful puckering that made him wish he could smooth every ridge away with his fingers. He gave himself a mental shake. This would not do. She was, after all, a mere female and one proven to be as determined to her own ends as any lady he had ever known. He could not trust such a woman. Such a woman had hurt him once very deeply, and he would never permit himself to be hurt in that manner again. Still, he could appreciate her beauty. What man would not?

"So, tell me, Lady Evelina, what precisely is 'the matter at hand.'"

"Oh, that," she said, laughing, settling her cup on its saucer. "I nearly forgot. I fear I have been enchanted with the weather."

"So you have," he said, smiling in return. If only she were not so pretty!

"Yesterday, when I met with our neighbors to tell them of Mr. Creed's tales and to inform them of your agreement to permit our treasure hunt, I was charged with the office of asking you to attend our next assemblies in Maybridge to be held on Saturday. The Crown has a generous hall on the first floor, and we never lack for gaiety. The invitation has been extended to Sir Edgar as well."

The whole of the invitation was a surprise, no less so than that Sir Edgar had been included. "Indeed? Whose notion was it to include Sir Edgar? For if you must know, I am quite stunned."

"I can see that you are," she responded. "As it happens, Miss Ambers took some pains to exonerate him."

"And now you have truly astonished me," he cried. "I had thought her lost to all proper feeling. Do you tell me she actually spoke kindly of him before all our neighbors?"

"Yes, very much so, though I believe it required some courage on her part. But she did not hesitate. Indeed, from all that was said, her mother may have been the author of the rumors that destroyed Sir Edgar's character before the world. Miss Ambers was shocked, for instance, to learn that no one knew he had offered for her."

Lord Rotherstone pondered this information. "I recall her mother most particularly. A veritable dragon. I can only suppose she took delight in destroying his position in society. However, I am glad to hear that Miss Ambers has finally made the truth known. Sir Edgar, you know, would never permit me to say an unkind word against her. It would now seem he was justified in his belief in her character. I have long suspected that my friend still holds her in a great deal of affection."

"She did not seem entirely indifferent to him, either."

He sighed. "I suppose this places me under some obligation to agree to attend the assemblies. I believe I could easily persuade Sir Edgar to join me were I to mention your opinion of her sentiments."

"Then you will come?" she asked, clearly surprised. She took a sip of tea, then settled the cup and saucer on the table before her.

"I have not said as much," he responded. He had already made his decision, of course. Attending the assemblies would be the perfect environment for lulling his enemies into a belief that he had forgiven them all. However, he could not seem to keep from teasing Lady Evelina. "Although I believe you might have it in your power to persuade me to attend if you truly wish it." He smiled.

"I would promise to dance with you," she offered cheerfully.

He thought he would like nothing better. "I should like a waltz," he stated, finishing his tea.

She rolled her eyes. "You know that waltzing is rarely performed at such assemblies."

He chuckled. "Then I think I had rather not attend."

"You will only attend if our little country band strikes up a waltz?"

"Yes."

"You are being absurd."

"So I am."

"The chamber at the Crown is not large enough for waltzing."

"That is not my fault."

"You are being ridiculous."

He laughed.

"Country dances are always a delight," she said, "though I begin to see what it is. You have probably not danced in ages, and you now lack confidence that you can manage the evening without disgracing yourself. What if I offered to practice with you?"

"Now you are making sport of me."

"A little," she said, laughing. "In truth, I think you are being abominably absurd for staying hidden in your castle."

"This is not a castle."

"You treat it as though it is castellated and moated, the drawbridge up!"

He could not help but laugh. "But I do not like my neighbors."

"What does that matter?" she cried boldly. "A man of your station is required to be engaged in whatever concerns your community. You cannot deny as much, though I feel certain you will try."

"You are intent on serving as my conscience." He liked watching her reactions pass over her face before she spoke. Almost it was as though he could read her mind. But could she read his? Did she suspect even in the smallest way the terrible plan that he had already set in motion, one that when completed might possibly tear her fine community apart?

"Your conscience? I do not know that that was my intention, my lord, but if it will bring you to the assemblies, where you might come to know your neighbors a little better, then so be it. They are not the monsters you believe them to be."

He regarded her closely. "My dear Lady Evelina, I beg to differ on the ground that you have not lived in Maybridge long enough to have determined all the truths about your new friends and acquaintances. Allow me some understanding, some discernment, some justification for my isolation."

"Yes," she said quietly, holding his gaze in a thoughtful manner. "I shall, though I cannot say in the least why I would agree to do so." She gave herself a visible shake. "However, I do not mean to be so terribly serious. An assembly can be a great deal of fun and," here she paused for a second and regarded him with a smile, "I would give you a hundred kisses if you would come to the assemblies."

"A hundred?" he cried. "My dear Lady Evelina, you do know how to tempt a man!"

Evelina looked into dark eyes that stared deeply at her. Why had she spoken such provocative words to him? They had left her lips before she had considered the consequences of them. She was aghast at her suggestion. How could she have said anything so . . . so wicked? What would he think of her? By the arrested thoughtful expression on his face, she believed she knew precisely what he was thinking. She began to laugh: at herself, at the absurdity of the situation and the suggestion.

The smile that he gave in response was crooked. "You should never say such a thing to a man, any man, even if you are just teasing. I hope you do not mean to make a habit of it."

She felt oddly disappointed that his response was so proper. "Of course I will not. It was a ridiculous thing to say, and I . . . I beg your pardon for having spoken so brazenly." She felt a blush begin to climb her cheeks.

He set his cup and saucer down on the table hastily. The cup rattled, even more so when he rose abruptly from his chair and jostled the table. He began to pace the room.

She turned to stare at him, not knowing what was causing him such agitation. "Have I distressed you?" She picked up her teacup and saucer again.

He stared at her and laughed outright. "Good God, no. It is merely that—Lady Evelina, I think you should go. I have the strongest presentiment that both of us have ventured onto dangerous ground, and I will warn you most particularly that were you to stay, you would soon find yourself in the basket!"

Evelina blinked. She realized he was marching about because of the hundred kisses, and she was no longer disappointed.

She swallowed her tea as he paced and scowled at her. Even in his scowls he was magnificent. Yes, he was magnificent. He was dark and brooding, a black stallion pacing the foothills, looking for his mares and stomping in his frustration. He was used to having his way; she could see that; she understood that part of him to perfection. That she had rattled him sorely was something of a pleasure to her.

"I do beg your pardon, Rotherstone," she said at last. "I have teased you mercilessly, and now I believe I must go." She finished her tea, settling the cup and saucer back on the polished silver tray and rose to her feet.

Rotherstone watched her preparing to take her leave and wished she would not go. He found he had enjoyed her rather wicked teasing but knew that nothing good could come of her staying a moment longer. Still, he did not want the moment to end. "It is still raining. I shall send for my coach."

Evelina wanted to refuse his offer, but her yellow bonnet forbade her to say anything but "Thank you. I am most grateful."

He rang for his butler and ordered the coach brought round. "Come," he said. "We may linger in the entrance hall for a time."

She strolled beside him, walking down a fine hall well lit by numerous large windows typical of the Elizabethan house.

"I hope you know," he said, "that you may say anything you wish to me."

She cast him a sharp glance, her expression once more alive with laughter, her green eyes twinkling merrily. He wished her beauty did not have this horrid effect upon him of squeezing his heart as though it were a soft plum in her hand.

"*Anything,* my lord?" she queried. "Those are by far the most dangerous words you have spoken, you know, for my tongue is not always tender."

He smiled. "By my experience, you are quite mistaken in that." She appeared confused for a moment, but when enlightenment dawned, when he could see she was remembering the kiss in the grotto, a rosy blush touched her cheeks just as it should have.

"How wicked you are! How . . . how incorrigible. No, do not speak! I forbid it. I hope your coach comes quickly before one or the other of us does something ridiculous. I will only say, " and here she straightened her shoulders, "that I hope you will come to the assemblies, and Sir Edgar as well. There is, however, one more thing I was to have asked you."

"You frighten me now."

"I can see that I have," she said, smiling anew. "Sir Alfred, that is, the entire party wishes to know if they might be included in further discussions with Mr. Creed."

"That I feel I must refuse." He lifted a hand when she opened her mouth to begin her arguments. "I beg you will say nothing further on the subject. Mr. Creed and I will decide what can be done, which holes will be dug, if necessary, and you shall be apprised of our decision one day to the next. Beyond that, I have nothing more to say."

"I suppose with that I must be content."

"Yes, you must."

"There remains only one last point of business. No, it is not a request. Our neighbors have agreed upon tomorrow at one o'clock in the afternoon to begin hunting for the treasure. Is this agreeable to you?"

"As much as your hunt will ever be."

"I mean the day and hour," she stated, lifting her chin.

He merely laughed. "Yes. Tomorrow at one. I shall inform Mr. Creed. Explore to your heart's content, but I beg you will do no digging at that time. You may call upon me the day after to apprise me of your success."

For the next few minutes, she chatted with him on inconsequential subjects, purposely avoiding even the smallest word of a flirtatious nature. In due course, his coach arrived.

She thanked him for his time, for the tea and for showing her the chapel ruins. With that, she quit his house.

On the following day, Evelina led her neighbors to the gate at the easternmost hedge bordering Blacklands.

With the map tacked to a large board, protected by a flap of buckskin and carried by a servant, the party aproached the very hedge and gate Evelina had explored some nine days earlier.

"Why do you suppose Jack Stub called it Devil's Gate?" Miss Ambers queried. "Are there any historical associations that would support the use of such a name?"

"Not that I know," Evelina said. She called to one of

her servants, who carried a ladder, and directed him to remove the vines above the gate to see if anything had been carved into the original stone.

Sir Alfred took charge of the map and led several of the party through the opened gate, passing onto Blacklands to begin their search. Evelina remained at the gate to see if the servant's labors would have a good effect.

In the end, several words did appear, but of so opposite a meaning to "Devil's Gate" that she found herself confused. Miss Ambers stood beside her equally puzzled as Stephen Rewell read aloud, "Where angels tread, lightly the soul passes."

"'Tis quite lovely," Miss Ambers cried, clearly enchanted.

"Beautiful, even tender," Mia said. She had asked and been permitted to join in the hunt. The younger Wesley children, however, were required to remain at Wildings. "Only, how could Jack Stub have called this Devil's Gate?"

"I must admit, it makes no sense at all," Stephen Rewell commented.

"What makes no sense?" his sister blurted as she suddenly appeared from the other side of the hedge at the gate. Passing through, she bumped the ladder upon which the servant was standing and nearly caused him to fall.

"Have a care!" Mr. Rewell cried.

"Oh, do stubble it!" Miss Rewell returned hotly. "What a cretin you are."

Evelina interjected quickly. "We have found an inscription in the stone above the gate. Do but look."

Miss Rewell read the carved poetic phrase. "I have no idea what that means," she said, wrinkling up her nose, "but there is nothing devilish about it, of that I am certain."

Evelina addressed the servant now holding fast to the ladder. "Do you see any more carving?"

"Nay, m'lady."

Evelina felt quite disappointed. She recalled Mr. Creed's warning that Jack Stub would not have made the finding of his treasure, even with a map, a simple process.

"Come, let us see what the others are doing," she said.

Passing through the gate, she found Sir Alfred near the stream, glancing first one direction then the other, then at the map. He surveyed the land as one in command. "There is a footpath," he said, gesturing across the stream. "Colonel Carfax, Mr. Rewell, Mrs. Rewell, Mrs. Huggett and Lady Monceaux have ventured in that direction. For some reason, Mr. Crookhorn and Mr. Fuller headed north around those hills. I have no idea why."

"Perhaps they are feeling adventuresome," Miss Ambers offered.

When Stephen Rewell, his sister, Euphemia and Miss Ambers began crossing the stream, stepping on stones carefully to avoid getting their feet wet, Sir Alfred drew Evelina aside. "I was hoping for a word with you. Did you have a chance to speak with Rotherstone?"

"Yes, of course I did. I had meant to tell everyone earlier, but there was so much excitement about beginning the hunt I quite forgot. As for Rotherstone allowing all of us to speak with Mr. Creed, he absolutely refused. He did not say why, but he was adamant on that point. He is, however, considering attending the assemblies with Sir Edgar."

"That at least is hopeful," he said, but he was frowning. At that moment, a shout rose from across the stream. "It would appear Mr. Rewell has discovered something of import."

Evelina picked up her skirts and made a careful if quick dash across the stepping-stones in the stream and walked briskly along the footpath she had traversed that first night. Sir Alfred followed behind.

A hundred yards down the path, she came upon Stephen Rewell and the rest of the party that had ventured in an easterly direction. Stephen Rewell held up a stone he had unearthed where the path diverged and the land sloped. "What do you make of this? Do you think it could be the ruin of the well mentioned in the riddle?"

Miss Ambers brushed the stone with her kerchief. The stone had been chiseled and a word written across the front. "I think it might be 'Edward' or something."

Evelina drew near the servant holding the map. "I think we are not far enough along to have reached the well yet."

"You are correct, Lady Evelina, inasmuch as these are not stones that once made up a well."

Evelina turned sharply and saw that Rotherstone had ridden up on his gray horse. He was very near the fallen log upon which he had been standing the night she had trespassed on his lands. She was transported backward in time so quickly that for a moment it was as though she could feel him kissing her again. The sensation was so profound that she could scarcely breathe.

This would not do, however. She collected herself quickly. "How do you go on, Lord Rotherstone?" she asked politely. Glancing about, she could see the tension in every person present.

"Very well, I thank you."

"And you are certain these are not from a well?"

"Very much so. They have been placed at this location to keep the soil from eroding, having been taken from the old garden where I can only suppose one of my forebears, in his youth, practiced a little stone carving of his own. There will be more of a similar nature if you keep digging, but I hope you will not."

Mr. Rewell set the stone back where he had found it. He knelt and felt through the thick grass. "He is right. There are any number arranged in a long row."

"A natural mistake, I am certain, Mr. Rewell."

Stephen Rewell rose up and tipped his hat to the earl.

"Are you known to everyone?" Evelina asked.

He glanced round the group. "I believe I am. Welcome to Blacklands."

As one, the group bowed or curtsied as was proper. Annabelle Rewell was heard to sigh very deeply.

"I will not detain your search," he said. "I came only to say that I am having my servants bring some lemonade to you. The day has proved rather hot, I fear, even though we had the nicest, most cooling rain yesterday."

"That is very kind of you, my lord," Miss Ambers said.

"Thank you. Well, good hunting." He inclined his head to Evelina, then turned his horse about and headed in the direction of the house.

Evelina watched him go and had the most ridiculous impulse to call him back, to beg him to stay for a few minutes. She hated that he had remained but so short a time. Good heavens! When had this happened, she wondered, that she had developed so strong a taste for his society? Any number of warnings rang in her head like a set of powerful church bells. It was one thing to kiss a man and to enjoy his kisses but quite another to actually prefer his company to that of any other gentleman of her acquaintance, particularly when he was a man whom she knew not to trust.

A few minutes later, Rotherstone's servants arrived with pitchers of lemonade and glasses for everyone. Evelina realized that in their haste to uncover the treasure, they had given little thought to how hot the day might prove or how long their search might actually be.

The lemonade was welcomed by all, but it was Mr. Crookhorn, returning with Mr. Fuller from their northerly jaunt, who spoke aloud the thoughts of all. "I would never have believed Rotherstone would be so kind." He removed his hat and wiped his sleeve over his forehead. His curly brown hair stood straight on end and gave him the look of a porcupine in full quill.

"It was very good of him," Miss Ambers said, taking great pains not to notice Mr. Crookhorn's hair.

Evelina had to bite her lip and turn away.

"I wish there was more sugar in it," Miss Rewell complained, staring into her glass.

Her brother rolled his eyes. "You ought to be glad their isn't, or are you hoping to lose another tooth?"

Poor Miss Rewell had already lost two, and these words served to send her in the boughs. "How could you say such a thing to me when you know how I have suffered!"

"Cook told you how it would be, eating all those biscuits and sweetmeats. It is only a wonder you have even one tooth left!"

Evelina could see that a sibling quarrel of no small proportions had just been engaged. "So tell me, Mr. Crookhorn," she cried loudly, "what were you hoping to discover by traveling up the stream?"

He took up her hint and, with a glass of lemonade in hand, moved to the map that the servant supported in his arms. "Mr. Fuller and I noticed that there were several marks on the map running in that direction, and we were curious as to whether there might be some geographical reason for it, a line of stones or trees or something."

"And what did you discover?"

He grimaced. "Nothing to signify. There were three oak trees on the hill, which you can see from here, but beyond that nothing that might correspond to the markings, of which there are five."

Evelina also drew near the map. "Can anyone tell me which direction we should go?" She turned around and gestured to the diverging paths, the upper path leading in the direction of Blacklands and the lower path toward the gatehouse.

This afforded the entire party an opportunity to scrutinize the map as well as the two paths. The elder Mr. Rewell, having finished his lemonade, settled his hands on his hips. "I would think the lower, because if I am not mistaken, the upper path is of more recent origin."

"How can you tell?" Miss Ambers queried.

"There are not nearly as many trees along the upper path as the lower, leading me to conclude that several may have been downed to cut the path."

"As reasonable a deduction as any of us could imagine," Sir Alfred said. "Well, shall we then explore the lower path?"

"What exactly are we looking for?" Mr. Fuller said. His sharp blue eyes were a trifle red-rimmed and deeply shadowed, quite telling signs of his vices.

Evelina gestured to the map. "This well," she said, pointing to a drawing of a stone well. "From there I believe we are to locate within thirty yards a marker of some sort, perhaps indicated in one of the riddles, that will give us the location of the treasure."

"It cannot be far," Lady Monceaux cried.

"Indeed," Mrs. Huggett said. "The map is so clear. We must be close."

Evelina smiled. "That is certainly my hope."

The party marched in a single line along the lower, more established path. Mr. Rewell and Mr. Fuller occasionally searched the areas alongside the path, but before anything of merit had been seen or discovered, Miss Ambers, at the head of the column, called out, "We have reached the avenue leading to the house!"

A groan of dismay rippled through the length of the line.

The next several hours were spent scrutinizing the vicinity from the avenue back to the creek in an ever-widening path of search, with the hope that some sign of an old well had been missed. Alas, by the time the sun was well on the wane, and more than one of the party was irritable for a need of nourishment, nothing of significance had been discovered. The party returning to Wildings was hot, tired and discouraged.

Fortunately, Lady Chelwood had had the foresight to have an array of food ready for the treasure seekers as soon as they arrived. By the time the weary searchers reached the long gallery, Will announced the treat in store for them. Once in the morning room, a feast was laid out, including refreshing ale for the gentlemen and peach ratafia for the ladies. The map was set up on an easel, and while everyone feasted on cold meats and a platter of fruit, each member took a turn once more studying the map.

"The answer must lie in the riddles," Sir Alfred said.

Evelina held her plate of food in hand and studied the old map. She was about to suggest that the party spend some time in trying to interpret the riddles, but she glanced about and saw so much fatigue writ in every expression that she held her tongue. Instead, she suggested that she confer again with Mr. Creed and set another date, Monday following the assemblies, when they might try again.

Not a single person objected, and she knew she had put forth the right plan.

Within half an hour, the carriages and horses were brought round that had delivered the party to Wildings. A few minutes more and the house was quiet again, save for Will begging to be permitted on the next hunt.

Chapter Eight

"I am shocked," Rotherstone cried facetiously. "You did not find Jack Stub's treasure yesterday? Incredible. And after an entire afternoon's search."

"Must you crow so loudly?" Evelina cried.

"Yes," Rotherstone stated, guiding her to the morning room, where Mr. Creed would soon join them. "For I remember quite distinctly that you appeared completely confident of success."

"In that you are utterly mistaken—merely *hopeful*."

He lifted a brow.

"Well, perhaps I did believe were we to search your land during the day, we would find the old well. If you recall, the well indicates the location of the treasure." She huffed a sigh. "You must not come the crab, my lord. I am excessively disappointed."

He merely laughed. "I see you have brought your map."

Upon entering the morning room, Evelina saw that Mr. Creed had already arrived. She immediately spread the map out on the sideboard and told him all that had transpired, the exact route that had been explored as well as Mr. Crookhorn and Mr. Fuller's exploration of the area to the northwest in hopes of explaining the slashing lines on the left side of the map.

Mr. Creed laughed. "I am persuaded these marks were a result of cleaning the quill and nothing more."

At that, Evelina burst out laughing. "Oh dear. And Mr. Fuller was breathing quite raggedly when he returned to us. I do not think he is used to so much exertion. He will not like being told he played the fool."

"No man does," Mr. Creed responded sagely.

"I suppose I have but one question, Mr. Creed. Was there ever a well on this portion of Blacklands?" She ran a hand over the southwest corner of the estate. "Or did we not cover a wide enough terrain during our search, although we were there for hours?"

Mr. Creed examined the map carefully. "As to a well, I never knew of one in that vicinity, nor do I recall my grandfather speaking of one, and he served as a stable boy on Blacklands and was later head groom. If there is a well, I cannot say where it might be."

"What do you recommend we do next?" she asked.

Mr. Creed thought for a long moment. "That you try again and do as you have said: extend your pattern of search to encompass a larger area. At the same time, set one or two persons to reviewing these riddles. Who can say what would have been in Jack Stub's mind when he wrote them, but there is a meaning, of that I am sure."

With that, Evelina felt she had to be content. "The entire group is anxious to begin again on Monday. Will that suit both of you?" When they agreed, she thanked Mr. Creed, who bowed and quit the chamber.

Rotherstone walked with her to the entrance hall and asked politely if she would care to stay to tea. She declined his offer. "For if you must know, Mama is permitting Euphemia to attend the assemblies tomorrow evening and she insists that I be with her when the seamstress comes this afternoon."

"Is this a first assembly then?"

Evelina nodded.

"Then she will want you near."

Evelina glanced up at him and saw an expression of understanding in his dark eyes. She wondered about him for the hundredth time. How could a man with so dreadful a reputation have such moments of real sympathy and comprehension? She was utterly mystified, but rather than succumb to her ever-present *tendre* for him, she chose to remind herself that the man who appeared so kind in this moment was also the man who had only acquiesced to the treasure hunt when she agreed upon demand to part with three things of great value to her. She wondered when he would make the first demand of her but decided not to ask. There was no sense in reminding him of their agreement.

"Have you decided whether or not you mean to attend the assemblies?" she asked.

He shrugged faintly. "Sir Edgar is not yet certain what he wishes to do, but whatever his decision, I shall abide by it."

"I would imagine it would be no easy thing for him to attend."

"Not by half, but the knowledge that Miss Ambers has defended him publicly may in the end have a happy effect."

"I shall choose to be sanguine," she returned, "and hereby express a hope that I shall see you both tomorrow evening."

He smiled and bowed but said nothing more.

With that, Evelina returned to her gig and made her way back to Wildings. If more than once her heart turned over at the mere possibility of dancing with Rotherstone, she ignored such musings. She could have no real interest in him, after all. On the other hand, what harm could there possibly be in a dance or two?

* * *

The following evening, Evelina went down her favorite country-dance with George Fuller. He was already half-foxed but danced so proficiently that he never once missed his steps. He laughed a lot, a circumstance that kept everyone around him amused, Evelina no less so.

She had arrived an hour earlier, and for much of the time betwixt, her gaze had shifted again and again to the entrance whenever a new guest would appear. A half hour past she had given up pretending that she was looking for someone other than Rotherstone.

She had dressed with greater care than usual. Even now, she admitted as much to herself. She should not have given a jot what Rotherstone would think of her new gown of light green patterned silk trimmed in Brussels lace, or of her long red curls piled atop her head and dotted with small white roses, or of the pearl and diamond earrings her mother had lent her. Yet so she did.

Would he come? Had she had any affect on him in the past sennight? Yet what useless thoughts these were, when he was a man not to be trusted.

Thus she had been tormenting herself.

Just as the set was drawing to a close, Evelina again glanced at the entrance to the rooms and saw that Lord Rotherstone and Sir Edgar had indeed decided to attend the assemblies. So shocking was the occasion, however, that at least two of the musicians simply stopped playing altogether and more than half the dancers ceased moving in midstep, causing several collisions. Fortunately, a few seconds more brought all the musicians to the end of the piece, otherwise there might have been a serious injury.

Mr. Fuller called out far too loudly, "By Jove and all that's wonderful, Rotherstone has come! Sir Edgar, too!"

Several titters followed behind hastily unfurled fans.

Evelina stood opposite Mr. Fuller in nothing short of shock. Rotherstone had come to the assemblies. She wanted to believe this was a compliment to her, but in truth she knew he had come to be of use to his friend.

As she watched him exchange pleasantries with Sir Alfred—a remarkable event in itself—Evelina felt much as she had when she first learned she was to inherit Wildings, that a strong wind of change was blowing through her life. She marveled at how much had already happened, that she was at an assembly in Maybridge with her mother and sister, that she was dancing and having a wonderful time and now Rotherstone had come. These were nothing short of miracles in her life. Her arrival at Wildings had made all things new. Jack Stub's map had captured her fancy completely. And Rotherstone had come. Everything now seemed possible to her.

When the dance ended, she rejoined her mother, who was sitting in her Bath chair. Lady Monceaux sat beside her. Together, the ladies sipped glasses of port.

"So, he has come," Lady Chelwood said as Evelina took up a seat beside her.

"So it would seem."

"Astonishing," her mother murmured. "And Sir Edgar with him."

"You seem to have some influence with Rotherstone," Lady Monceaux whispered to Evelina.

"As to that, I do not think his presence here is due to my influence. My sense is that he chose to attend entirely on behalf of Sir Edgar."

"Ah," Lady Monceaux murmured. "That would indicate a graciousness in him quite at odds with Sir Alfred's opinion of his character. I have often wondered . . ." Her voice trailed off.

"Perhaps his character has been mistaken all this long while," Lady Chelwood suggested.

Evelina had begun to wonder the very same thing.

Lady Monceaux whispered, "Do but look at Miss Ambers."

Evelina glanced in her direction. Like everyone else, her gaze was fixed to the entrance. However, her complexion was quite high, and there was a longing in her expression that was unmistakable. "She must love him," she said. The ladies murmured their agreement.

Turning to look at Sir Edgar, she saw that he was presently conversing with Colonel Carfax and Mr. Fuller. Mr. Crookhorn joined them, and very soon all the gentlemen were laughing, Mr. Fuller the loudest, of course.

"A propitious beginning," Evelina murmured.

Euphemia crossed the room to them in that moment. She was beaming as she approached her mother. "Did you see me dance with Mr. Crookhorn? I did not even have to mind my steps."

Lady Chelwood took her daughter's hand. "You performed beautifully, my dear. I was never more proud."

Evelina looked up at her sister and smiled. "I would advise you, however, to try to avoid Mr. Fuller if you can. He is wretchedly addicted to drink and will certainly grow less secure in his steps as the evening progresses."

"I would have to agree with your sister," Lady Monceaux added quickly. Since Mr. Fuller in that moment took a glass of wine from a nearby servant, the ladies laughed together.

Euphemia said, "Lord Rotherstone appears quite handsome this evening. I believe he may be the most elegant gentleman here tonight."

As one, the ladies shifted their gazes to the earl, and almost as one, they sighed. Evelina would have been amused had she not realized that one of the sighs had been her own!

Mia, however, was quite right. She was herself struck with how he looked in formal blacks and whites, his neckcloth tied to perfection, his coat designed so perfectly that it appeared molded to his broad shoulders, the tails of his coat neither flared nor bunched as some were. He quite cast the other men around him in the shade.

As she watched Rotherstone begin looking about the chamber, her heartbeat quickened. When he found her, his gaze settled on hers and he smiled, if faintly. All the air seemed to leave her chest in that moment. She simply could not breathe.

"He is indeed a handsome man," Lady Chelwod murmured, turning to her daughter.

"Very much so," Lady Monceaux agreed, also shifting to look at Evelina.

For herself, she was still struggling for air. "Indeed," she said, but again a sigh followed. She might have been embarrassed to have made such a display, but for the present her attention was so fixed on Rotherstone that even a blush could not find its way to her cheeks. Even when her mother and Lady Monceaux exchanged a meaningful glance, even when her sister smiled broadly, her complexion remained unchanged.

After a few minutes, he began making his way toward her. His cousin introduced Rotherstone to several young ladies, and she could see that he was asking as many to dance. She began counting and very soon realized that he would have no dances left for the next hour and, if he continued in this fashion, none at all for the entire evening by the time he reached her. The chamber was horridly filled with ladies desirous of partners. She felt wretchedly panicked and a little sick at heart and all for a silly dance or two! She was a woman grown, but in this moment she felt to be little more than sixteen.

"You are trembling," her mother whispered.

"Am I?" she queried softly. She glanced down at her gloved hands and saw that she was. Meeting her mother's gaze, she found so sweet an understanding in her eyes that she asked quietly, "Am I lost?"

Lady Chelwood smiled. "Perhaps. Is he a good man? You have been now in his company several times. Have you yet formed a proper opinion?"

She shook her head, her gaze reverting to Rotherstone, who was but a few yards away. "I do not think I have."

A moment more and he was descending upon them, Colonel Carfax by his side. He greeted Lady Chelwood and Lady Monceaux first. Only after making a few polite observations and queries did he turn to Evelina.

"The musicians are about to strike the first note." He extended his hand to her. "You did promise the first set to me, or have you forgotten?"

Evelina laughed, relief flooding her as she placed her hand in his. "Most certainly I did promise."

When she rose and took his arm, he leaned close and whispered, "Your fingers are trembling."

"It is the most ridiculous thing," she said, looking up at him and smiling. How was it just being close to him could cause her heart to beat so rapidly? "My hands always tremble at a ball."

"Every ball?" he queried, guiding her to an empty place in the line of dancers.

"No," she responded, chuckling. "Just this one." She left him to stand opposite him. She could see that a quizzical look was in his eye as he watched her. She wondered what his thoughts were.

Rotherstone realized he was all at sea. He had come to

the assemblies in order to support his friend as well as to begin establishing himself with his neighbors. What he had not been prepared for, however, was the way he had felt a few minutes earlier when he had caught Lady Evelina's gaze from across the room. How was it possible that merely looking at a female could cause every muscle in his body to flinch and tighten? From that moment, he had had but one object: to be with her, to dance with her, the sooner the better.

The entire trip across the ballroom beside his cousin, greeting half a dozen young ladies and requesting their dances, had seemed to require hours of precious time. Every dance he solicited was one less he could ask of Evelina. Every word that fell from his lips was one that would not fall on her ears. When had she become so necessary to his enjoyment?

He realized the evening would be a struggle. He would be caught between desiring to be with her yet knowing he should not, hoping he might somehow dance three or four sets with her yet knowing if he did he would set every tongue to wagging. Good God, his mind had become a boy's mind. Worse still, every other thought was about how he could steal her away from the assembly and possess her lips again.

Of course, as he stood opposite her waiting for the music to begin, it did not help that she was by far the most beautiful creature in the room. A lovely green gown clung to her exquisite figure, white roses were tucked among her red curls and large pearls adorned her earlobes. Even in London, he had not seen so much beauty combined in one lady.

The music began, they came together and his arm was about her as they turned to the music. "I would have something of you tonight," he said in a low voice.

The music parted them. Together again, he continued, "The first of three demands."

He watched the color in her cheeks fade, for he knew he had shocked her. However, since her green eyes glittered like emeralds, he knew she was not offended. The music drew them apart.

Once more together, she whispered, "What would that be? What do you require?"

He could only smile in return, for he meant to tease her, to alarm her, to torment her, at least so long as her eyes appeared as though fire danced in them. Of course, he wished for nothing less than a kiss from her, but he would not say as much in the middle of a dance.

Together again, he said, "You must wait until the set is concluded." He smiled and watched as she offered a playful glare then smiled in return.

"You mean to torture me," she murmured.

"Very much so."

The remainder of the set was spent in just this sort of light banter. Nothing could have pleased him more. When the dance drew to a close, he could not remember having laughed so much at a ball.

He led her from the floor and would have continued his assault on her senses, but he noticed that her attention was caught by something else and that she appeared distressed.

"What is it?" he asked.

"Mama," she returned.

Rotherstone glanced at Lady Chelwood and saw that she was leaning forward slightly, her elbow settled on the arm of her Bath chair, her hand resting on her forehead and her fingers shading her eyes. Evelina hurried toward her.

"Mama," she cried. "What is the matter? Are you in pain? Of course you are. I can see that you are. I knew you should not have come. I knew the assembly would be too much for you. Come! I insist on taking you home this instant."

Lady Chelwood lifted her head, her eyes narrowed in what Rotherstone could see was a great deal of pain. "What nonsense is this?" she asked. "I am perfectly well, and I most certainly will not leave the assembly."

"Mama, I can see that you are very ill."

"Perhaps I have been feeling a twinge here and there, but nothing I cannot manage. Perhaps if you were to bring me another glass of wine."

"No, we are leaving. Let me fetch Euphemia." She turned to do so, but Lady Chelwood caught her hand.

"I beg you will not," she whispered urgently, pulling on her daughter's hand. "Mia has been looking forward to the assemblies for so long. You cannot disrupt her pleasure now. I will not allow it. I am her mother and I am yours. You will do as I say, at least in this instance."

She spoke forcefully, but it was clear to Rotherstone that in her debilitated state she was unable to withstand her daughter's overbearing kindness.

"Mama, we are going. Now. I shall brook no refusal."

Rotherstone saw the pinched line of Lady Chelwood's lips, and he thought he understood. He drew close to Evelina. "You shall not leave," he whispered in her ear.

"I most certainly will," she returned, meeting his gaze firmly.

He smiled. "No, you shall not." He turned to Lady Chelwood. "Will you excuse us, my lady?"

"Of course," Lady Chelwood said, a little shocked.

Rotherstone then drew Evelina aside and asked quietly, "Do you recall what I mentioned to you earlier?"

She searched his eyes, and when enlightenment dawned, that she was obligated to him, an appalled expression overtook her entire face. "You cannot be serious?

You would not ask this of me: to jeopardize the health of my parent? You would not be so cruel?" Her words were spoken in a harrassed whisper.

"I believe it is you who are being cruel in your sympathy."

Lady Evelina glared at him. "How dare you?" she hissed.

"I dare because in this circumstance you are wrong. However, to continue debating the matter would only bring an unwanted attention to either of us, so I will only say again that this is my first demand, and you will heed it or I shall happily make it known that you are a woman who will not keep her word."

He had struck home on all counts. The fight left her entirely. She was angry; he could see that. "Very well. Have it as you will, but if you think I will not have a word or two for you when next we are in private . . ."

"I look forward to it, my lady," he murmured, smiling. "Now, pray tell your mother you have changed your mind." He guided her back to her parent.

Lady Chelwood leaned back in her chair. "Whatever is amiss? Why were you quarreling?"

Evelina said, "Rotherstone refuses to permit me to take you home."

Lady Chelwood stared in some wonder at him. He smiled at her in response. "How very kind of you, my lord," she said, tears touching her eyes. "I . . . I thank you."

"You are most welcome."

"Only, how did you manage it when she will never listen to me?"

"Mama," Evelina said softly, as one wounded.

Lady Chelwood addressed her daughter. "I know you love me and you wish the best for me, but, my dear, sometimes it is as though you are my master. In truth, I miss my daughter, my friend, and at least a small degree of freedom with which to dictate my course."

"But I am always thinking of your health."

"I know that, my darling."

"But surely . . . Mama, do you truly see me as a tyrant?"

"At times, yes," she responded candidly.

"Oh dear," Evelina said, dropping into a seat beside her. "It is merely that . . . I detest seeing you in even the smallest amount of pain."

"I know that you do, dearest, but this is my cross to bear, not yours. And I cannot bear it well if you cosset me. I know you do not understand, but were I to leave tonight and destroy even a particle of Mia's happiness, then the pain I am experiencing has seen another victory."

Evelina took her mother's hand gently in hers. "You are the most courageous woman I have ever known. If this is indeed how you feel, I will do better. I promise you that, Mama. I will do very much better."

Rotherstone excused himself. "Forgive me, but I am to dance with Miss Rewell. I can see her waving her kerchief to me quite frantically." He bowed and moved away.

Evelina watched him go. She was stunned by all that had just transpired. She still held her mother's hand and felt a responsive squeeze.

"I am beginning to think," Lady Chelwood whispered, "that Rotherstone may be an exceptional man. From this moment, you have my leave to love him as much as you wish."

Evelina once more looked at her mother. "It is just that it is so unfair that you should suffer, especially now when so much good fortune has come to us."

"Pray do not cry, my darling, or you shall reduce me to tears as well. And that will not do in the least!"

She gave her mother's hand a squeeze and released it.

At that moment, a sudden hush came over the assembly. Lady Chelwood murmured, "Do but look, Evie."

Sir Edgar was leading Miss Ambers onto the floor. "How tenderly he holds her arm," Evelina said.

"I have never seen her smile so sweetly."

"It is a love match indeed," she whispered.

"So it would seem."

When Mr. Crookhorn asked Evelina to go down the next set, the assembly took a more normal course. Evelina danced until her feet ached, as did her sister, Rotherstone fulfilled his obligations to a proper number of the young ladies present and Sir Edgar gave rise to a great deal of speculation when he asked Miss Ambers to go down a second set. Finally, the assembly ball ended with several groans of disappointment.

Because of the natural flow of the evening, Evelina did not have another occasion to speak with Rotherstone until it was time to leave. As she gathered several servants to assist her, he begged to be allowed to help Lady Chelwood down the stairs. The servants carried the Bath chair down first, while he supported her arm as she made her way to the stairwell. She moved quite slowly, her pain much in evidence. She was a frail woman, and before she attempted even one stair, he murmured, "Permit me, my lady." Without allowing for her permission, he gently lifted her into his arms.

Evelina was behind them and gasped, but much to her surprise her mother merely laughed and said, "So I have come to this!" she cried. "Very well. You certainly seem sufficiently strong."

"I am," Rotherstone responded, smiling broadly.

Evelina trailed behind them, aware that from this moment she would think very differently about both her mother and Rotherstone.

Once her mother and Euphemia were settled in the

barouche and the footmen were struggling to secure the Bath chair to the back of the coach, Evelina drew Rotherstone apart from the coaches, horses and guests. In the dark shadows of the inn, she thanked him for his wondrous kindness to her family.

"You are very welcome. Do I apprehend you do not intend to give me a dressing-down for exacting the demand I did from you earlier this evening?"

"How could I do so when you must know you have changed our lives for the better tonight?"

Even in the shadows, she could see that he was greatly struck by her gratitude. For herself, her heart was so full, so warm. She wanted to give greater expression to her gratitude but was not certain how. "You showed me how blind I was to the deeper needs of my mother, and for that I shall always be grateful." She did not know what possessed her in that moment, but she took sudden hold of the front of his coat, gripping it tightly. "Thank you, Gage, more than I can ever say." She then kissed him hard on the lips for a very long moment.

When she released him, he reached for her, but the coachman came into view. She turned swiftly and moved in his direction. "Are we ready then?" she called out.

"Yes, m'lady."

"And the Bath chair is quite secure?"

"Very much so. I checked it over more than once."

"Excellent. Let us depart." She climbed aboard the coach and saw that Mia was worried. She held their mother in her arms. Her eyes were closed.

"She should not have come tonight," Mia said, her face twisted in anxiety.

Evelina drew in a deep breath. "She would not have missed it for the world. She wanted nothing more than to see you dance at your first assembly. I, too, as it happens.

Tell me who you favored dancing with the most, and were you able to forestall Mr. Fuller?"

Lady Chelwood spoke. "Yes, Mia, you must tell us everything. I want to hear it all."

Mia glanced at Evelina, and she gave her sister an encouraging nod. The journey home was a sweet, delightful discourse of all the events of the evening, from Euphemia's first dance to her last. She dwelt especially on what everyone had come to believe was the renewal of love between Sir Edgar and Miss Ambers. Nothing, it would seem, held greater value in her young mind than the fulfillment of love between two people each of whom had endured society's censure for the past several years. She spoke of dancing with nearly all the gentlemen present, save for Mr. Fuller, who had been on the brink of asking her to go down a set when he suddenly collapsed into the chair beside her. "He actually leaned his head back against the wall," she cried, "and began to snore! I was never more shocked!"

The sisters laughed heartily together, and even Lady Chelwood chuckled, if faintly.

"Of all the gentlemen with whom I danced, I must say I found Lord Rotherstone to be the most enjoyable. He made me laugh nearly the entire set. He kept teasing me about having cast a spell on Mr. Fuller, thereby relieving the entire assembly of his loud voice."

"I am glad to hear it," Evelina said. "I know I have been given reason to think ill of him, but more and more he is proving himself to be a man of some good parts."

"Besides being so handsome," Mia cried. "I only wonder he has escaped marriage for so long."

"Some gentlemen," Lady Chelwood said, "wait for exactly the right lady before venturing to the altar. He is such a man and very wise, I think."

This was more than she had said the entire journey. Evelina believed these words were meant for her. The coach finally arrived at Wildings, and the next several minutes were devoted to tending to Lady Chelwood's comfort and care.

The housekeeper saw her supported with a blanket and tucked into the Bath chair then carried slowly upstairs by three of the strongest footmen. Seeing her mother released at last to her abigail, whom Evelina knew to be devoted to her mistress, she could finally breathe a sigh of relief.

Only then did she bid Mia good-night and retire to her chamber. She was greatly fatigued, but in the most wonderful way.

As she lay in her bed, she was overcome with the sweetest, happiest reflections. She had seen Rotherstone and Sir Edgar take part in an assembly. Sir Edgar had danced with a woman he had once asked to marry him. Rotherstone had engaged fully with his neighbors. She had even seen him conversing amicably with Sir Alfred. The neighborhood was improving, and she took great pleasure in knowing she was part of those changes, which appeared to be of benefit to Maybridge and the attending gentry. She had even kissed Rotherstone, an act that had been as impulsive as it had been innocent, for she had only meant by it to give some expression to the gratitude she had felt toward him. Everything, indeed, seemed to be changing, but she could only wonder what Rotherstone thought of her now.

Later that evening, Rotherstone paced the library. He felt completely and utterly undone by all that he had experienced during and immediately after the assembly. Having taken strong control of the animosity he felt for many of his neighbors for the purpose of advancing his revenge upon them, he had unexpectedly found himself in the middle of a very fine assembly. He had not expected to be so well entertained, so welcomed, so involved in the lives of people he had kept at such a great distance.

He was of course not in the smallest degree fooled by Sir Alfred's attempts at warm civility. His father's explanation of the events of seven years ago placed Sir Alfred in a terrible light. He was no child to be misled by the baronet's attempts to engage him in conversation or his offers to see his wine glass refilled. No, he knew what Sir Alfred was, and that knowledge continued to drive him regardless of how pleasant the evening had proved.

The ladies he enjoyed very much. There was an artlessness among them all that indicated an excellent sort of breeding shared among the ladies of Maybridge. Lady Euphemia in particular had charmed him with her wit and innocence. She knew how to laugh, a quality shared amongst the entire family.

Lady Monceaux had intrigued him. As the wife of his enemy, he had been naturally suspicious of her. But she had conversed at length with him and in a manner so devoid of criticism or arrogance that he soon formed the opinion as to which in her marriage was the superior partner.

Her words were thoughtful and kind. "I wish that we might have known you earlier, my lord. But you were a typical youth, away at school most of your years and intent on your own interests at university and beyond. I wish you to know that I always had a deep admiration for your father and that I was infinitely regretful that something occurred to separate our families. Sir Alfred, of course, did not share the particulars with me, but I hope you will find it in your heart to forgive the incident that has kept you from our circles these many years and more."

He had narrowed his eyes at her, trying to determine if she was dissembling, but he saw nothing in her expression or her manners to indicate deception of any kind. "I know my father was very sad to have lost the friendships that he did."

"Perhaps you will be able to set everything to rights," she said, smiling. "I was especially grateful when you allowed Lady Evelina to persuade you to permit our treasure hunt. That, I believe, will prove to be a good beginning—for all of us, I trust."

He had returned an appropriate response, but he had also wondered if she knew even in the smallest amount that his efforts were not toward reconciliation at all, but rather toward exposure and revenge. He felt sorry for her, because it was her husband who was his primary object and she did not seem to be deserving of injury.

He stopped his pacing, sat in a comfortable chair beside an empty hearth and sipped a fine glass of brandy. The one surprise of the evening had been Lady Evelina, almost from start and certainly to finish.

Initially, he had thought to exact a kiss from her as one of his requisite three demands. Instead, he had insisted she relinquish control over her mother, a circumstance that had altered probably forever the relationship between parent and child. The tenderness that had resulted between them, in word and in action, which he had witnessed, had been so moving that his own heart had come to ache almost painfully in his chest. He could not have left Evelina's side in that moment had he wanted to.

Later, when he had attended to Lady Chelwood himself, carrying her down the stairs and seeing her settled in Mia's arms within the family barouche, his growing opinion that her ladyship was an excellent woman had been confirmed again. He had known her husband, and there could be no two opinions that the former earl of Chelwood had not been the equal of his wife. Nor was their eldest son worthy of his family. As much as he had disliked Lord Bramber, he began to believe that the baron had made a very wise choice in bestowing Wildings upon Lady Evelina.

The greatest surprise of all, however, had been the very last moment with Evelina in the shadows of the inn, when she had kissed him so purposefully. Once before she had kissed his cheek, but that had been a friendly salute. This time there had been something more in the way she kissed him. He understood her purpose, to express her gratitude, but he felt all the strength of her character in that moment.

What she could not know, perhaps would never know, was that he had been more affected by that kiss than by any single event in the course of his life.

He was, in fact, undone.

Chapter Nine

On Monday afternoon, just past one o'clock, Evelina stared at Rotherstone, unable to credit that he, as well as Sir Edgar, had come to join in the treasure hunt. The earl had not given her the smallest hint at the assembly on Saturday that either of the gentlemen had meant to do so.

She was not the only one to be a little shocked. Even the younger Mr. Rewell had cried out, "What the deuce?"

Lady Monceaux came forward immediately and offered a small curtsy. "You are very welcome, my lord, I am sure. And you, Sir Edgar."

The remainder of the party followed suit, and the next several minutes were spent in gathering round the map and engaging in a discussion as to which areas of the southwest corner of Blacklands had not yet been explored and what the party's strategy ought to be. Mr. Creed's advice to expand the area to be searched was put forth, whereupon Mr. Crookhorn suggested they divide the land in segments that would then be explored in small groups. When no objection was raised, several clusters of treasure seekers went off in various directions to explore every hillock, ravine and wooded copse within a half-mile radius of the original path. An ancient well, or the remnants of one, was the object.

Evelina's party consisted of her sister Mia, Rotherstone,

Sir Edgar and, not surprisingly, Miss Ambers. That the interesting pair found it imperative within the first few minutes of the exploration to venture down an entirely separate path from their own also did not surprise her.

Mia smiled broadly. "Did you chance to see how he looked at her when he first arrived?" she queried.

Evelina thought her sister was addressing her, but when she turned to give answer she saw that Mia was looking at Rotherstone. The earl also smiled. "Smitten, very badly so."

"Very badly indeed!" Mia cried. "Oh, but think! We may have a wedding breakfast to attend before the summer is out. I do not think I could be happier. And do you believe they are a good match?"

Rotherstone gestured for her to precede him down a narrowing footpath and said, "It certainly does not matter what my opinion is. Sir Edgar will do as he pleases. However, I believe Miss Ambers to be a young woman of excellent character and not a little courage. Her temper is certainly sweet. She is the sort of lady whom I believe would make any man a good wife. That she appears to love Sir Edgar is his good fortune."

Evelina, having joined them from a different path a few feet away, said, "These are very fine compliments indeed. I am quite envious of Miss Ambers in this moment. I did not know it was possible for any young woman to secure your good opinion."

"Is this true?" Mia asked, as Rotherstone allowed Evelina to pass him as well. "Are you so severe upon our sex generally?"

"Your sister would have you believe so."

"And that is what disturbs me, for if you must know, I value Evie's opinion above anyone's."

Rotherstone fell silent for a moment. Evelina turned to regard him, wondering what next he would say. The spirit of the entire exchange had been quite light-hearted, so that she did not expect anything of a serious nature to fall from his lips.

"I believe, Lady Euphemia, that you have quite put me in an intolerable position. If I protest Lady Evelina's criticism of me, you will be required to doubt her opinions, yet if I do not, you may begin to find as much fault with me as she does."

At that, Mia laughed in great delight. In just such a way the hunt continued. As their small group headed south, nothing more was seen of Sir Edgar and Miss Ambers. Occasionally, Evelina would espy Lady Monceaux, Mrs. Rewell and Mrs. Huggett, who were exploring to the east.

Back and forth they wandered, climbing more than one small hill, searching out every thick copse that barred their path and pressing on until the drystone wall was reached that separated Blacklands from the lane beyond. Across the lane was one of Rotherstone's tenant farms.

"I know I should not be," Evelina said, leaning against the wall, "but I confess I am greatly disappointed." She settled her gaze on several sheep clustered near a ruin of a stone shed on the farm beyond the lane. One of the ewes was scratching her side against the wall and leaving tufts of wool behind.

Mia leaned down to retie her half boot. "As am I," she said. "Lord Rotherstone, are you certain you do not know of a well anywhere on your property?"

"Alas, I do not, and as you may imagine, I was used to play in these woods since I was a boy."

"Then what is the point of our searching?" Mia asked reasonably.

"You must place that question before your sister."

Evelina smiled broadly. "For the pure pleasure of it," she responded happily.

"You have your answer, Lady Euphemia."

"I wish you will not address me so formally," she said, wrinkling her nose. "I have come to think of you as an elder brother. Oh dear, have I offended you? Do you think it improper of me to have said so, for now you are frowning."

"Then you must forgive me. I have no experience in the matter, having no siblings of my own. However, I would like very much to address you in a manner you would prefer, but only if *Lady* Evelina does not mind."

Mia laughed at the emphasis he had placed on "lady." Not yet being seventeen, she did not censure herself overly much, a circumstance that Evelina thought had made their time together quite enjoyable. She smiled in return. "I can have no objection to Rotherstone addressing you as he would a sister. However, with me I fear I must insist on some formality." She turned her laughing countenance to Rotherstone and saw that a warm light had entered his eye.

He said, "You are not always entirely formal with me. As I recall, there was a moment on Saturday night when you were not formal in the least."

Evelina bit her lip.

"You mean when Evie kissed you?" Mia cried, unthinking. She clamped a hand over her mouth and a blush instantly suffused her cheeks.

Evelina was also blushing and said, "I was not certain you had seen my, er, indiscretion."

"I thought it very sweet," Mia said, "and not undeserved, for he had been so kind to Mama. However, I beg you will both forgive me for having been so completely thoughtless in having reminded you of it."

"You are not to blame," Rotherstone said, appearing entirely nonplussed by the exchange. "After all, I hinted at it first."

"Are you in love?" Mia asked, glancing from one to the other.

"Mia!" Evelina exclaimed. "You have just gone beyond the pale for a second time."

For some reason, Mia did not seem in the least penitent. She merely smiled and turned on her heel. "I have something I would ask Annabelle, and if I am not mistaken, she is exploring with her brother just beyond Lady Monceaux's position. I will leave you now." She turned once to wave then hurried away.

Even though Evelina suspected that Mia had matchmaking designs in leaving her alone with Rotherstone, she did not bother to call her back. She had begun to fear anything else that Mia might take into her head to say. "You must forgive her, you know. She is still quite young."

"There is nothing to forgive. We have been indiscreet and have given rise to all manner of speculation in her young mind."

"If I recall, you were not indiscreet, I was."

He chuckled. "I could have prevented the kiss, but then it all happened so very quickly."

"The hour was late and the night dark. You could hardly see me coming at you."

He chuckled again. "I am grateful then that I did not have a moment to decide. I do not think I have enjoyed a kiss more. But come, let us return to some others of the party. I begin to be afraid that you might accost me again."

"I would never do so, not with those sheep continuing to scratch themselves against the stones. Could anything be less romantic?"

Rotherstone watched them for a moment and shook his head. "I suppose not," he said, laughing.

As they started up the path, a shout was heard from a

distance to the northeast. Evelina recognized Stephen Rewell's voice.

"What is he saying?" she asked.

"I believe it is, '*I have found the well.*'"

"Indeed?" she cried, a burst of excitement coursing through her. She did not wait, but picked up her skirts and began to run. Rotherstone's laughter followed her.

Fifteen minutes later, most of the party was gathered about what the younger Mr. Rewell had proclaimed was the well.

"But are you absolutely certain?" Evelina asked, quite despondent, as she glanced up at Rotherstone.

"Indeed, Carfax will tell you. Here he comes now."

"The devil take it," the colonel grimaced. "I see Rewell found our old fire pit."

"Well," Sir Alfred said, huffing a sigh, "how very unfortunate, for I vow this ring of stones is the most promising thing I have witnessed all day. I am coming to believe that Jack Stub's treasure is nought but a hum."

So dominant was the air of discouragement that Evelina recommended they return to Wildings for some refreshment. Not a single person offered an opposing suggestion, and everyone began moving in a northwesterly direction toward where the map had been left with one of the Wildings servants.

Once gathered at the map, Evelina asked if Rotherstone and Sir Edgar would like to join them. Sir Edgar, gazing fondly at Miss Ambers, agreed at once and that so enthusiastically that a round of chuckles passed through the group. Rotherstone also accepted, a circumstance that set Evelina's heart to fluttering anew.

An hour later, after platters of fruit, cheese and biscuits had been consumed, as well as a proper quantity of ratafia, lemonade and ale, the party gathered closely about the map once more. Each of the riddles was read aloud again.

A variety of solutions were put forth as they had been before, but with little success. Colonel Carfax addressed the heart of the matter. "Other than the fact that we have not found a well at this location on Blacklands," here he gestured to the map, "another difficulty arises in that there are no flat stones about this area of Rotherstone's property that might fit this riddle: '*Some stones flat, others tall, a bridge in death, to any wat fall.*'"

Rotherstone suggested, "If you remove the riddle that would indicate the treasure had been buried on Blacklands, and ignoring the large X on the map as well, do the remaining riddles suggest another location?"

The party fell silent. Miss Ambers read aloud all five riddles.

'Time is lost, a smuggler's weary end, the world is upside down, walls that will not mend.

"*'Devil's Gate wat opens, black the land will be, down a path, a treasure ye will see.*

"*'Cross the stones, cross one to dare, pearl and gold within, small and rare.*

"*'Ye olde well, draws water deep, of ale and mead, made honey-sweet.*

"*'Some stones flat, others tall, a bridge in death, to any wat fall.*'"

"How many wells are there in the vicinity of Maybridge?" the elder Mr. Rewell queried.

"A score, no doubt," Mr. Crookhorn responded. "One might as well ask how many *stones* there are." He ran a hand through his thick, curly locks so that once more he looked like a porcupine. When Mia and Annabelle Rewell began giggling together, he rolled his eyes and cried, "The deuce take my hair!"

This set everyone to laughing. After a minute or so another lengthy discussion of the riddles ensued, resulting in no conclusions whatsoever as to where a new hunt for Jack Stub's treasure ought to commence. Evelina could see that the party had grown weary. She watched Rotherstone confer quietly with Sir Edgar, after which both gentlemen rose to take their leave.

First, however, Rotherstone begged to have a word with William. Evelina led the gentlemen to the garden, where the younger children were plotting out a large maze that Evelina had decided to create on a portion of the expansive grounds. William ran to the earl, exchanged a few words that Evelina could not hear and gave a shout of triumph.

"We are to go fishing tomorrow!" he shouted.

Evelina felt her heart expand as she looked at Rotherstone. "How kind of you. I am exceedingly grateful."

Time and place were arranged, after which the gentlemen took their leave.

When Evelina returned to the drawing room, she found Sir Alfred standing before the map, shaking his head, his hands slung behind his back. "What a puzzle," he said. Turning to Evelina, he added, "Well, well, I suppose you will want to speak with Mr. Creed again."

"Aye," she responded, smiling, but she was feeling a trifle blue-deviled. "I will take the map to him again and see what next he recommends, but I will be very surprised if he suggests we once more comb this area of Blacklands." She could not credit that with even a quite specific map, they had not yet located the treasure.

Everyone rose and began gathering bonnets, hats and gloves, and the group slowly progressed to the entrance hall, a few stepping out of doors. Evelina had just expressed her enthusiasm to Lady Monceaux about several of her plans to decorate Colonel Carfax's ballroom for his upcoming *fete*, when she overheard the colonel say, "I heard he recently lost over a thousand pounds at one of the East End gaming houses."

"That seems unlikely," Mr. Rewell said. "I was at Brook's a fortnight past, which Rotherstone frequents, and heard it bandied about that he will scarcely ever sit down to a game of cards, and when he does he always wins."

"Yes," Mr. Fuller interjected, "but you have just described two very different establishments. Perhaps he means to give one appearance to the *beau monde* and another to a set of persons who do not give a fig for his birth and breeding."

Sir Alfred frowned. "Sounds like he's following in his father's footsteps, eh?" A silence fell among the group. Evelina noticed that an odd exchange of glances ensued. She felt uneasy.

Next to her, Lady Monceaux had begun to frown quite deeply.

"Whatever is the matter?" Evelina asked quietly. "Are you not well?"

"I am perfectly fine, thank you." She gave herself a shake. "The afternoon has been rigorous. I actually walked up and down more than one hill. At my age, 'tis not an easy thing. Ah, the carriages have arrived." She bid Evelina good-day and moved out of doors.

After a few minutes, Evelina was left standing alone in the entrance hall. She felt utterly downcast, but she knew her lowness of spirit involved more than the fact that the treasure was still undiscovered. As she began to climb the stairs to her bedchamber, she recalled the discussion several of the gentlemen had had about Rotherstone. *He recently lost over a thousand pounds at one*

of the East End gaming houses. She shuddered suddenly
and clapped a hand over her mouth as though to hold
back her thoughts and feelings.

The sensation was so familiar. How many times had
she learned that her own brother had lost a thousand or
even two at some "hell" or other? She had heard Rotherstone went often to London, even to game, but until this
moment she realized she had been forgetting this about
him, or perhaps choosing to forget.

She felt foolish and sick at heart. Was it true? Was it really true? And what had Sir Alfred meant that
Rotherstone was following in his father's footsteps?

On the following day, Evelina descended the stairs
and burst out laughing.

"Mama, whatever are you doing?" she cried. Her parent was spinning her Bath chair in circles in the large
entrance hall.

Lady Chelwood, her eyes shining, responded, "I only
learned about an hour ago that I could do this. It takes
some skill, but I am getting better."

Evelina drew on her gloves and chuckled a little more.
Since the night of the assemblies, when she had been
so chastened by Rotherstone's insistence that she permit
her mother to have her way, she had striven to continue
allowing her parent to make her own decisions. Though
she had been amused to see her mother twirling the
chair in circles, she had still found it quite difficult to
keep a stream of orders from passing her lips. She
wanted her mother to cease her spinning, to take more
care that she did not injure herself, to rest, to not exert
herself overly much; in short, to be more of the invalid
she knew her to be.

At the same time, there could be no denying that her

mother had been happier in the past three days since the assemblies than she had in the past twelvemonth.

Of her own accord, her mother suddenly stopped. She was breathing hard but smiling. "Are you off to see Mr. Creed?"

"I am," Evelina returned, pushing each finger of her gloves snugly into place. She wore a walking dress of a serviceable blue calico, half boots of sturdy brown leather, a snug spencer of twilled dark blue stuff and a straw bonnet trimmed with crocheted lace and artificial silk bluebells.

"Well, you look very pretty."

"Very pretty indeed!" Mia called from the doorway to the drawing room. "Will Rotherstone be with you when you discuss with Mr. Creed our unsuccessful hunt of yesterday?"

Evelina knew what her sister was about and lifted her chin. "No, for if you have forgotten, he is fishing with Will in one of the trout streams this morning."

"I have every confidence," Mia said, smiling broadly, "that if you were to take a very long time with Mr. Creed, his lordship would probably return in time to see you. After all, he will not want to be angling with William all day."

Evelina had thought as much herself, but she had also recollected yesterday's account of Rotherstone's gaming losses; consequently she was not so enthusiastic as she might have been. To her sister, she said, "You seem to have settled everything in your own mind on the subject, never once taking into account the possible feelings of your sister."

"I know my sister's feelings even if *she* does not!"

"Now you are being absurd, and I intend to leave."

Evelina did not hesitate but slipped past her mother, who had once more begun twirling in her chair. She opened the door and a fine summer's breeze blew over her. She could not keep from smiling. Whatever her concerns, fears or even disappointments, there could be no disputing that the blue sky overhead was exquisite. She would have no need of either horse or carriage today. The weather was very fine and a walk to Blacklands, by way of the lanes, suited her to perfection.

An hour later, she was seated in the morning room sipping a cup of tea that Mr. Creed had very kindly provided for her. He sat adjacent to her, the map this time spread before him on the table. He scowled and shook his head, grumbled over the five riddles, and shook his head a little more.

"I was convinced from the first," he said, tugging at his white hair just above his ears, "that Jack Stub was up to snuff. He no more would have made this map simple to follow than he would have cut off his other arm."

"Have you even the smallest notion what he meant by his riddles?"

"Nay." He sighed heavily. "I have thought on this map a score of times and more since first seeing it. Sometimes I feel that close to solving the mystery." He held his fingers in a narrow pinch.

"I have as well," she confessed. "Though I brought the map today, I must say I have every portion of it memorized. I have even sketched in my mind the streams that are drawn on the map and their names."

He lifted his gaze from the document still protected by the velvet and smiled. "I see we have a similar mode of solving a problem. Do you know what intrigues me the most about these configurations?" He pointed to the map.

Evelina leaned forward in her chair. "What?" she asked.

He traced his finger over several of the waterways.

"How Halling Stream when it enters River Rother intersects closely to Buckstee Stream here to the east. Then how Nettles Stream merges with the Buckstee and together—"

Evelina interjected. "Together they form a striking S pattern. I noticed it as well. Indeed, I believe that Mr. Stub forgot that Buckstee and Nettles actually intersect. Rather, he drew Nettles in such a manner that it connects directly with the River Rother. Do you think that error in particular is of significance?"

Mr. Creed sighed. "I cannot say. I suppose we will not know until the treasure is finally found." He turned the map sideways so that east was now in a northern position. He turned it again and again, then righted it once more. "There must be something that we are not seeing." He grew silent again, and set to studying the map further.

Evelina's attention drifted. As she sipped her now-cold tea, she thought about Rotherstone and wondered just how much time had elapsed thus far during her meeting with Mr. Creed. Surely, if she stayed much longer she would be forced to see Rotherstone before leaving Blacklands. Because she was still distressed by the most recent gossip about him, she realized she would rather not meet with him just yet.

Another minute passed, then another. Suddenly, Mr. Creed threw back his head and laughed quite heartily. "I have it!" he cried. "Or at least I think I do. By Jove, I believe I do!"

Evelina's heart jumped. "You do? Tell me at once."

He laughed again. "I fear you will despise me, but I cannot."

"Whatever do you mean?" she asked, aghast.

"My master instructed me that if I ever solved it, I was not to inform you."

She was so shocked and dismayed that she sat back in her chair with a thump. "He cannot have said so," she cried. "What manner of beast is he to have made such a wretched decree?"

"I would agree 'tis very cruel. On the other hand, my lady, you have a keen intelligence, and I am persuaded that given a little more time you will discover the answer for yourself. I will give you a hint, though—concentrate on the shape of the streams and rivers."

She was so angry that she could hardly keep one proper thought fixed in front of another. All that seemed to dominate her mind was her desire to see Rotherstone put in the village stocks. What a vile man he was to have done this to her! And what of the others?

She decided she could hardly say anything to her neighbors. She only wished Mr. Creed had not told her he had solved the mystery.

She rose to her feet, thanked him crisply for the tea, rolled up the map and realized she had yet one more reason for being grateful his lordship had not returned from his fishing expedition with her brother. She rather thought that had she seen him in this moment, she would have boxed his ears.

She quit the chamber, her head high and her entire being on fire with aggravation. She marched down the drive, the map securely beneath her arm and began scuffing at the rocks beneath her boots. She could not remember the last time she had been so angry.

Rotherstone whistled as he walked in a southeasterly direction on the circuitous lane that serviced both Blacklands and Wildings. He was returning from a summery fishing expedition with Lord William that he had enjoyed very much. His young friend had reminded him of happier times in his own childhood when he and his cousin, Colonel Carfax, would fish and hunt nearly every day.

He realized he was happy in this moment, and there was no doubt in his mind that his present contentment had a great deal to do with his comings and goings at Wildings. He also knew that Lady Evelina would by now have finished conferring with Creed. He was also well conversed with the fact that she would only take the path connecting their properties if she had received prior permission from him. On this occasion, such permission had not been sought. He had every hope, then, of meeting her, particularly round the next bend, after which the lane straightened out for a considerable distance.

He whistled more loudly still, competing with the incessant chatter of the sparrows, of which there must have been a thousand in the nearby woodland. A sound not far distant, however, caught his attention: a whelp, a scuffling and a frightened cry. He was running before he had ordered his boots to pick themselves up. As he rounded the bend, he saw a woman's figure in blue rolling slowly into the deep, weed-strewn ditch that separated the lane and Blacklands. Her bonnet came off in the tumble and a shock of red hair bespoke her identity.

"Evelina!" he shouted.

He reached her within seconds, slid down the bank of the grassy ditch on his boots and turned her over. She was limp in his arms.

"Evie," he whispered to her, using her family's pet name. "Darling, can you hear me?"

He sat against one wall of the ditch, drew her onto his lap and propped his legs against the opposite wall in order to better support her. Her complexion was chalky, her red curls littered with leaves and debris, her eyes closed. He felt over her head, and his fingers were soon wet with blood.

A sick feeling of panic came over him. "Evie," he whispered urgently again. "Please, dearest, can you hear me? Evie, Evie? Please answer me."

Her eyelids began to flutter and several short and quite pitiful moans passed her lips. She began to struggle. "No, no, do not! Do not!"

"Evelina, 'tis I! You are safe! Calm yourself!"

At that, her eyelids fluttered open. "Gage," she whispered. He watched as sudden tears streamed down her cheeks. "Is he gone?"

"Indeed, he is," he responded, holding her gently. "But he has done you injury. You are bleeding from your head."

"Yes. I remember now. I was walking toward home and I heard whistling. I smiled, thinking that the day was so lovely that of course any sensible person would be whistling. Suddenly, a blur of brown came out of the woods. I saw a small log. I know I cried out; then I was falling. The next thing I knew, I was struggling against you. Oh, my head hurts dreadfully."

"As it should. Hold still. Lean against my shoulder and let me find my handkerchief." She did as she was bid, and he tilted sideways in order to reach his pocket with his free hand. He found his kerchief and held it to her wound. She moaned anew.

He cradled her for some few minutes and instinctively rocked her. Once in a while he could hear her sniff.

"The map," she cried suddenly. "Where is the map?" She sat up quickly and instantly regretted doing so and leaned back again. "Oh, my poor head. Only, Rotherstone, where is my map?"

The ditch being quite deep, and seated as he was, he

saw only what was along the length of it. "I do not see it. Perhaps it is on the road."

"I believe whoever hurt me wanted my map."

"Undoubtedly. Why else would you have been attacked?"

"There can be no other reason."

"Come. I must take you home."

"I shall try to stand, with your help. I am persuaded I can walk, if I try."

He did not believe her, but he allowed her to sit up slowly and to gain her feet. She looked down and chuckled. "Do but look." She pointed at the bottom of the ditch.

The map was beneath his boots, dirty and partially torn. He reached down and picked it up.

"Where is . . . the velvet . . . I had been using to . . . to protect . . . it?" Her voice sounded quite strange, as though she had spoken from a great distance.

Fortunately, he glanced at her in time to watch her eyes roll in her head. She would have toppled over then and there but he caught her. Once more, she was entirely limp in his arms. He fought the tears that tightened his throat, and a wave of anger flowed over him so profound that had her assailant been within arm's reach, he would not have been able to answer for his actions. The murderous rage that infected every limb had the happy effect of charging him with great strength and purpose. She felt as a feather in his arms. He climbed easily from the ditch and began a quick progress in the direction of Wildings, a full mile distant.

His thoughts were varied as his boots ate up yard after yard of road. He was angry and frustrated. What would have happened to her had he not been nearby?

Only then, as he allowed his mind to imagine the worst, did he come to realize that after all his intentions of keeping Lady Evelina at bay, she had somehow managed to invade his heart. For the first time, he considered the possibility that he might be in love with her.

Evelina made her way back from a very deep fog. She did not know where she was or why her head ached so fiercely. Opening her eyes became a painful process until at last the deed was accomplished. She met Dr. Dungate's concerned gaze. He was holding her wrist and counting her heartbeats, his lips forming each number.

"Ah, Lady Evelina," he murmured softly. A warm smile suffused his face. "You have returned to us."

"Was . . . I gone so very long?" Her throat felt very dry.

"You must be thirsty," he said.

He held a cup to her lips and supported her neck. She gulped the water gratefully. Only then did she glance around the chamber. Her family smiled at her: William, Sophy, Alison, Euphemia and her mother. "Where is Lord Rotherstone?" she asked.

"Here." He emerged from the shadows beyond her bed.

"Have you the map?"

At that, everyone laughed, though she did not quite understand why.

Her mother, sitting in her Bath chair, which had been pushed close to the bed, stretched out her hand to her. "The very last thing any of us give a fig for is that horrible map."

Evelina knew she had been struck a hard blow to her head, for she still could not understand why her mother would speak so. Mia moved closer as well. "Evie, we thought you might . . . well . . . die."

At that, Will's face crumpled.

"No, no, my love!" she cried, gesturing for her brother to draw near. "I would never do so." He threw himself on her chest, a sudden movement that made her wince for the pain that shot through her head. She held him tightly, however, and waved the doctor away. "I merely had an adventure," she explained. "And it was very exciting. I should do it all over again did I have the chance."

"You would?" he asked, lifting a wet face to hers.

She tousled his red hair. "Of course. Only, I wonder if you might do me a very great favor."

"Anything," he said.

"I beg you will make certain that Lord Rotherstone has had a proper meal and at least one tankard of ale before he leaves Wildings." She lowered her voice. "I fear your sisters will not know to be attentive to a man in that way."

"Of course I will!" he cried, straightening up at once. He turned to Rotherstone. "Come with me."

"With pleasure," the earl responded.

Evelina called to him before he parted the chamber. "I wish to speak to you before you leave."

He met her gaze but lifted a teasing brow. To William he said, "Your sister found her tongue quickly enough. She has already begun ordering me about. I begin to think she was merely *pretending* to have been hurt."

Evelina delighted in her brother's sudden burst of laughter as the pair quit the chamber.

Over the next half hour, Dr. Dungate examined her and told her what she might expect from having taken so fierce a blow to the head. He recommended that she rest a great deal in the coming days and said that he would call on her each afternoon to see how well she progressed, until he was satisfied her recovery was complete.

He soon took his leave, and she was left to speak with

her sisters and her mother. She reassured them as best she could about the attack but promised that until the business of Jack Stub's treasure had been resolved, she would travel the lanes about Maybridge only if she had at least one footman to offer some protection.

Mia finally shook her head in some wonder. "Are you aware, Evie, that Lord Rotherstone carried you for well over a mile?"

Evelina frowned slightly. "I suppose he must have," she said slowly. "I know I was looking down and laughing because the map was beneath his boots, dirty and torn. The next thing I knew, I was looking into Dr. Dungate's hazel eyes. And he really carried me all that way? I am astonished. Was he greatly fatigued when he arrived?"

The ladies intoned as one, "No."

Lady Chelwood said, "You were as a bird in his arms, I swear it is so."

"I was very angry," Rotherstone called from the doorway. "So much so that I believe I could have carried her another fifty miles."

Evelina turned to look at him and was suddenly overwhelmed with all that he had done for her. "My lord, how shall I ever repay you? I begin to think you saved my life."

He drew close and would have answered her, but Lady Chelwood withdrew her hand from about Evelina's and said, "My dear, I am feeling a little fatigued."

"Mama, I am so sorry to be a worry to you."

"Stuff and nonsense. However, the children have not eaten their dinner. I should like to see them all fed. Cook will be sending you her special broth very soon, I am sure. Even if you are not hungry of the moment, I hope you will eat something of it. She will take a pelter if she thinks you have stopped eating."

"Of course, Mama."

"Come, Mia. Sophy, you may push me if you like. No, Alison, do not pull a face. You pushed me all about the garden this afternoon, remember?"

Their voices faded as they left the chamber and creaked the wooden floors all the way down the hall.

Rotherstone came to stand close to the bed. "Whatever am I to do with you?" he asked, clucking his tongue and shaking his head. "I should never have allowed you to remain even five minutes at Blacklands that first day, for you have been trouble ever since."

Evelina could not help but smile. She extended her hand to him. "You have proven yourself a friend in so many ways. But this! Did you truly carry me all the way to Wildings?"

He nodded.

"You will be sore for days!"

"I certainly shall!" he cried, rubbing his arm.

She could only smile a little more.

The amused expression on his face faded in quick stages. "I do not suppose I could persuade you to give up this ridiculous treasure hunt?"

She shook her head. "What a poor creature I would be were I to permit a trifling bump on my head to disrupt our hunt."

"I wish you would be a little more serious," he said firmly.

Her heart sank. She could see he meant to be difficult, but how was she to explain her determination to him?

He suddenly squeezed her hand, which she only now noticed he was still holding. "Enough," he whispered gently. He leaned down and kissed her forehead. "There will be sufficient time in the future for us to brangle over our disagreements. For the present, you must rest and make yourself well."

"Thank you," she murmured, sighing deeply.

"I shall take my leave, but I promise I will call again very soon."

"I should like that."

He bowed and turned to quit the room.

"My lord!" she called out. "Only tell me first, where is the map?"

He rolled his eyes, reached into the pocket of his coat and withdrew the torn and tattered parchment. He crossed to her and she took it from his hand, once more thanking him.

He merely scowled his displeasure in response and in two seconds more had left the chamber on a quick tread.

Evelina unfolded the torn map gently. It nearly hung in two pieces now. She was a little surprised at how she felt about having it back in her possession. She had already memorized the entire map; however, tomorrow, when she felt better, she intended to draw a new one, copying everything exactly as Jack Stub had created it.

For now, however, she merely touched it with the tips of her fingers, grateful that she was still alive and even more grateful, though she did not understand entirely why, that the map had not been taken from her.

Chapter Ten

The next day, Evelina lay quietly in her bed. Her head still ached, probably a little more so because her mind had become occupied by the attack. By now, everyone in a ten-mile radius of Maybridge, both highborn and low, would have known that she had found Jack Stub's map and that a treasure hunt was in progress primarily at Blacklands.

In her naïveté, she had never considered for a moment that she might be in some danger. The hunt was for her an adventure, and if it truly did yield a fortune, she rather thought their small community could donate the whole of it to the orphanage at Studdingly. She had never truly had a thought beyond this.

Now, however, she had to consider the possibility that someone, though probably not a member of their party, was desperate to have the treasure.

She had discussed the situation at length with her mother, but Lady Chelwood had been at a loss as to what ought to be done next. "Certainly if you had seen your assailant," she had said, "we might know better how to proceed. However, I should tell you that yesterday Rotherstone sent Mr. Creed about the entire neighborhood to make inquiries concerning anyone who might have been seen in the lane where you were attacked. Not a single individual, muchless a suspicious sort of person, was witnessed in the vicinity that day. Not one."

"And Rotherstone did this for me?" she asked, astonished. "Is this indeed true?"

"Of course. I would have expected nothing less of him."

"Is this your true opinion of our neighbor? You perceive his character to be so worthy?"

"Very much so." Her mother had tilted her head. "You do not hold him in as much esteem as I, do you?"

"I confess he is doing much better of late, but you must admit that his reputation among our neighbors was previously quite shocking."

"So it was," she had said, a deep frown between her brows. She then gave herself a shake. "Well, I suppose we cannot know all the particulars, especially from Rotherstone's point of view these many years and more. That is the true difficulty of coming so late to a neighborhood." She paused and appeared to consider the situation again. "On this other matter, Evie, I beg you will take to heart what happened to you yesterday. You will promise not to go about by yourself again?"

"I most strongly assure you I have no intention of doing so." She had touched her head quite gingerly in that moment. "I cannot tell you how ill I was yesterday, and today I vow I am as weak as a kitten. No, I have no interest in making it easy for my assailant to hurt me again."

Over the next two days, Evelina received visits from nearly every one of their party. The horror with which the attack upon her person had been received always dominated the initial part of each call. Shortly afterward, however, the frustrating conclusion followed that little could be done in light of Mr. Creed's investigation.

Her neighbors were in agreement on two fronts: that Evelina refrain from going out in the lanes alone, and that the hunt continue, but with a greater urgency, if possible, to see it brought to a speedy conclusion. The sooner Jack Stub's treasure was found and disbursed, the better.

Evelina of course agreed with the general consensus, for the more quickly the treasure was discovered, the more certain no further injury could befall any of the party. She realized she had not as yet discussed with Rotherstone the fact that Mr. Creed believed he had solved the map's secrets. Were he to be prevailed upon to allow the solution to be made known, there was an excellent chance that the treasure could be recovered almost immediately. She hoped he would be reasonable the next time he called, for she fully intended to persuade him to release this most valuable information to the community.

On the third day of her recovery, Colonel Carfax, Mr. Crookhorn and Mr. Fuller called. Each was particularly solicitous.

"And you are certain you are well?" the colonel asked. "I have been anxious for your health from the moment I learned of the attack."

"Indeed, you must tell us how you fare," Mr. Crookhorn added.

Mr. Fuller nodded as well.

Evelina gestured for them to sit down. When they were settled, she said, "I am so much improved that even Dr. Dungate is surprised."

Colonel Carfax smiled. "That is excellent news, although I will not be in the least offended if you must absent yourself from my ball on Tuesday next."

Evelina pretended to appear affronted. "I should think myself a poor creature indeed if a small bump on the head should prevent me from attending your *fete*.

Indeed, knowing that such a pleasure is in store for me has elevated my spirits more than you can know."

"Then I shall claim a country-dance even now and hold you to it."

"Done," she returned, smiling.

His expression, which had been affable, now dimmed, a concerned frown marring his brow. "But when you were attacked, you truly saw no one?" he asked.

"Not in the least," she responded. "Merely a blur from my right, and though I knew I cried out, the next moment I awakened to Rotherstone's voice."

"Too wretched by half," Mr. Crookhorn murmured, his face twisted with distress. "But are you, that is, are you absolutely certain this person was intent on getting the map? Could there have been some other reason for the attack?"

Evelina sighed. "I believe my assailant had only the map in mind. The velvet with which I protected the map had disappeared, but the map itself had slipped unawares to the bottom of the ditch. If the attacker had not wanted the map, the velvet would have been in the ditch as well."

"Very true," Mr. Crookhorn commented.

"I also suspect that he may have heard Lord Rotherstone's whistling, become frightened and may not have ascertained that he actually had the map in his possession before fleeing. There would be no reason for the person who did this to take the length of velvet otherwise."

"No, indeed," Mr. Fuller said. He cleared his throat and glanced around the drawing room as though searching for something. He tapped his throat. "Very hot day. Deuced uncomfortable."

Evelina laughed at him. "Would you gentlemen care for a little ale?"

Mr. Crookhorn nudged his friend and rolled his eyes.

Mr. Fuller in turn ignored him. "You are very kind, Lady Evelina, but I would not want to put you to any trouble."

Euphemia rose. "I shall tend to it at once." She gave a tug on the bell-pull, and within a few minutes the gentlemen had their ale.

By the fourth day, Evelina found that her head was no longer giving her even the smallest pain. The day was fine, and she was permitted to be out of doors. She reclined with Will on a chaise that had been brought to the foot of the garden and settled beneath an apple tree. Several chairs were scattered about in anticipation of the family spending some time during the day in the garden, but instead of making use of one of them, her brother had stretched out beside her. Together they were looking at a leaf collection he had made the summer prior.

"Hallo!" Rotherstone called from the terrace. He waved and held up his fishing tackle.

Will bolted from the chaise before Evelina had a chance to stop him. He began to run.

"William!" Evelina called after him. "One moment, please!"

Will skidded to a halt and turned to face her. "What is it, Evie?"

"You will not want to wear your new shoes to Scrag Stream."

He looked down at his feet. "No, indeed! Mama would have my head, and Mia, too, for she told me not to wear them outside!"

With scarcely more than a hurried bow to Rotherstone as he shot past, William disappeared into the house.

Rotherstone laughed and continued in her direction.

"Good morning," she called out.

"And to you," he responded. "A perfect day for lying on a chaise in the garden. How are you feeling? I must say your complexion is greatly restored."

"I am feeling very well indeed," she said. Her heartbeat quickened as it always did when he drew near. Even in garb designed to take the hardship of traveling up and down a creek bank in search of trout, his presence still affected her feminine heart. He wore a low leather hat that appeared to have been in use since he was a young man, a coat of brown stuff she was certain would be shed as soon as propriety would allow and aged buckskin breeches tucked into serviceable top boots. Even though his attire was more useful than elegant, his neckcloth was a work of art, the fine white linen setting to strong advantage his dark eyes. She took a deep breath, trying to settle her heart, and continued, "I have not had even the smallest bit of a headache since yesterday. I believe Dr. Dungate will permit me to begin going about in society very soon."

"I am glad to hear it," he said, laying the tackle basket and rods on the grass nearby. Drawing a chair close, he sat down. "I brought you some roses from my garden. Your sister is putting them in water. I believe she means to bring them out to you."

Her heart turned upside down. "You brought me a bouquet?" she asked, smiling broadly. "How very romantic!"

He narrowed his eyes at her. "I believe flowers to be a proper offering to the sickroom."

She laughed. Then, reclining as she was, she let her gaze drift upward. Through the branches of the apple tree, she watched a single puffy cloud pass over a deep blue sky. "Could anyone want for a finer sickroom than this? They have quite spoiled me, you know." Shifting her gaze back to him, she added, "I am brought soup and tea every half hour—yes, I swear it is so, or very nearly—and all our neighbors have called upon me at least once. You are right about the flowers, however. My bedchamber now resembles the hothouse."

He laughed. "Well, I am glad to hear our neighbors have been attentive to you."

"I fear the news of the attack has had quite a sobering effect on everyone but I have been attended to with great kindness. Indeed, I have never known such a wonderful group of people, a circumstance that makes me very happy you are at last coming to enjoy the society about Maybridge. This of course leads me to ask whether or not Mr. Creed has discussed with you his belief that he knows where the treasure—"

Rotherstone lifted a hand. "Forgive me. I do not mean to be discourteous, but I have no wish to discuss anything about Jack Stub's treasure today. I have come to inquire after your health and to take your brother fishing. Anything more, I fear, will have a very unhappy effect upon me."

Evelina wanted to press him, but there was such a look of genuine concern in his eye that she chose instead to honor his wishes. "Very well," she said quietly. Giving the subject a turn, she said, "Miss Ambers tells me you are having some of the gentlemen to your house tonight."

"I am," he said.

She could not help but smile. "I take that as a sign of progress, and I confess I am very well pleased."

Rotherstone took great delight in the warmth and contentment on Lady Evelina's face. From the time he had stepped out onto the terrace, he had become fully aware that she was recovering from her ordeal exceedingly well. He felt in that moment a great deal of admiration for her and, yes, affection.

He might have agreed to take Lord William angling again, but he was not so certain his motives were entirely pure. After all, an opportunity to see that the lad had some amusement in the company of someone other than his nurse or his sisters and mother held the decided advantage of allowing him to converse with Evelina again. That he wished to converse with her, indeed, that a day without her company somehow seemed sadly flat, were circumstances that might have troubled him had he allowed it. He was not looking for love or even a wife. No, he had greater concerns than setting up his nursery.

From the time that he had learned of Sir Alfred's perfidy, an act that had been sanctioned by the gentlemen of the neighborhood, he had been committed to avenging the wrong done to his father. For five years, from the time of his death, he had had but one objective. Ironically, it was because of the lady before him that he was very near to succeeding in his plans.

Guilt pierced him suddenly. He knew Evelina was coming to trust him more and more. He also knew that he valued her trust, her belief that he might just be in possession of a proper character after all. What would she think of him, therefore, if she knew his true intentions in having allowed himself to be drawn into the local society? Worse still, what would she think of him were she to know his purpose in bringing the gentlemen together tonight?

He felt a powerful urge to tell her all, both the truth about what had happened so many years ago and just what his intentions were now.

"What is it, Rotherstone? You seem suddenly distressed. If you are concerned for me, I beg you will not be. I am quite well, I promise you."

So strong was the impulse to speak that he opened his

mouth and was ready to begin when William suddenly cried from the terrace. "I have proper shoes on now!"

He came running at a gallop. Rotherstone rose to his feet, an immense feeling of relief washing over him that he had been spared telling Evelina the truth.

"So you do," he called back. To Evelina, he turned, smiled and said, "I confess I have been worried, but I will no longer be if you promise you are truly recovering as well as you seem."

The sweet smile that overspread her lips and that was reflected in her sparkling green eyes caused a powerful feeling to take hold of his chest. He felt a strong urge to touch her, to hold her, and if Will had not been racing toward him he might have possessed himself of her hand, kissed her fingers, or perhaps kissed her full on the lips!

How grateful he was that Will had arrived and was picking up the rods. He bowed to Evelina, took the tackle basket in hand and told Will to lead the way. He watched as the boy cast his sister a broad grin, and on a happy step they set off to the west in the direction of Scrag Stream.

Two days later, Evelina was in the library on the first floor of Wildings studying the map. The ancient document had suffered badly in the attack. Besides being torn, more of the edges had crumbled away, and because Rotherstone had stood on it while in the ditch, dirt had been ground into the center, nearly obscuring the place where Halling Stream joined the River Rother.

She had found a new piece of velvet, red this time, upon which to lay the map. For the past hour, she had been reviewing her last conversation with Mr. Creed. They had been discussing the fact that the rivers and streams formed an S, when he came to understand the map's meaning. However, she could not place the smallest significance on this fact. She did not see how the position of the local waterways could possibly affect the location of the treasure.

She recalled that he had turned the map, so she did as well, only this time she carefully shifted the velvet instead, keeping the map safe. One turn, two, three and back again—she saw nothing that gave her even a hint as to where the treasure might be buried. Blacklands was still Blacklands, only why did the riddles not seem connected overly much to the map?

If only Rotherstone had not forbidden Mr. Creed to tell her what he knew.

She had not spoken with the earl since the day before, when he had again taken Will fishing. She wished he had been willing to discuss the matter with her then, for he had seemed quite happy to see her. She smiled, recalling how light and easy their conversation had been. He had brought roses and had expressed concern for her recovery.

Just before Will had emerged from the house wearing proper shoes, however, the earl's expression had grown rather grim. His thoughts had been drawn inward, so she could not know precisely what he had been thinking. She supposed he had been worried for her health. Once Will had returned, the moment had passed.

She breathed a heavy sigh. Rotherstone had been on her mind a great deal of late. No matter how hard she tried, she could not seem to reconcile his good parts with his bad parts. He was kind to her family in every respect and attentive in ways that none of her neighbors had ever been. Yet he was a gamester and was known to frequent the East End gaming houses. On the other hand, he had probably saved her life by carrying her all the way back to Wildings when she had fainted from the attack. At the same time, he could be so deucedly mulish, particularly where the hunt for Jack Stub's treasure was concerned. On that score, he had been resistant from the very beginning.

As she perused the map again, she was a little surprised by the sudden appearance of Bolney in the doorway. "Forgive me, my lady, but Lord Rotherstone has arrived and wishes to know if you are receiving company."

Evelina felt her heart leap. Since her mind had been so full of thoughts of him just now, she was certain Providence had brought him to her door. Now she could address with him the matter of Mr. Creed 's knowledge of the map's secret. She felt certain that given the recent attack, and therefore the need to find the treasure as quickly as possible, Rotherstone would be reasonable.

The moment he appeared in the doorway, she said, "This is a bit of a chance, for if you must know, I have spent the past two hours looking at Jack Stub's map, reading and rereading all the riddles, and still I have not the smallest notion what it was Mr. Creed saw. He must have told you by now that he believes he knows where the treasure is truly buried."

Rotherstone, who had been smiling warmly, now began to frown. "I see you are fully recovered, for you have not even greeted me as would normally be considered proper."

Evelina blinked. "I do beg your pardon. You are quite right. How do you go on?"

"Very well, thank you." He eyed her suspiciously.

"And how is your health?" She clasped her hands in front of her as if to hold back her impatience.

"I am in excellent form." He moved several paces into the chamber, but he was still watching her carefully.

"And you? I have come to inquire if you are indeed well and whether or not you still mean to attend the ball tomorrow night."

Evelina moved to stand before the map. "I must confess I had not given the ball a single thought for the past day or so, but yes, I will be attending with my sister Mia." She glanced at Rotherstone and saw that he was regarding her intently. "Is there something else you wish to say to me?"

"Let the treasure lie," he said quietly. He stood opposite her, the table and the map separating them.

She was shocked by the suggestion. "How can you say such a thing when you must know how close we are to discovering it?"

"What good can come of continuing the search even if there is a fortune to be had? You have already been hurt once because of the treasure. Perhaps Mr. Creed and I had been joking you about a curse, but I am come to believe there is always a curse attached to those who pursue any object greedily."

Evelina found her temper rising. "You think me greedy? Is that what you are saying?"

He narrowed his eyes. "Well, are you?"

Evelina watched him for a long moment. She was angry that he was so completely hostile toward the treasure hunt and had been from the first. "I do not understand you at all, only this time I will say to you what you once said to me: You must determine for yourself if my prior actions prove whether or not I am a woman of character, a woman to be trusted."

He remained silent.

She chose to address a different aspect of the subject. "However, if you are still concerned that we will encroach further on your lands, I can relieve your mind on that score. I am persuaded the X marked on the map is a ruse of some sort. I no longer believe the treasure is on your property."

"The possibility that the treasure may have been buried somewhere on Blacklands might have been my concern at the outset," he stated, "but no longer. I am persuaded you are in danger. You should give this up now, before something else befalls you."

"Nothing will happen to me," she said forcefully. "We have all taken care to see that it will not. I have already promised not to go abroad alone until the treasure is found, and if you would but listen to reason and order Mr. Creed to inform me of what he knows that I do not, then we may be done with this hunt on the instant. You have that power in your hands even now."

She watched a stubbornness enter his eye. She knew the answer before ever he spoke.

"No," he stated. "I have been opposed to this hunt from the first, and a sennight past, when I was forced to find a woman in a ditch whom I happen to . . ." He paused as though searching for the right word.

"To what? Despise? Loathe?"

"I have grown to care for you," he said sharply. "As a neighbor and as a friend."

She leaned forward, placing her hands on the table. "Then prove yourself a good friend, a good neighbor, and give permission to Mr. Creed to enlighten us all, or do you know the solution to the puzzle yourself?"

"I do not. I was not in the smallest degree interested."

"You seem unreasonably set against this. I vow I do not comprehend you in the least. I never have!"

"And I do not comprehend why you must be so set on this course!"

Lady Chelwood and William suddenly appeared in the doorway. "My dears," she called out, maneuvering her chair to the doorway. "Your voices can be heard to the rafters. Do calm yourselves." She glanced meaningfully at William, who was clearly overset.

"Oh dear, were we so very loud?" Evelina asked. "I do beg your pardon." She glanced at Rotherstone. "I fear his lordship and I have been having this argument for the past three weeks now."

Rotherstone shook his head. "This was quite unforgivable. I do beg your pardon, my lady, Will." He bowed to them both.

"I do as well," Evelina added. To Rotherstone she said, "I am sorry for what I have said. I believe I spoke in my frustration. Forgive me?"

"Of course."

Evelina could not help but smile. "You have been so kind to me and my family, and my demands have been unreasonable. I shan't press you further on the subject."

Lady Chelwood, satisfied that peace had been restored, asked Lord Rotherstone to stay for nuncheon. He agreed, and the remainder of his visit was quite pleasant. Of course, they both gave the subject of Jack Stub's treasure a wide berth.

When he was ready to go, Evelina chose to walk with him to the door and once more apologized for coming the crab.

He frowned anew as he regarded her. "I am sorry you have just said so."

"I beg your pardon?" She looked into his dark eyes and wondered if he had just gone mad. "Do not tell me you intend to begin brangling with me anew."

"That remains to be seen," he said quietly. "I have been pondering since the attack just how I might make the situation safer for you, and my conclusion is this— for the second of the three demands you agreed upon over a fortnight past, I must insist you give me the map."

She felt dizzy, almost as though she would faint. "Th-the map?" she asked, unable to credit her ears.

"Yes. Though I do not need to offer even the smallest explanation, I shall do so. If it is known that the map is in my possession, whoever tried to hurt you will not do so again; there will be no need. You will then be perfectly safe, and more persons than just myself can be at ease."

Evelina knew he was speaking sensibly, but she felt like bursting into tears. Naturally, she would not consider for a moment becoming a watering pot in front of Rotherstone, so instead she asked, "Even if your motivation is my safety, how can you require this of me when you must by now have some sense of what the map means to me?"

"How you feel about the map is wholly unreasonable," he countered in a whisper, clearly not wanting to disturb the family again. "It is just a map and probably a fraud at that, and I mean to have it no matter how many arguments you put forth."

She clamped her lips shut for the longest moment. They had already overset both her mother and Will with their brangling, and she did not want to do so again. Besides, there was little point in trying to argue him out of his position. By all that was honorable, she had to forfeit the map to him. She had promised to give him three things upon request, and so she must, but never would she have thought he would demand the map of her.

"One moment, then." She turned on her heel and mounted the stairs. Once in the library, she carefully rolled the map up in the red velvet and secured the resulting roll with two ribbons.

Returning, she handed him the velvet case. "I just want you to know that I have this map memorized in every detail, so do not congratulate yourself on any score that you have separated me from my objective, for you most certainly have not."

He did not give her answer but merely bowed as if to take his leave.

"Do you not wish to see if the map is truly within?" she asked angrily.

At that, a crooked smile twisted his lips. "No. I trust you."

"At this moment, I consider that an insult, but there is something more I would say to you. You think my interest in the map unreasonable, but do you not understand that for the first time in my life I feel fully and truly alive?"

His expression grew arrested, and a flash of understanding passed over his face. A moment more, however, and the fleeting expression vanished. He bowed again and was gone.

On the following morning, Evelina had been deciding which gown to wear to Colonel Carfax's ball when she received a surprising visit from Lady Monceaux and Mary Ambers.

She knew something must be afoot because Lady Monceaux should have been fully engaged in helping Colonel Carfax's housekeeper prepare for the ball. She had her butler, Bolney, show them into the library and at the same time requested tea for them all.

When she entered the chamber, she was careful to close the door. "That we might have a comfortable coze," she said, smiling. "Do sit down."

The ladies took up seats beside one another on a settee of rose silk damask. Evelina sat down opposite them in a winged chair of striped cream silk. Lady Monceaux glanced at Miss Ambers before beginning. "I suppose you must be wondering what has brought us here today."

"Of course I am surprised, since the ball is but a few hours away. However, you both seem rather distressed. May I ask the cause?"

Still neither lady spoke. Miss Ambers watched Lady Monceaux carefully while her ladyship sighed heavily several times.

Evelina said, "I hope you do not think me easily offended and are thereby refraining from offering a criticism by which I might receive some benefit."

"No, no, not in the least," Miss Ambers said, leaning forward in her seat. "Indeed, this subject has so little to do with you that we both feared we were succumbing to a terrible piece of gabblemongering in bringing this particular information to your notice."

"Well, I hope one or the other of you will now relieve me of my suspense, for I vow I am all curiosity."

Lady Monceaux said, "Very well. You know that on Saturday night Lord Rotherstone held a party just for the gentlemen."

"Yes, I thought it quite generous of him to have done so."

"Indeed, that is what Miss Ambers and I believed as well, but an alarming report has come to our attention through Sir Edgar."

"Sir Edgar?" Evelina queried glancing at Miss Ambers. "He confides in you, then?"

She nodded. "I do so hope that I am not breaking his trust, but indeed, you and Lady Monceaux are the only two people I would even consider consulting. I hope I may rely on your discretion."

"Of course." Evelina grew uneasy. She could not imagine what next she was to hear, but she could think of nothing of a happy nature that would have brought either lady to her door this morning. "Pray continue."

Miss Ambers nodded to Lady Monceaux. She picked up the thread of the subject. "Sir Edgar said the party quickly turned to gaming, hazard in fact, but that at first the stakes were unexceptionable. However, the more the port, brandy and rum punch was passed round, the stakes increased until every roll of the dice at hazard was for ten pounds—"

"Ten pounds!" Evelina exclaimed. "Good God."

"There is worse," Miss Ambers said. "Before the gentlemen quit Blacklands—" She could not continue.

Lady Monceaux intervened. "Before the festivities drew to a close, my husband was wealthier by five hundred pounds. But that is not all. Mr. Crookhorn by three hundred and Colonel Carfax by another two."

The uneasy feeling sharpened. "You mean to say that Rotherstone lost this amount?"

The ladies nodded together.

"How could this have happened?" she cried. "I had heard rumors that he was gambling while in London, but I confess I wanted to believe they were just rumors, a great deal of useless gossip."

"Not so useless, we fear," Miss Ambers said. "However, Sir Edgar was adamant that Rotherstone did not generally give himself to reckless gaming in this fashion, nor has he ever heard that the earl previously sustained such enormous losses."

"What is there to wonder in that?" Lady Monceaux observed sadly. "How many gentlemen have we known in the past who are able to control their appetites to a point, and then one night they lose an entire fortune? I do believe that some are even capable of contriving such situations, the sharps we hear of so frequently. However, this among neighbors—! It is all too familiar, I fear."

Evelina's thoughts turned to her brother, whose addiction to gaming was severe. "Chelwood," she said. "You have described my brother completely."

"I do beg your pardon," Lady Monceaux said, "but in truth I was not thinking of him."

"Of whom, then?" Evelina queried.

Lady Monceaux seemed perplexed. "I was speaking only in generalities, of gossip heard through the years."

"I see." Evelina became lost in her thoughts. Rotherstone was a gamester, then. She did not want to believe it was true. Even though she had been given hints over the past fortnight, indeed, over the past eight months, still there was so much good in him that she simply could not believe he was as capable of wasting his fortune as her own father and brother.

"There must be some mistake," she said, glancing from one lady to the other.

Mary Ambers shook her head. "Had I heard this news from anyone but Sir Edgar, I should have set it down as the grossest falsehood. Indeed, even now, having come to know Rotherstone in these past several days and particularly in light of the service he rendered you, I would not have believed him capable of anything so irresponsible."

Lady Monceaux looked out the window. "My husband was extraordinarily happy this morning. I thought perhaps his contentment was due to how well the breach had seemed to be healed between himself and Rotherstone. I was so very encouraged. When Miss Ambers called on me just before I was to go to Darwell Lodge that I might be of assistance to Colonel Carfax, I must confess I was completely dashed in every hope. You see, this feels very familiar to me."

"To what precisely are you referring?" Evelina asked.

"For I can only presume that you are not speaking of my brother or general experiences."

Lady Monceaux shook her head. "For the present I cannot say, since I have only my suspicions, and until they are born out I refuse to create a whirlwind when only a little breeze might be blowing."

Evelina felt a shiver go through her. Lady Monceaux's distress was evident, and her instincts told her that something of an unfortunate nature was afoot. She did not feel at liberty to pursue the subject, however, so she queried, "I appreciate very much your having told me of what happened last night. However, I cannot help but wonder to what purpose you have come to me." She glanced from one lady to the next.

Lady Monceaux sighed again. "It has been lost to none of us that Lord Rotherstone has a certain preference for your company, that he has even to some degree taken an interest in your family. Both Miss Ambers and I thought that in view of the earl's recent involvement in our community—which we feel has been an excellent beginning—you might be willing to give his lordship a hint."

"About his gaming habits?" she asked, astonished that they would even propose such a thing.

"Someone ought to make a push," Lady Monceaux said. "Sir Edgar will undoubtedly give him a dressing-down, but I am convinced that your opinion could have a beneficial effect as well."

"You flatter me exceedingly, but I do not believe I have such power with Lord Rotherstone. However, if the opportunity should arise, you may trust me when I say I most certainly shall not withhold my opinion."

Lady Monceaux smiled suddenly. "That I believe very much to be true. You give me hope, Lady Evelina, indeed you do, more than you know."

Evelina was not certain to what precisely she was referring. However, she had her own questions and asked, "I
hope I do not seem impertinent, but beyond your concern for Rotherstone, what are his gaming habits to you?"

"It has merely been my experience that if such events
occur in a neighborhood with increasing frequency and
to such an end that one neighbor loses a great deal of
money to another, friendships are ruined. We are just
now experiencing a wonderful renewal, and I for one do
not wish to see our neighborhood troubled again, and
certainly not for such a reason as gaming."

"I see," Evelina murmured. "I commend your motivation very much."

The tea arrived, and with the subject of Rotherstone
having been discussed to Lady Monceaux's satisfaction,
the subject turned quite naturally to the forthcoming
ball. Evelina could not help but ask of Miss Ambers,
"And are your first two spoken for already?"

Miss Ambers blushed, but she smiled happy. "Yes, indeed they are," she said.

"I am very happy for you," she said. "I liked Sir Edgar
from the first. I met him by accident when I called on
Rotherstone to first speak to the earl about Jack Stub's
map and treasure. Sir Edgar was an absolute delight, and
he was very supportive of my efforts when Rotherstone
was not."

The remainder of the visit involved finishing the entire pot of tea, listening to Lady Monceaux's descriptions
of the decorations for the colonel's ballroom and offering as many accolades to Mary about her beau as could
make her blush again and again.

That evening, as Evelina dressed for the ball, her
thoughts turned to Rotherstone. She refused to be

blue-devilled about his apparent gaming problem, although she felt she had every reason to be overset.

She had come to value his presence in her life more
than she had thought possible. He was kindness itself to
William, and all her family enjoyed his teasing and banter when he took part in their small family circle.

For all that, however, he was still something of a beast.
There could be no two opinions on that score. His having taken the map from her had been the cruelest thing
he had yet done; that is, until this morning, when she
learned he had lost one thousand pounds at hazard to
Sir Alfred, Mr. Crookhorn and Colonel Carfax.

She still did not know what to make of it. The more
she thought about his having done so, the more she
sensed something was amiss, something she could not as
yet understand.

Her maid bid her sit before her dressing table and
began arranging her long red curls into a riot atop her
head. "I think I should like to see the pearls looped
through tonight. Could you manage that, Sarah?"

"Aye, miss," her abigail returned, smiling. "I always
like the pearls with your fiery locks."

Evelina smiled, but her thoughts were soon drawn
back to Rotherstone. She had known him such a short
time, after all. What could she possibly know of him that
was wholly true? Sir Edgar had told Miss Ambers that his
gaming of last night was not at all like him, and yet it was
known, or at least believed, that he went to London for
the purpose of gambling. She simply did not know what
to think. One thing for certain: Should the appropriate
moment arrive, she would not hesitate to speak to him
tonight at the ball!

Chapter Eleven

"Evie," Mia said, addressing her just as the family coach turned down the lane that led to Darwell Lodge, "are you not feeling well? Have you the headache?"

Evelina was drawn from her reveries to regard her sister. "Not in the least, I assure you. Indeed, do not be troubled, I am perfectly well."

"But are you certain? You have scarcely spoken three words to me since we quit Wildings. Perhaps you should not have come to the ball, after all."

Seated beside her sister, she took Mia's hand in her own. "I promise you, my head does not hurt in the least."

"Then what is it?"

Evelina regarded her sister hesitantly. She wasn't certain whether she should confide in her or not.

Mia tilted her head. "I am no longer a child, Evie, if that is why you are frowning at me. I hope you may trust me to be both discreet and understanding."

Evelina could not help but smile. "You are very right. I know you to be both these things. Very well, I shall tell you what has caused me so much distress of late, but I do depend on your discretion. As you know, I had a visit earlier from Lady Monceaux and Miss Ambers."

"Yes, you were closeted in the library with them for some time. I confess I was intrigued and not a little concerned."

"As it happens, they informed me that there had been a great deal of gaming at Blacklands on Saturday night."

"Oh no," Mia whispered. Though she was only sixteen, she had not been ignorant of their eldest brother's misdeeds. "I am very sorry, indeed grieved, to hear it."

"As am I. However, I promise you I do not intend to remain silent on the subject. I have had many years to think what I should have said to Robert when he first came into his inheritance. However, by the time I saw that something should be done, I believe it was already too late. His character was fixed, his habits unmovable. Still, I regret remaining silent. As for these present circumstances, I must say I am quite prepared to ring a peal over one or several heads if I must."

Mia was silent but met her gaze with a smile.

"What is it?" Evelina queried. The expression on her sister's face was quite odd.

"You are greatly changed, Evie, since our coming to Kent, and all for the better, I believe."

"I have never been happier in my entire existence," she returned thoughtfully. "Even if I still do have a bump on my head."

Mia laughed.

Evelina watched the passing scenery. The hour was just past seven, but a warm twilight still lit the countryside in a glow. The evening was very fine, not a cloud in the sky, a perfect night for a ball. Or for a quarrel, Evelina thought.

From the time Lady Monceaux and Miss Ambers and bid her good-day, Evelina had been fretting over just what she should do next where Rotherstone was concerned. She was aggravated with him on so many points that she hardly knew which of the several infractions she ought to address first: his gaming, his high-handedness in demanding the map or his refusal to allow Mr. Creed to be of use to his neighbors. If he thought for one moment that she would permit even one of these subjects to rest, he was quite mistaken.

Only, where to begin in taking him to task for his mistakes?

When the coach turned up the drive, Evelina glanced at the trees, flower beds and shrubbery. She confessed she was a little shocked at what she saw. She knew that the colonel had been in possession of his property for nearly a decade, having inherited as she had from a more distant relation than was usual. She had always understood there to be a fine income attached to Darwell, so she could not understand why the estate had such an overgrown, untended appearance.

Of course, the colonel had never married, a circumstance that might have accounted for the untidy nature of the property. Some gentlemen were not as interested in the care of their estates as others.

Her mind immediately reverted to Rotherstone. He was not such a man. His property, even his house, showed a level of care and husbandry that was beyond pleasing. His cousin, it would seem, was not so gifted.

After waiting behind a train of carriages, she alighted with her sister at last at the entrance. Darwell Lodge was a fine brick manor house, but as she glanced up at the numerous windows, she was surprised to see that several shutters were missing.

Upon entering the house, the sound of music flowed the distance from the ballroom to the entrance hall.

Mia leaned close. "My first ball! I only wish Mama was with us tonight."

"As do I. She will be sorely missed."

Greeting Colonel Carfax and Lady Monceaux, she moved with Mia down a long hall to the ballroom.

"Do but look," Mia cried. "I vow everyone I have ever known in my life is here tonight."

"I daresay there are no fewer than two hundred persons present."

As Evelina's gaze moved over the wonderful array of gowns in every shade of silk, satin or finely embroidered muslin possible, a sweet sensation of pleasure flowed over her. Like her sister, she knew most everyone present, a circumstance that warmed her heart. This was the first time she had been so nearly connected to an entire community, and she found herself extraordinarily grateful. How dear so many faces had become to her!

She searched for one in particular and found him conversing with Miss Ambers. As so many times before, she found herself nearly incapable of shifting her gaze from him. She sighed inwardly. If only he were not so wretchedly handsome besides being quite strong and tall, his shoulders broad, his waist narrow. Even his leg was well turned.

She gave herself a shake. Regardless of his many physical beauties, she promised herself that tonight she would not be moved from her mission of making him realize how seriously he had erred!

He turned just at that moment, saw her and caught her eye. She lifted her brow and her chin for the purpose of giving him a hint and moved in a direction quite opposite from him.

Lord Rotherstone could not keep from smiling. He watched Lady Evelina, clearly on her high ropes, move across the ballroom floor, intent it would seem on speaking to anyone but him.

"How beautiful she is," Miss Ambers said. "And the strangest thing of all is that she does not seem to be aware of her beauty."

"I believe it to be one of her greatest charms," he said.

"She has many, not least of which is the ability to make a guest feel welcome. I am always at ease in her company. But there is something greater than even this, I think. Do you know, I believe she has inspired me with courage. Yes, that has been her greatest gift to me."

He looked down at Miss Ambers. "Indeed?"

The lady before him nodded, and her light blue eyes sparkled. "She always speaks her mind. Once I decided to follow suit—which I did a fortnight past nearly to the day—I cannot tell you how handsomely I was rewarded."

He smiled at her. He realized he liked his friend's choice very much. "I believe I understand," he said.

When Sir Edgar came to claim her for the next country-dance, he remained where he was. He had a clear view of Lady Evelina, for Mr. Fuller had led her out. He could see that she was still angry with him since she steadfastly refused to look at him.

Not that he cared, for of the moment he desired only to watch her. She was gowned in a lovely lavender silk ball dress. She wore pearls in her coiffure that complimented both her red hair and her fair complexion quite to perfection. Her neck was beautifully sloped, and his heart began to ache as it often did when he settled his gaze on her.

Good God, he thought suddenly. *I am in love with her!*

There it was, the truth he knew he had been denying for the last three weeks. He loved her and had been in love with her since he had first held her in his arms. He recalled that moment to mind, of discovering her on his estate at a late hour. She had been wearing a cloak and carrying a lantern. Even then her beauty had worked strongly on him. He recalled something she had said to him that night.

"How did you do that?" she had asked. *"How did you make me desire what I had no intention of desiring?"*

He now wondered the same thing of her. How had she made him love her, particularly when he had been so completely disinterested in love?

He moved along the side of the ballroom floor, matching the distance she traveled down the dance so that he was always opposite her. He realized she was like no other female he had ever known. Beyond her beauty, she was good and kind. He had believed her to be determined to the point of selfish interest, but now he was no longer certain. What was there of selfishness in how devoted she was to her family or even in the manner in which she extended herself to her neighbors without judgment or criticism? What did she expect in return save the pleasures of friendship?

He felt uneasy suddenly, not about her but rather about how much he had made use of her, particularly over the past sennight. If all were to proceed as he had planned, this very evening he would achieve his object, the ruining of Sir Alfred Monceaux. He had had only one purpose in agreeing to reenter the local society: to engage Sir Alfred in play that he might destroy him. He knew what most of his neighbors did not, that Sir Alfred was deeply in debt. In losing to him on Saturday night he had meant only to whet his appetite for a new, final game tonight, and he had every confidence Sir Alfred would oblige him.

The only question in his mind, however, was whether or not he should tell Lady Evelina the hard truth about Sir Alfred first.

Evelina knew that Lord Rotherstone had been following her progress down the dance, but she had steadfastly refused to acknowledge him in any manner. She was still too angry to speak to him and feared that were he to engage her in conversation, she would be unable to keep from raising her voice to the rafters. She had not truly

understood just how incensed she was until his continued presence brought all her objections to his latest
conduct forcibly to mind.

As the set ended, Mr. Fuller returned her to the side
of the room opposite Rotherstone. She thanked him for
the dance, but when she saw, over Mr. Fuller's shoulder,
that Lord Rotherstone was bearing down on her, she
dropped a quick curtsy, excused herself and walked
briskly from the chamber.

As she rounded the corner to the hall, she nearly col-
lided with Colonel Carfax, who immediately begged
pardon.

"No, 'tis my fault," she said. "I fear I am trying to avoid
your cousin."

The colonel laughed. "What has Gage done now to
have so set up your back?"

"Too many things," she responded. "Only, I beg you
will walk with me awhile."

"Of course," he responded. "Come, let me offer you
some refreshment." He led her to one of the antecham-
bers, in which several servants were found dispensing a
variety of drinks. A number of gentlemen were present,
draining tankards of ale, and more than one lady was
seated nearby sipping a glass of ratafia.

"Do you care for champagne or would you prefer
ratafia?"

"Champagne, if you please."

Once sipping the cold, bubbly wine, Evelina thanked
him for giving the ball. "For I do not think anything is
quite so pleasant for a country neighborhood."

"'Tis my pleasure," he responded, inclining his head
to her. "Only, I do not see your mother. I had hoped she
would feel well enough to attend."

"In truth, Mama is very well, but she did not like leaving William and the twins."

"I suppose the servants tend to them as well."

Evelina did not know what he meant. "I beg your pardon?"

"Well, how do you manage an evening when part of the family is at an event such as this? Are there servants enough to prepare and serve dinner, for instance?"

"Of course." She thought his question extremely odd.

He nodded, then laughed. "I do not know what I was thinking, as though you would give your servants a holiday because you are here. A bachelor's establishment is a very different thing. I have often wondered how I might manage things better. So all your servants are in attendance?"

"Well, as to that, Mama insisted that Bolney have the evening to himself, and I believe two of the upper maids are gone to visit their families in Studdingly. Otherwise, Cook and her staff, my able housekeeper, as well as the head groom and the stable boys, are performing their usual duties."

He shook his head and appeared dismayed. "I believe I have been taken sore advantage of for a very long time. In truth, I do not know if everything is being done properly. I suppose I should have had a wife long before now. You ladies always seem so capable. How late, for instance, does your staff remain at their duties? Do you permit them to retire early?"

Evelina still thought these questions a little odd, particularly since they were being asked in the middle of a ball. At the same time, she had no difficulty in comprehending his ignorance of housekeeping matters. "I leave all to my housekeeper, but it is my understanding that since most of the staff rises before dawn, they are between the covers by eleven o'clock."

"I see. Well, that would make a great deal of sense." He eyed her carefully. Lowering his voice, he queried,

"And are you truly recovered from your ordeal of a week past?"

"Very much so," she responded cheerfully.

"I must confess I was never more shocked. I could not imagine what manner of desperate creature would do harm to a lady."

"Nor I," she returned.

At that moment, Lady Monceaux appeared in the doorway, waving to the colonel. He turned to Evelina. "I beg you will excuse me, but it would seem my hostess has need of me."

"Of course."

When he had gone, she left the antechamber, intent on returning to the ballroom, but was suddenly accosted by Rotherstone. He took hold of her arm and guided her in a swift movement into the drawing room. "You cannot ignore me all evening," he said. "I apprehend that you are for some reason disenchanted with me, and I thought perhaps were you to give voice to your feelings we might be friends again. Although I imagine you are still taking a pet that I have your map."

Evelina lifted a brow. "At the very least I am distressed because you have the map."

"At the very least?" he queried. "This is not at all hopeful. You seem to be holding a basket full of my misdeeds tonight."

"You know that I am," she responded hotly. She turned as if to go, but he would not let her.

"Lower your voice," he whispered, hooking her arm and preventing her from quitting his side. "The entire chamber is staring at us."

"And I do not give a fig if they are," she retorted.

He smiled, leaned close and whispered, "Will you come with me that I might hear your complaints, then?

If I can find a private location, I promise you I will permit you to give full expression to them all."

"Are you certain you have sufficient courage?" she asked haughtily.

He merely laughed. "I believe I do, though I vow you make me quake in my shoes."

"I see you mean to be facetious. Very well, but remember that I have warned you."

He led her to the music room, but there were still several persons scattered about the chamber. Beyond was a hall leading to a billiard room and a small chamber reserved for card play. Both he soon found were overflowing with guests.

"This will not do by half," he stated. "My cousin must be pleased to have so many people in attendance at his ball, but where the deuce are we to find a proper place to quarrel?"

She glanced up at him. "I see you think it all a great joke," she stated.

"Not precisely," he returned. "Just a large misunderstanding. Ah, I have an idea. I believe there is a conservatory beyond the billiard room."

Evelina continued to walk beside him and whispered, "I would hardly call any of what has occurred between us a misunderstanding."

He leaned close and spoke again in a low voice. "You are right. I would never use such a term as 'misunderstanding' to describe any of the kisses we have shared."

She cast him a sharply depressive look. "The last thing you will ever receive tonight, my lord, is a kiss," she returned, her voice equally low, "if that is how I am to interpret this last absurd remark!"

A burst of laughter erupted from the billiard room and followed them down the hall. The doors to the conservatory were closed. Rotherstone opened one and ushered her within. The air smelled damp and earthy.

Unfortunately, this chamber was in use as well. Several younger persons including Annabelle Rewell, were playing a game of blind man's bluff in the center of the chamber.

"I suppose we must go outside," he said.

Evelina nodded her acquiescence. Sidestepping the laughing and jumping group, Rotherstone guided her from the conservatory. A path led to the north, and with a full moon glowing strongly over the dark, shadowed landscape, he suggested they take the path. She moved briskly in front of him, a circumstance that made him laugh a little more. She most certainly had taken a pet. He wondered if she had learned the results of his party on Saturday night. He thought it quite likely she had.

Evelina could not believe Rotherstone's *sangfroid*. Had he no conscience at all?

In the distance, she saw a low drystone wall and a tall iron gate. "Will that small garden be far enough, do you suppose?" she asked, glancing at him.

"I am not certain," he responded. "I believe that would depend on how much of a fishwife you intend to be right now."

She ground her teeth. "The loudest one you have ever heard, I expect."

When he chuckled, she grew angrier and once more set her feet along the path. Why would he not be serious? How could he have committed so many crimes against her and think it all a great joke? But beyond this, did he not even suspect she had learned of his losses and that she might be outraged that he had been so utterly irresponsible?

As they reached the gate, she began, "I received a very

unexpected visit this morning from Lady Monceaux and Miss Ambers. What do you have to say to that?"

He faced her. "Oh dear. I suppose you know all, then?"

"Yes, I do," she responded with some asperity.

He drew open the gate, and a long, loud grating ensued. "I daresay no one has been here in a very long time."

"We perhaps should beware of snakes." She passed through the opening and saw that there was a great deal of tall grass scattered among narrow gravel paths. "I had thought this was some manner of garden, but if it is, I vow I have never seen anything so wretchedly unkempt."

"I would agree, but I do not think it is a garden."

"What, then?" She peered at something gleaming brightly in the moonlight and drew back instantly. "That is a gravestone! Gage, I fear we have stumbled into an ancient graveyard!"

He chuckled very low against her ear. "Frightened, Evie? Do not tell me you are afraid of a ghost or two? Although you may cling to my arm for safety if you so desire."

She did not stand either on her pride or ceremony and quickly took hold of his arm. Glancing up at the trees to the northeast, she said, "Why, that must be the church tower at Gildstone, so very close. Do you suppose this graveyard is connected?

"It is not so far distant. I imagine it is or was at one time. Only the trees separate the church by little more than a hundred yards."

Evelina was appalled that a graveyard would be so poorly cared for. "Have you noticed," she said, glancing about at all the fallen stones, "that your cousin's property is quite badly maintained?"

"As it happens, I have."

"Earlier, he was complaining to me that he did not always know how to manage his property and that he should have taken a wife. At first, I agreed with him, but then I recalled that you do not have a wife and that Blacklands is a perfect model of excellence."

He stopped her in their progression and turned her to face him. "That is the first kind word I have had from you this evening. Thank you very much. Ah, I see you are still angry with me. Well, perhaps now would be the proper time to come the crab. You may commence, if it so pleases you."

She tried not to laugh, for he was being ludicrous. However, she had but to recall to mind that he had lost one thousand pounds to Sir Alfred and the others and her amusement vanished entirely. She did not begin her complaints with that, however. Instead, she dwelled on his numerous sins, how from the first he had been unwilling to oblige his neighbors, how he had obstructed the finding of the treasure by not permitting Mr. Creed to reveal the solution to the map, how he had been a perfect cretin in demanding three things of her merely for the right to explore his land for the treasure, and finally how he had taken the map from her in the name of honor! Yes, she spoke eloquently, damning his character here and there as it pleased her, until she was ready to broach the most recent, critical subject.

"And after all these terrible things," she stated strongly, "you must add to your faults by losing one thousand pounds at hazard! What do you have to say for yourself?"

He shrugged. "Well, 'twas not one thousand."

Hope rose in her breast. "Was this merely a vicious recounting, then, that I had from Lady Monceaux and Miss Ambers?"

"No, for I do not believe either of these ladies capable

of the smallest viciousness. As it happens, I lost one thousand and eleven pounds."

She drew in a sharp breath. "How vile you are to speak so lightly on a subject you must know ignites my rage. You must know I despise gaming of every sort."

He opened his eyes as though innocent. In the moonlight, they were as dark as the night. "But I recall Will telling me you often played at cribbage with him for a tuppence a point. I think you a very great hypocrite to take me to task for something you engage in yourself."

She growled. "You know very well there is a vast difference between the two."

"Very true. Cribbage is played with little pegs while hazard is not."

"Ooooh!" she shouted. "You would try the patience of a saint."

"I think you a saint," he said.

"What? Now you will mock me?"

"On no account. As it happens, I do think you a saint." His smile grew crooked. "I have thought so ever since I saw you reclining on the chaise beneath the apple tree with William cuddled in your arms. I thought you a saint then, or at least one of the most virtuous ladies I have ever known."

Her mouth was agape. She could feel the cool night air passing over her lips and teasing her throat. What a beast he was to have said something so . . . so splendid to her! She did not know what next to say, indeed, all her desire to keep reading him the riot act seemed to dissipate.

In the next moment, he slid his arms about her waist, and she did not protest, not even in the slightest. "I was never more grateful," he said, "than when Sir Edgar made it all but impossible for me to refuse that first invitation to dine at Wildings, for then I was able to watch you amongst your family."

She placed her hands on his chest. "Gage," she said, only faintly aware that she had addressed him again by his Christian name, "of what are you speaking? You are making no sense."

He drew her a little closer. "I am speaking of you," he responded, leaning down to kiss her on the forehead.

"You are trying to make me forget why I am so angry with you," she said.

"Am I succeeding?"

"No," she retorted, but already it seemed she had forgotten.

"Then I must do a great deal better!"

Without so much as a by-your-leave, he pulled her tightly against him and kissed her hard on the mouth.

Evelina was stunned. How had it happened that the dressing-down she had given him had turned quite masterfully into a kiss? Oh, yes, now she remembered. He had called her a saint. Her traitorous arms slid up his chest and wrapped themselves tenderly about his neck.

Rotherstone was kissing her again. It had been far too long, ages and ages. How delicious his lips felt against hers. Somewhere deep within her mind she knew she should not be kissing him, but she could not for the life of her recall why that was.

He drew back slightly, and because the moonlight was slanting just so across his features, she could see that he was smiling. "Am I doing better now?"

"Better than what?" she asked dreamily.

His smile broadened. "Definitely better."

He kissed her again and again, a minute passing and then another. Evelina drifted away from Darwell Lodge and Maybridge, away from Blacklands and Wildings. She was sailing to a sweet distant land that had never before been explored and one she was certain she would not want to leave for a very long time.

Adventure was in the feel and taste of his lips, in the strength of his arms as he held her, in the way his tongue searched out the depths of her mouth.

"Evie," he whispered against her lips.

"Mm," she responded softly.

"Can you trust me?" he asked.

At that, she opened her eyes, drawing back just enough to look at him. His words had brought her sharply back to earth. She could not read his expression clearly since the moonlight played tricks on whatever object it touched. "What do you mean?" she asked. She drew back a little more until her hands were clasped loosely at the back of his neck.

"It is true that I lost a great sum on Saturday night, but I want you to know that it was to a purpose."

"I do not understand," she said.

"I am not at liberty to explain further, which is why I am asking you whether or not you can trust me."

She searched his face for a long moment. "I cannot say," she said at last. "I have known you but a little while, only three weeks, and what I do know of you is so mixed in intention and result."

"I am in love with you," he said abruptly.

"Wh-what?" she cried.

"I am fully, completely and desperately in love with you."

"But you cannot be!" she cried. "That is quite impossible!"

Now he grinned. "You have changed everything for me, from that first night on Blacklands, and I love you."

"I believe you have gone mad."

"Wondrously so."

Evelina still could not believe she had heard him correctly. Rotherstone was in love with her?

"Besides, what is it you think I am doing right now?" He kissed her full on the lips and drew back.

"You mean in kissing me?"

He nodded.

"Flirting?" she asked, mystified.

"I tell you again, I am in love with you, Evelina. More than you will ever know."

Now he was so serious that her limbs began to tremble. She recalled what her brother had told her before she had come to Wildings. *Your heart is a rusted gate! What man will ever want you?*

She understood now that there was nothing rusted, stuck or otherwise unusable about her heart. She had merely been waiting for Rotherstone all these years.

"Is there even the smallest chance," he asked, "that you might return my regard?"

"Yes," she whispered. "Though I know I should not, I do. I love you, Gage, but I am still not certain if you are a man to be trusted."

He did not in any manner mock her. Indeed, he appeared more serious than ever before. "More than anything, I want you to be able to trust me."

She released him. "Last night, you lost over a thousand pounds. My brother and deceased father ruined the Chelwood estate because of gaming. How am I ever supposed to trust a man who would lose so vast a sum in a single night.

Rotherstone touched her cheek with his hand. "I do not know, but I sincerely hope in time you will be able to." He released her cheek and offered his arm. "Come, I believe we should return."

Evelina took up his arm and glanced at the graveyard. The careful mistress of Wildings could not keep from saying, "This is truly dreadful. Look how many stones are lying flat, and an equal number broken."

"Indeed," Rotherstone murmured as he guided Evelina toward the gate. His thoughts became fixed suddenly on his cousin, on the unkempt appearance of his grounds, on his habits of gaming frequently in London, on the part he played in helping Sir Alfred to rob his father seven years ago.

He addressed Evelina. "And you are very certain you did not see the man who struck you down?"

She glanced at him sharply. "What made you think of that now?" she said, passing through the gate.

"I believe that only a desperate individual would have risked so much by attacking you. Of late, I have begun to wonder if that person was one of your party."

Evelina gasped. "No, that cannot be!" she cried.

Rotherstone laughed. "You still have such confidence in the goodness of all your neighbors, to the last man?"

"I do," she responded. "And I know your opinions to have been softened a trifle of late, for I believe you have been more content than ever to be going about in our society."

He smiled, if sadly. "I am content because I have been so often in your company."

"Rotherstone," she said. "You should not say such things to me. That is, I am not in the least persuaded that you and I, that we should ever truly suit."

"You may be right," was all he was willing to say on that score, particularly since there was every possibility that she might desire to have nothing to do with him after tonight.

Rotherstone said nothing more but turned his attention instead to another matter. If what he suspected was true, he needed to inform his cousin that Evelina was no longer in possession of the map.

* * *

Shortly after supper, as a majority of the dancers were returning to the ballroom, Rotherstone kept a keen watch on his cousin. The more he considered the possibility that Carfax had attacked Evelina, the more he saw that of all the treasure seekers, his cousin may have had the strongest motivation to do what he could to secure the treasure. Attempting to steal the map would have increased the chances that he could discover Jack Stub's treasure first and even dispose of it before anyone was the wiser. The giving of a ball would provide a perfect opportunity to make a second attempt to secure the document. The entire neighborhood was here, imbibing a great deal of champagne, dancing, playing at cards and billiards, and were he to slip from the house during the later hours, who would be the wiser? Returning, were his absence even noted, he could claim any number of excuses to account for it.

If such were true, Rotherstone felt his cousin to be a great deal more clever than he had ever before understood.

As the evening progressed, Rotherstone went about as though he was half-foxed, tripping over things, bumping into people and talking with a slur to his words. He did this for his cousin's benefit, hoping to lull Carfax into a belief he could do what he wished without interference. All the while, he followed after him.

Just before midnight, his cousin stole from the house and headed in the direction of the northwest wood. Rotherstone crept after him, taking great care not to be seen. Once Carfax entered the wood, Rotherstone hurried after him. He heard a horse whinny and was just in time to prevent Carfax from heading down a northerly and quite narrow lane.

"Hallo, cousin," Rotherstone said, slurring his words a trifle as he took hold of the bridle. "Leaving your own ball? This is quite mysterious conduct. Where might you be going at this hour," he hiccoughed for effect, "and with your house full of your neighbors and guests? You will be sadly missed."

"What the deuce are you doing here?" Carfax cried.

Rotherstone squinted his eyes. "Damned dark in these woods. Can scarcely see you. Are you poaching? Wait, I know what it is. You have taken up the smuggling trade, although I think you ought to have established yourself much nearer the coast."

"You are being ridiculous, Gage. You are quite foxed. Go back to the house."

"I mean to know where you are going," he said, his words forming a single slurred string. "Where are you going?"

"If you must know, to see my little 'bird of paradise' in Maybridge."

"Are there any such creatures in Maybridge?" Rotherstone asked, weaving on his feet. "I always though it the dullest village in the world. Besides, this lane travels north and Maybridge is southwest."

"The devil take you!" Carfax cried. "I have an assignation in Maybridge and felt it would be safest to take this route. You may follow if you like."

Rotherstone, still holding the bridle, shook his head. "I think not. In fact, I intend to engage Sir Alfred, Mr. Crookhorn and Mr. Fuller in a game of hazard. I had thought you should join as well, since I mean to have my thousand pounds back tonight."

The woods were dark, but still he could see the considering glitter in Carfax's eyes. Believing he understood his hesitation, Rotherstone dropped his voice to a whisper and added, "There is one more thing I feel I ought to tell you. I confide in you because, well, damme, you are blood, after all."

"What is it?" he asked, now sitting quietly in the saddle.

Rotherstone whispered, "I have the map. I forced Lady Evelina to give it to me. I mean to find the treasure for myself!" He hiccoughed loudly. "Good God, I am foxed. Well, well, have your bit of fun. I am returning to have my game of hazard. Although I certainly hope the night will clear my head."

With that he turned around, weaving slightly as he left the woods. He was not in the least surprised that Carfax followed after him.

Chapter Twelve

"This cannot be happening," Evelina murmured as much to herself as to Lady Monceaux, who stood beside her.

"I fear that it is," she responded.

Evelina felt so ill at what was going forward that tears kept burning her eyes. She was standing in the billiard room surrounded by at least three score of guests. The chamber was hot even with the windows thrown open. With every toss of the dice, she was jostled back and forth like an ocean wave that could not make up its mind in which direction to go.

Five of the neighborhood gentlemen played at hazard: Rotherstone, Sir Alfred, Mr. Fuller, Mr. Crookhorn and Colonel Carfax. Rotherstone had gathered a considerable stack of vowels before him, both Mr. Fuller and Mr. Crookhorn as well. The colonel, however, was known to have lost over a thousand pounds, and Sir Alfred's losses were at this point beyond measuring.

Rotherstone continued to accept the vowels from both gentlemen, all the while appearing as though he were in his altitudes. Evelina, who had come to understand his habits well, knew he had scarcely imbibed a full cup of champagne, muchless a sufficient quantity of any spirit to account for his slurred speech, lazy eyes and tendency to laugh and talk far too loudly than he ought. She believed he was merely pretending to be foxed. She recalled her conversation with him earlier, when he had said that he had lost the thousand pounds on Saturday night to a purpose. Understanding began to dawn.

"We must stop this madness," Evelina said, addressing the lady next to her.

Lady Monceaux glanced at her. "No, I think not," she said, appearing strangely calm. "I now see my husband for the first time. I see what he is."

Evelina turned to hold her gaze. "What do you mean?"

She leaned close to her ear and said, "I believe Rotherstone has been planning this night for a very long time."

Evelina drew back and met her gaze. "What do you know that I do not?" she queried.

"Come and I shall tell you."

With some difficulty, Evelina pushed her way through the crowds, Lady Monceaux following close behind. At last, free of the enrapt crowd, she was able to lead Lady Monceaux to the drawing room, which was now quite empty. The chamber was soothingly cool.

Removing to the far side of the room, Evelina sat down on a small settee. Lady Monceaux joined her. There were tears in her eyes.

"Sir Alfred was never one to keep me informed of estate matters. Sometimes the housekeeping budget was plump in the pocket and at other times I would be required to wait weeks or even months before I had the funds with which to pay my servants or to discharge the tradesmen's bills. This has been a pattern since we were married nearly five and twenty years ago.

"However, seven years ago an event occurred that settled our affairs for a long time after: several years, in fact. I never knew what it was, I only had my suspicions, but this I did know—from that moment, the elder Lord

Rotherstone was no longer a friend to my husband, nor was he a friend to any of the gentlemen now playing a deep game of hazard with his son."

Evelina understood it all now. "I am deeply shocked. However, your history explains so very much, everything in fact. Do you, that is, have you any notion what amount the elder Rotherstone lost that night?"

"I once heard the sum of forty thousand pounds mentioned between Mr. Fuller and Sir Alfred. They had been quarreling, I believe because Mr. Fuller's conscience was hurting him."

"So the gentlemen shared in this robbery?"

She frowned and shook her head. "I do not think so. The game occurred at Pashley Court, and at one point I went into the room to see if the gentlemen had need of anything. I saw Mr. Crookhorn and Mr. Fuller both asleep in chairs while the elder Lord Rotherstone, his nephew Colonel Carfax and my husband continued to play. I thought Rotherstone looked rather foxed, which he never was to my recollection, and I was about to intervene, but my husband physically removed me from the chamber. He told me that this was a matter between gentlemen.

"When I think on it now, I blame myself. I knew some misdeed was occurring, but I did not have the strength to withstand my husband's overbearing manner.

"I retired to bed, the gentlemen went to their various homes and for several years there was a financial surplus in my home. Perhaps that was why I closed my eyes to what I knew must have happened. For the first time, I could be at ease. What a coward I was!

"So you see, Lady Evelina, Rotherstone is playing to take back that which was stolen from his father, that which separated his father from Maybridge society until the day he died."

Evelina felt several tears seep from her eyes. "Rotherstone must have thought me a fool," she said, sighing heavily.

"Why do you say that?"

She laughed harshly. "If you only knew how I championed the neighborhood to Rotherstone. When I think I had actually come to believe that it was by my persuasiveness that he began to take part in the community again, I confess I feel exceedingly foolish indeed. Although I am not in the smallest amount gratified to know that he made use of me quite freely for the purpose of rectifying an old wrong."

Lady Monceaux took her hand and patted it gently. "You love him, do you not?"

"Horribly so," she returned. "But what manner of man is he that he would take up so vengeful a course? I must ask myself again, can such a man ever truly be trusted?" Evelina straightened in her seat. "Do but listen."

"What is it?" Lady Monceaux asked, mystified. "I hear nothing."

"That is my point. There was used to be a great deal of shouting and laughter; now there is only silence."

Evelina rose to her feet, as did her companion. Together, they hastened to the billiard room. The crowd in the hallway appeared stunned.

"What is it?" Evelina asked Stephen Rewell, who was standing in the doorway.

He appeared to be in shock. "Rotherstone just beat his cousin and Sir Alfred all to flinders. Carfax owes him over two thousand, but Sir Alfred's vowels are so great in number that Rotherstone has declared that he requires nothing less than the deed to Pashley Court as payment."

"*What?*" the ladies intoned together.

Lady Monceaux immediately begged to be permitted

to enter the chamber. The crowds parted for her. Evelina entered as well by means of following closely in her wake.

Permitted to the side of the billiard table where the two men were locked in silent battle, Evelina wondered what next would happen. She knew Sir Alfred to be a hard, even disagreeable man who was not likely to relinquish his property merely because it was demanded of him. At the same time, as she glanced at Rotherstone's stubborn jaw, she understood quite well there would be no relenting in him. She feared that a challenge might ensue.

From her side vision, she watched the lady beside her lift her chin. "You must give him what he asks for, Alfred," Lady Monceaux said in a clear, crisp voice Evelina had never heard her use before. "It is the only honorable thing to do."

A single enormous gasp rose from the crowd surrounding the table.

"Silence!" Sir Alfred thundered, directing all his present venom and frustration at his wife.

"No," she answered simply. "I will not permit this farce to continue a moment longer, and please close your astonished mouth, it is not in the least attractive."

Titters moved through the crowd.

Amazingly, Sir Alfred shut his mouth.

Lady Monceaux continued, "You will put in writing this very moment that you agree to give Pashley Court to his lordship in payment for your vowels. If you do not, I will make known that which ought to be kept secret."

Gasps and murmurings swept round the table.

Evelina stared at Lady Monceaux. Never would she have believed so much strength could be born in a creature that a mere fortnight past had cowered beneath her husband's cold stare. Right, however, was on her ladyship's side, and the evil that had been playing itself out in her husband's dissolute habits could not stand.

"You have gone mad," he said to his wife, but fear reigned in his eyes.

"Perhaps I have," she returned, her own eyes blazing. "But you will write your promise even now, and tomorrow you and I together will take the deed to Blacklands."

He shook his head. "This is utter madness."

"Nevertheless. You will do as I have said. You made this bed a long time ago, and now you will lie in it."

Tension filled the air. Carfax's guests stared at Sir Alfred. He took a quick glance around. "I require a pen, paper and ink."

Not a single soul moved while these items were brought to him. He did not sit but rather laid the paper out in front of him. He scrolled his name, *Sir Alfred*, and began to write.

Evelina's gaze, however, became transfixed by the unusual manner in which he had written the S of his title. She tilted her head, and a bolt of excitement suddenly coursed through her. She had it! Most certainly she knew now where Jack Stub's treasure was buried.

As Sir Alfred continued to write his promise, the five riddles on Jack Stub's map flowed through her head.

"*Time is lost, a smuggler's weary end, the world is upside down, walls that will not mend.*

Devil's Gate wat opens, black the land will be, down a path, a treasure ye will see.

'Cross the stones, cross one to dare, pearl and gold within, small and rare.

Ye olde well, draws water deep, of ale and mead, made honey-sweet.

'Some stones flat, others tall, a bridge in death, to any wat fall.'"

Sir Alfred handed the paper to Rotherstone. Evelina

watched him read it. All the while, her mind was engaged in what she believed would prove to be the solution to the riddles.

Carfax tossed his vowel to Rotherstone as well. "I hope you are satisfied," he exclaimed.

Rotherstone merely smiled.

Evelina suddenly spoke. "Colonel, is there a well at Gildstone?"

"What?" he asked, clearly confused.

"Is there a well, an old well, at Gildstone?"

"Yes. A very old well, but what does that have to do with anything?"

"Only that I believe I know where Jack Stub's treasure is buried."

All eyes turned to her, and instantly the combined questions and astonishment of the guests filled the small chamber.

"There is another question I would ask," she said loudly, rising above the excited chatter in the room. Silence fell.

Evelina queried, "Did Jack Stub have a daughter, perchance?"

Miss Ambers suddenly cried, "I see it now. Of course, he must have. Yes, of course."

Evelina smiled at her. "Do you have it?"

"Yes, I have it! I have it!"

"Anyone else?" She glanced round, but not a single soul in the party could respond.

Rotherstone met Evelina's gaze. "Why do you not show us where it is, for I apprehend it is very close."

"Then you have guessed it?"

He nodded.

"Very well. Colonel, if you will send your man to fetch a shovel, several lanterns and perhaps even a few rushlights, we will proceed."

"But where is the treasure to be found?" he asked intensely.

"I will not say, for I believe I should cause a stampede otherwise. No, you must wait until we have sufficient light and a shovel."

"Perhaps we should have several shovels," the elder Mr. Rewell suggested.

Evelina shook her head. "We require only one, of that I am certain."

When Colonel Carfax, his complexion extremely heightened, went in search of one of his servants, Evelina was besieged with questions. She refused, however, to answer even one of them. "You must wait until our host has returned," she cried.

A general roar of conversation ensued. Evelina watched in some dismay as Rotherstone folded up Sir Alfred's note and tucked it between his shirt and waistcoat. His expression was rather serious as he approached her, squeezing his way among a dozen guests, for the billiard room was still uncommonly thick with people.

In the excitement of having suddenly solved the map's mystery, she had forgotten that the reason she had suddenly understood the meaning of the riddles was because of the manner in which Sir Alfred had written his S on a most horrid document.

When Rotherstone reached her, she opened her mouth to protest what he had done, but he was before her. "Yes, yes, I know you are in the boughs, but all will be well, I promise you. All that is required now is that you trust me but a little."

She was astonished at his audacity. "You cannot possibly be serious."

"More than in my entire life. I have but one question," he added, raising his voice. "Will you marry me?"

The entire chamber fell silent again. Evelina felt every

eye upon her and gave Rotherstone so scathing a look that he immediately threw up his hands. "I can see what the answer is. You have no need to say a word." Since he laughed as he spoke, the crowd laughed with him.

When the general conversation in the room once more rose to a dull roar, she leaned close to him. "You have gone mad," she said. "Or do you think I could possibly accept the hand of any gentleman who would gamble as you have just now?"

"You have spoken sensibly," he said, his resonant voice playing havoc against her ear. "To that, I fear, I have no answer, but I refuse to be hopeless. Indeed, I have every confidence that before the night is through, you will agree to be my wife."

Evelina shifted to look at him. "Mad as Bedlam indeed," she reiterated.

Only then did Evelina, glancing at Lady Monceaux, become aware that Sir Alfred had made his way to his wife. He was speaking to her in a harsh undertone. Evelina knew that in previous times Lady Monceaux would have been cringing, but now she wore the expression of a warrior as she turned slightly and merely stared her husband down.

Sir Alfred leaned back and clamped his lips shut. "Madame," he whispered. "You forget yourself."

At that, Lady Monceaux smiled. "You are mistaken, husband. I believe I have just *remembered* myself, and high time." With that, she turned toward Evelina. "I fear this chamber is too warm for me. I believe I shall retire."

"I shall accompany you, my lady. Indeed, we ought to fetch our shawls, for in a few minutes we shall be taking a walk on the colonel's property."

The ladies hooked arms, and when the crowd parted for them, they quit the chamber. The journey to find their shawls required mounting to the second floor in order to find the ladies' withdrawing room.

By the time Evelina was in possession of the garment and had descended the stairs, she found the entire party, some two hundred souls, crushed inside the entrance hall and spilling into the various adjoining chambers.

She could not help but laugh. "Has the colonel arrived with a shovel and lanterns?"

The answer was a resounding "Yes!"

Draping her shawl about her shoulders, she descended the stairs, and upon seeing that Colonel Carfax was working his way amidst the throng from the back hall, she directed him to return from whence he had come. "For we shall be walking in that direction."

The crowd as one began to flow toward the northerly rooms. Several doors and more than one low window at the back of the house opened. Like a flood, people began pouring from each door.

Once Evelina made her way out of doors, she approached the colonel, who was surrounded by several servants each carrying either a lantern or a rushlight. The colonel himself had a heavy shovel slung over his shoulder.

"Lead the way," he said.

Evelina began the same journey she had made with Rotherstone earlier. This time, those of the local gentry who had been involved with the treasure hunt were clustered near Colonel Carfax and the lightbearers. After that, nearly two hundred people trampled the lawn and then the path leading to the graveyard.

Before the gate, the party stopped, as did all conversation.

"You believe the treasure is buried here?" the colonel asked, shocked.

"Yes," Evelina responded. "I am convinced of it. I do

not think, however, that in such a small space everyone should go in. We would not be able to move about at all otherwise."

The colonel arranged for only the original treasure seekers, and his servants, of course, to enter the graveyard. Once assembled, Evelina addressed Miss Ambers. "If you would be so good, will you tell us where you believe the treasure to be buried?"

"Do you really wish for me to explain?"

Evelina nodded. "If you please."

"Very well." She glanced about the original party, meeting each gaze. "First, the most telling riddle, the one that offers the key to the map, is the riddle that speaks of the world being upside down. Blacklands and Darwell are situated in nearly exact locations were the map turned upside down. That is the real trick."

All those who knew the map so well immediately murmured a joint "Ah" of understanding.

Miss Ambers continued, "Next, we are not far from the hamlet of Gildstone. Indeed, if you look in a northeasterly direction you can see the church tower not a hundred yards distant." As one, the entire party looked through the tall trees. "And we all know there to be a fine old well near the church."

"I see the church!" someone cried out in a great slur of words. Laughter spread through the onlookers.

Miss Ambers laughed as well, then explained. "The riddle speaking of ale and mead and honey I believe refers to the hamlet of Gildstone. I cannot say what the original meaning of the word 'gild' might have been, but in this case I believe it refers to the color gold."

The group expressed another sage "Ah."

"Next is this gate." She gestured to the wrought iron. "Remember the reference to *'some stones flat, others tall, a bridge in death, to any wat fall*? What better way to describe a derelict graveyard, particularly this one."

Lady Monceaux interjected, "That is precisely what I said on the very first day of our reviewing the map together!"

"So you did," Evelina cried enthusiastically. "We ought to have heeded your opinions more."

Lady Monceaux smiled. She appeared happier than Evelina had ever known her to be.

Mrs. Rewell said, "But where is the treasure, then? Are we expected to unearth all these poor dead persons?"

Evelina laughed. "No, not at all. There is one more riddle that I believe tells us where we are to look. Miss Ambers, you have taken us thus far, pray take us to the end of the journey."

Miss Ambers took a deep breath. "The final riddle goes, *'cross the stones, cross one to dare,'* which I take to mean that we will find a cross on one of the gravestones."

Mr. Crookhorn said, "Of course. That is quite obvious now. And the last bit?"

Miss Ambers said, "*'Pearl and gold within, small and rare.'* If I have understood correctly, there should be a gravestone with the name Pearl written on it, or, if not, 1652, since that date appeared on the map. My guess would be that a cross will appear somewhere on the stone."

"That must be it!" Colonel Carfax called out. "But let my servants search for the grave. Over half the stones will need to be lifted in order to read them."

"I believe that is an excellent notion," Evelina said. She nodded for him to thus instruct his servants.

The search commenced.

Evelina watched as Colonel Carfax orchestrated a careful and thorough search of gravestone after gravestone. So many had fallen over and shattered that a number of them had to be pieced together to determine the inscription. Finally, the grave was located, tucked away in a far corner, quite small, the date 1652 chiseled at the very top, a cross beneath and the name and dedicatory words, *For Pearl* carved below.

The original party of treasure seekers gathered round.

A solemnity overcame the group assembled round the grave. At the same time, a hush settled over the larger party now drawing closer to the perimeter of the graveyard.

Again, the colonel instructed his men, and the shovel was set to work. Slowly and carefully the grave was disturbed.

The first object found wrung Evelina's heart, a small coffin not three feet long. Colonel Carfax looked at her and asked if she thought the grave should be opened. Evelina nodded. A deeper hush fell upon the crowd. Not a soul breathed as the lid was removed.

Within was a small skeleton bearing a mass of wispy red hair. The remnants of a gown covered the bones. "Close it," Evelina said. "I daresay this is Jack Stub's dear little Pearl, *'small and rare.'*"

The lid was placed back on the coffin.

"There would be appear to be only earth below," Sir Alfred said, staring into the depths.

The colonel directed one of the servants to hold a rushlight overhead. The party moved back and again the colonel directed his question to Evelina. "Should we dig further?"

She nodded. "Yes, for I am convinced that he left a treasure here for his daughter."

The only sound during that early morning hour was of a shovel thumping against damp earth. Several minutes passed until at last iron struck iron.

A gasp and a sudden cheer went up among all who

heard the sound. Evelina's heart seemed to explode with excitement. From the time she had found the map, she had envisioned this moment, but never would she have thought to feel as she did now, as though the sky had just burst all by itself into an array of fireworks.

A few minutes only saw the small iron box pulled from its grave. The colonel's servant was ready to slam the shovel down on the lock that secured it, but Evelina stayed him.

"One moment," she called out. "If you please, I would that Pearl was returned to her resting place first."

"Yes," Lady Monceaux agreed. "That would be proper."

"Hear, hear," several of the gentlemen agreed.

Little Pearl was placed in her grave, her coffin settled deeply into its earthen vault. The vicar of Maybridge was asked to bless the burial, a service he performed readily and which lent a proper air to the strange proceedings. Afterward, a servant shoveled more earth, this time refilling the grave.

Only once the gravestone was reset did Evelina nod for the servant to perform the last task. He lifted the shovel high and brought the head clanging against the lock. Three times he struck, and on the last the lock broke and fell away from the small iron box.

The colonel started to lift the lid, but Rotherstone stopped him. "I believe that this privilege belongs to Lady Evelina."

He was not alone in this sentiment, as several of the party said, "Hear, hear." Evelina did not hesitate but trembled as she approached the box. How odd to think that all this had begun because of a map hidden in the floor of her great-uncle's attic. Even odder to think that the map had indeed proved genuine.

Evelina knelt down, not caring that her gown would be dirtied. She lifted the lid and could not prevent a gasp. The trunk was full of gold sovereigns. On the top of the pile, however, was a scrolled document.

Evelina carefully removed it. Age and damp had made the paper fragile and the script scarcely legible.

"A lantern, please." She gestured to the nearest servant. He drew near and lowered his lantern to the ground beside her. "I can just make this out," she stated loudly. "'For widows and' . . . yes, I see what it is . . . 'orphans.' 'For widows and orphans.' I believe it refers to a scripture about true religion being the care of widows and orphans."

"What?" Carfax cried, almost indignantly.

"I believe I understand," Miss Ambers said. "Pearl was his child, perhaps the very reason for his existence. I believe he loved her very much and wanted to honor the joy she had brought him. Even the epitaph suggests that this treasure was to commemorate her life."

"Surely you are being overly romantic about a smuggler's brat," the colonel cried. Several guests expressed shock at his speech. Still, he continued, "If he had truly wished to honor her, he would have given his treasure to a worthy establishment at the time of his death."

Evelina could not help but notice the wild look in the colonel's eye. She said, "But you are forgetting that at the time, the smugglers were being hunted down and destroyed. What dying wish of his would have been honored by a mob ready to tear him from limb to limb? No, I believe his plan was sound. Besides," and here she eyed him carefully, "he probably understood quite well that with such a treasure in hand there would likely be a great deal of squabbling over ownership. We, of course, have a very different view tonight."

"We have no such thing, if you mean to suggest that the treasure be given away. I wish it made clear at the outset that the treasure was found on Darwell land and will belong to the estate. There can be no two opinions about the legalities involved. Jack Stub's treasure is mine."

Evelina was shocked and appalled by Colonel Carfax's attitude. She opened her mouth to voice her strong disagreement, but the earl was before her.

"Well, cousin," Rotherstone said in a rather bored drawl, "I beg to differ with you."

Evelina watched in some bewilderment as the colonel turned to stare at him. "Your opinion hardly matters," he said. "I intend to retain a solicitor, and I believe the King's law will prevail."

"We should all like to see the King's law prevail," Rotherstone said quietly. He paused for effect before adding, "*In every possible respect.*"

Evelina saw the hard look in the earl's eyes and wondered what he could mean by emphasizing these last few words in particular.

Colonel Carfax shifted on his feet. "I do not take your meaning."

"Oh, but I think you do, and if you are wise now, you will permit these good ladies to determine what ought to be done with Mr. Stub's treasure."

The colonel looked about him wildly, seeking some recourse. Evelina could not know what threat Rotherstone was making that had set Colonel Carfax on his heels, but he had all the appearance of wanting to run but not knowing where to go.

"Good," Rotherstone stated. "Then we are of a mind—or is there anyone else here who feels they have a claim to the treasure?"

Evelina thought Rotherstone had never appeared more masterful than in this moment. Given the gambling habits of more than one of the gentlemen present, she rather thought there were several who wanted desperately to argue the point of ownership. However, no one stepped forward to contest him.

"Excellent," he stated, almost angrily. He then picked up the quite heavy box and approached Miss Ambers. "You once asked me to contribute to the refurbishment of the orphanage in Studdingly, and I callously refused. I was very wrong to have done so. I believe we would do well to make certain that Jack Stub's treasure is allocated in a manner he has already made plain to us. There is probably sufficient money within this box to build a new wing, one that might be named after Pearl."

Tears brimmed in Miss Ambers's eyes. Sir Edgar, standing beside her, said quietly, "Well done, Gage. Well done indeed."

A cheer suddenly went up round the gathered guests.

"I would give this to you even now," he added, "but I fear I am having difficulty holding it. For the present, would you have an objection to my seeing it stored at Blacklands until we can see it safely delivered to the orphanage's bank?"

"None at all," she responded cheerfully. "In fact, I would be greatly relieved."

As Evelina regarded Rotherstone, warmth swelled in her heart. Was such a gentleman, who would give a fortune to an orphanage, a man she could trust?

He turned to her. "I believe there is now but one matter of business to conclude," he said, setting the heavy box down.

Evelina smiled, her heartbeat quickening. "Indeed?" she queried. Was this a man she could trust?

In a quiet voice, he said, " For the last of my demands I require your hand in marriage."

"You *require* my hand in marriage?" she returned archly.

"Yes," he said, narrowing his eyes. "According to the terms of our agreement."

A general muttering swelled over the crowd. "What agreement?"

"It is a private matter between myself and Lady Evelina."

Sir Edgar challenged his friend. "I do not believe you have the right to require anything of Lady Evelina."

"You must ask the lady herself whether I do or not."

Sir Edgar turned a questioning gaze to her. "Is this true?"

Evelina sighed. "I fear it is. I suppose there is nothing for it. We are now betrothed."

Rotherstone took her hand. "You will not honor me with even one small argument?" he queried, a crooked smile on his lips.

"I am a woman of honor," she responded, lifting her chin. "I will abide by our agreement. However, there is one thing I would ask of you as a wedding gift, but it is not a small thing."

His smile broadened. Almost he was grinning. "I will give you whatever you ask for, though I strongly suspect I know what it is already. Do I, for instance, have it in my power to give it to you now?"

"Indeed you do, my lord."

He sighed. "Oh, very well. Have it, if it gives you contentment." He withdrew Sir Alfred's note containing his written word that Pashley Court now belonged to Rotherstone. He handed it to Evelina.

She took it with a smile, opened it and read the contents. "Excellent."

Sir Alfred stepped forward at once. "Eh? What's this?" He moved close to Evelina. "Well, well, I knew you to be a good girl. Now give it here and all will be forgiven amongst friends." He extended his hand to her.

Evelina held his gaze. "You presume too much, Sir Alfred. Your wife told me the whole of your history, and if there is forgiveness to render, I believe it is you who must beg forgiveness of Lord Rotherstone."

He bristled, and his anger appeared as two bright red spots on his florid cheeks. He made as if to intimidate her, his expression darkening, his fists clenched, but suddenly Lady Monceaux cried, "Enough, Alfred! Enough or you will have me to answer to." Her eyes sparked fire.

The crowd gasped and cheered.

Sir Alfred took a step backward, stumbled and fell. As he lay propped on his elbows, he stared at his wife but said not a word.

Lady Monceaux jerked her head toward Rotherstone. "Do as Lady Evelina has bid you. Now."

Sir Alfred addressed Rotherstone, "I do beg your forgiveness, my lord."

The earl regarded him for a long moment, and though there was much whispering among the crowd as to what this exchange could possibly mean, the earl finally said quietly, "Done."

"Thank you, Rotherstone," Lady Monceaux said. Turning to Evelina, she added, "Do whatever pleases you with that document. I should not care if you sold the estate and gave the money to Miss Ambers's orphanage. Indeed, I would be greatly satisfied." Sir Alfred showed a little sense and chose to remain silent, though he slowly gained his feet.

"I have but one intention, my lady," Evelina said. She then offered the note to her. When Lady Monceaux took it, albeit slowly, as one stunned, Evelina added, "Rotherstone will have his solicitor draw up the proper documents making the estate yours. We will not lack for witnesses." She glanced about the crowd that in turn had been hanging on her every word. Many gasps of astonishment and a few huzzas again passed round the crowd.

"This is a very great kindness," she said. "I shall never forget it. But as Miss Ambers has done," here she turned to Rotherstone, "I would leave this in your safekeeping until all might be handled by your solicitor." She offered the document to him. "For I trust you."

Rotherstone beamed. "As you wish. It shall be done."

Lady Monceaux, still the hostess, called out, "And now, what about a little more music and dancing, a little more iced champagne, another round of whist or two before we part for the evening?"

The crowd agreed with a cheer and began working its way back to the house. Sir Edgar, with Miss Ambers on his arm, stayed Rotherstone for a moment. "We desire that you be the first to know. We are engaged."

"I can hardly be surprised," Rotherstone said, "when you have scarcely been at Blacklands since the assembly at the Crown."

"I confess I have been a very poor guest," Sir Edgar returned, smiling broadly.

He clapped his friend on his shoulder. "I am happy for you both. This is a proper ending, after all."

Miss Ambers cried, "And a most excellent beginning."

"Just so," Sir Edgar murmured, covering Miss Ambers's hand with his own.

With that, the happy couple also trailed the crowd.

After a few minutes, Evelina saw that the only persons remaining in the graveyard were Carfax and his servants, herself and Rotherstone. The servants were awaiting orders from their master, but he was now sitting on a fallen gravestone. Rotherstone dismissed the servants. One by one they filed out of the graveyard and headed in the direction of the house.

Carfax looked up at Rotherstone. "What am I to do now, for you must know I am ruined?"

"I have not the faintest notion," Rotherstone said. "Although I shall be happy to purchase passage for you to either the Colonies or to New South Wales."

"And an allowance?" he asked, his expression somber.

"You do not deserve one. I will, however, offer a gift of two hundred pounds and a promise to settle your tradesmen's debts, but nothing more. As for Darwell, I will see that your estate is sold, the proceeds to discharge any that remain of your debts, honorable or otherwise."

He rose to his feet. "Done."

"You know you deserve to hang," the earl stated.

The colonel glanced at Evelina. "Yes," he responded.

Evelina felt a chill go through her. "You mean . . . *you* were the one who wanted the map?"

"Of course," he said without the smallest hint of remorse.

Rotherstone took up her arm. "If you wish these terms to be otherwise, you have but to say the word. In this matter, I will defer to your judgment, your desire."

Evelina felt tears sting her eyes. To Carfax, she said, "I accounted you a friend." She then gasped, "Is that why you were asking me all those odd questions about which of my servants were at Wildings tonight?"

His jaw worked, and he lowered his gaze, but he said nothing.

"Were you intent on going to my house tonight?"

When he remained silent, Rotherstone said, "I found him in the woods to the north astride his mount. I believe he had but one object—to try a second time to steal the map. However, he changed his mind when I let it be known that the map was now in my possession."

Evelina did not know which affected her more in this moment, a real fear that Colonel Carfax might have done harm to her family had he succeeded in reaching Wildings, or her profound anger that he had so deceived and betrayed her as a friend.

"Go, Colonel," she cried, "and do not return to England. I will not be so generous should I ever see your face again."

He did not wait, but offered a mocking bow and walked swiftly in the direction of the house.

A moment more and Evelina was left alone with Rotherstone. For a very long time indeed, long after the colonel had disappeared into the house, she remained very quiet. Finally, she said, "I cannot believe he nearly killed me. And I trusted him so implicitly. I begin to fear I shall never be able to trust my judgment again."

He covered her hand with his own. "I believe he ought to have been an actor. He deceived everyone, not just you. Though I knew something of his unfortunate habits, even I did not for a moment suspect him of having been your attacker."

She looked up at him. "This has been a very strange night."

He smiled faintly. "Very."

She then dropped his arm and turned to face him. "Besides which, you have actually forced my hand in marriage. Do you know, I am come to believe you are a horridly unromantic creature."

"I thought my proposal quite romantic. A graveyard and moonlight—"

"And two hundred people! Besides, it was not a proposal: It was a demand!"

He chuckled. "So, my dear Lady Evelina, will you do me the honor of accepting of my hand in marriage?" he asked.

"I have no choice."

"I give you the choice now. I hereby end our agreement, and you are free to reject me if you so desire."

"I believe I do not like it so well when you are being noble in this manner."

"I see," he murmured, slipping his arms about her waist. "You prefer that I embarrass you in public?"

She smiled. "I was embarrassed by nothing you did tonight, Gage. You set so many things to rights and proved that you were worthy of my trust and my love."

"You love me then?" he asked, drawing her close.

"Yes, I have said so," she cried, lifting her chin.

He nodded. "You are not very romantic, either. You were supposed to say, 'My darling Gage, I love you more than the sun, moon and stars,' at the very least."

"You would not have believed me had I said as much."

"Very true."

He did not hesitate, but leaned down and kissed her tenderly on the lips. She responded as she had so many times before, by sliding her arms about his neck and giving kiss for kiss. How dear he had become to her in so short a time, how necessary to her happiness.

She remained with him in the graveyard for a few minutes more, until the strangeness of the surroundings began working on her. She drew back and said, "We should leave this place."

"I could not agree more."

"However, there is one thing I should like to do first."

"What would that be?" He seemed curious.

She crossed to Pearl's grave and offered her thanks for the treasure her little life had provided not just to their community but to her own heart as well. Once this was accomplished, she took up Rotherstone's arm, and he guided her from the graveyard.

As she walked beside him back to the house, she said,

"I think I shall venture into the attics tomorrow. If I am very fortunate, I may find another map."

"I forbid you to ever return to your attics. No more maps, Evelina, I beg you, no more maps!"

At that, she could only laugh. "But it was a lovely adventure, was it not?"

"For whom?"

"For me, of course, although you must admit you took some enjoyment from it as well."

"I will confess there were times when I took a great deal of enjoyment from it!"

She heard the provocative tone in his voice and gave his arm a squeeze. "I hope you mean to be equally ridiculous once we are married."

At that he laughed, but he would not permit her to enter the house. Instead, he drew her into the shadows and spent the next several minutes proving just how *ridiculous* he intended to be.

More Regency Romance
From Zebra